And on
the Eighth Day
She Rested

JD Mason

Sadorian
PUBLICATIONS

Published by Sadorian Publications, LLC

Cover Design: John Riddick, Jr.

© 2000 by JD Mason

All rights reserved. No part of this book may be reproduced, stored in or introduced into a retrieval system, or transmitted in any form or by any means without the expressed written consent of the Publisher of this book.

Library of Congress Card Catalogue Number: 00-112003
ISBN 0-9700102-8-1 (pbk)

Second Printing, July 2001
10 9 8 7 6 5 4 3 2 1

Published and printed in the United States of America

This is a work of fiction. It is not meant to depict, portray or represent any particular gender, real persons, or group of people. All the characters, incidents, and dialogues are products of the author's imagination and are not to be construed as real. Any resemblance to actual events or persons, living or dead, is purely coincidental.

www.Sadorian.com

God told me once in a dream:
to get to the inevitable, the burden is
not on me
…but you.

ACKNOWLEDGEMENTS

So many people have come to my rescue on this project that to include them all would result in another book. But there are some very special people I would like to express my gratitude to. First and foremost, to Cynthia and Collinus Newsome. You've turned out to be some of the best little sisters in the world. Not once did either of you ever tell me I couldn't do this. I love you both. I have to thank my best friend and partner for life, Carol Henton for reminding me of just how determined God can be when you set your mind to him. Much love to my first reviewer, critic, and all around cheerleader Tonja Medlock who never let me get away with saying "I give up!".

To Lisa Cross, who believed in me before I ever did and who has aspirations of turning me into the next Oprah despite my best efforts to just write books. You're enthusiasm is contagious and I adore you for it. I'd like to thank Zane for giving me the time of day and allowing me into her world where the sky's a slightly different color than everyone else's. Her perspective is invigorating! To my friend and mentor Linda Dominique Grovesnor who's grace and determination are priceless. I will admire you forever. Thank you. To the most dynamic publisher on the planet, John Riddick Jr., who's vision for the future of black books and authors is extraordinary. Thank you for allowing me the privilege of taking this journey with you.

And on the Eighth Day She Rested

Even when I was young
I had choices
Only I misunderstood them
Got them mixed up with fate
And instead of making my choices
I let them make me
So, here I am

Truth & Consequences

Domestic violence. There's nothing domestic about the violence in my world. My husband beats my ass and that's been my truth for the past 14 years. Being slapped across the face or punched in the stomach isn't as neatly choreographed as they make it look in the movies. Not everybody is a pretty white woman who cries on a cue or falls just right, landing seductively on the kitchen floor. Swollen eyes and cheeks can't be covered up with a little extra mascara and rouge. And I've never seen a movie that's shown what it's really like to get your ass whooped with a leather belt while you crawl around on all fours with snot running out of your nose trying to hide behind tables, chairs, or underneath the bed begging this man not to hit you anymore. When he does stop, it's only because his arm is tired or he's got somewhere to go and your ignorant ass ain't doing nothing but wasting his damn time anyway.

I never had children. Came close though. I miscarried shortly after finding out about the baby and I swore I'd never get pregnant again. Losing that child was devastating and it meant losing every aspiration I'd weaved together in my mind about my marriage. That child was to be my savior, my retribution and my new beginning. He was the answer to every hope I held and the realization of every dream I prayed would come true. Maybe having a child would change things, change him and me. Maybe he'd see how wrong he'd been and want to set a good example for his kid. Maybe my ass was smoking crack and didn't even know it. Any ideas I might have had about having children with this man disappeared and I later concluded that no man like Eric deserves to be the father of my children and no child deserves to have a father like him.

Momma's name was Karen. She was a beautiful black woman with skin the color of caramel, long, dark brown hair that hung down her shoulders and soft, full lips that held captive a smile that could warm a frigid Colorado winter. Only thing was, she never saw herself as beautiful without a man in her life. Karen was afraid of loneliness, and desperately clung to any stray with a few kind words and a dick. She was in and out of relationships for as long as I could remember, ultimately settling on some fool who threatened to leave her if she had the baby she was carrying, which was his. She used what little money we had to get an abortion and bled to death. I was 13 years old.

The experts say I'm perpetuating the cycle of abuse. But I say bump what the experts say. I say that's a lame ass explanation and nowhere near good enough to justify hell. The truth is, my need for reassurance or companionship hasn't kept me in this marriage. Love hasn't kept me with this man. Financial dependence isn't the reason I've stayed. Insecurity? That's not enough of a reason either. Fear. It really is that simple. Fear has kept me right here all these years. Sure, I've left him. But he's come after me promising me the moon, then making me see stars by hitting me so hard up side my head it was all I could do not to pass out, daring me to leave again. Fear threatens that I'll go from bad to worse. Fear warns that he'll hit me if my attitude isn't quite right or my sex isn't good enough. Fear promises me that he'll kill me one day. I've lived in fear for so long, it's all I know. But being afraid all the time isn't how I want to spend the rest of my life and nothing else has ever motivated me until now. The last time Eric threw his plate at me because he wanted his pork chops fried instead of baked motivated me to get out of this marriage. The last time he emptied my checking account and all the checks I'd written for bills bounced, motivated me to put him out once and for all. The last time he crawled on top of me and demanded I scream his name then call him "daddy" motivated my ass to get as far away from him as possible. Freedom motivates me, the concept, the idea, freedom from my husband and my fear.

Three weeks ago I woke up another year older and tired. Sick and tired to be more precise. So sick and tired that nothing else matters but to not be sick and tired anymore. For years I've accepted that my life is my life and that's all. I work, eat, sleep and try really hard not to upset the delicate balance of power in my household. Do I really want to continue to live my life under the umbrella of my husband's dictatorship? Hell no! So what's the difference between this moment and five years ago? Five years ago, I was ready to get away from his ass, but I'm still here. What's changed now? Me. I've changed, and honestly, I don't care anymore. What can he do to me that he hasn't already done? Make me cry? Hurt my feelings? Humiliate me? I know. Maybe he can force me to fuck him again? There's nothing else he can do to me he hasn't already done. Short of killing me, Eric's made all my worse nightmares come true, and I have nothing else to be afraid of.

Despair has become my sustenance and it's been with me so long, I've almost forgotten how to live without it. Isn't that ridiculous? These past few weeks I've taken advantage of his absence and every hour, minute, second of the day that I haven't been working or sleeping, I've gone over it a thousand times in my mind questioning myself. Why would a woman choose to live like this? Why would this same woman be so afraid of dying when, in fact, she's been dead ever since she first laid eyes on the son-of-a-bitch? For the life of me, I don't know. Eric is the only man I've ever been with. I was 18 years old and as naive as they come. He saw that and he wanted that so that he could mold me into exactly what I am.

Nothing.

One

I hate being a secretary, but unfortunately I'm great at it. Have been for almost 15 years. The usual five o'clock quitting time has eluded me again and I'm on my way home exhausted and drained, which is nothing new. They've finally finished construction on the Buckman Bridge and traffic isn't nearly as bad as it used to be. Of course this time of night it's not bad anyway because all the smart people are home by now digesting dinner and watching television. Reflections dance off the St. John's River, creating elusive images of a world that's so much better than the real thing. Nothing more than illusions float on top of this river but they're seductive enough to make me wish I could be an illusion too and not some tired, worn out administrative assistant on her way home from a hard day at the office. Actually, I don't mind the drive. It's relaxing and helps alleviate some of the tension I've been drowning in all day. Sometimes I wish time stood still. Sometimes I wish this bridge would never end, my car wouldn't run out of gas and I'd be the only one on the road listening to a jazz station that played nonstop with no commercial interruptions.

I swear, I've been working so much I see dancing contracts and depositions when I close my eyes. My hours are nine to five, but lately it's been more like nine to nine. Somewhere along the line, McGreggor, my boss, decided that the abolition of slavery doesn't apply to Legal Secretaries on a salary. Now don't get me wrong. I've never been afraid of hard work. I love productivity and excel under the pressure of deadlines. But like most people, I enjoy getting a pat on the back from time to time too. I can't remember the last time I heard a simple, "Thank you, Ruth" or "Great job, Ruth." McGreggor isn't big on gratitude or appreciation, but he's larger than life in his demands and expectations.

It's almost eight-thirty when I turn down my street and all I want to do is enjoy a quiet evening alone. Tonight's agenda includes soaking in a hot bath, giving Gerald Albright the privilege of serenading me and sipping on a hot cup of plum tea. Not exactly the most exciting evening, but that's my idea of heaven on earth. I know tomorrow's not going to be any better than today was and the best I can hope for is that it won't be worse, so I just want to relax and peel out of this stress.

I pull into the driveway next to my husband's big, black Pontiac and all of a sudden I don't feel very well. My peaceful thoughts slither down through my stomach, into my intestinal tract and escape from my behind in the form of gas. I haven't seen or heard from Eric in weeks and this time I savored it. This time, it didn't matter where he was or what he was doing or who he was doing it with. This time, I refused to trip or allow myself one jealous or insecure thought. I even backed away from feelings of inadequacy. No, this time was different. It was a vacation.

In retrospect, every time Eric's taken off on one of his little hiatus' from our marriage has been a blessing, but it's taken me 14 years to finally realize it. God realized it though. A long time ago he realized that I've needed this time away from Eric even more than he's needed to be out fucking around. This brief separation has served as an example to me of how life could be without Eric...really cool, full of ocean blue peace. Since he's been gone, no one's called me a bitch or cussed me out about the drycleaners putting too much starch in his shirts. I didn't have to have sex or lie that I couldn't have sex because of the persistent period I've suffered from all these years that my gynecologist can't seem to find a reasonable explanation or cure for. If he was smart, he'd know that no one can bleed as long as I've been claiming to bleed and still be alive. But...

I've just turned 33 years old and the fantasies I used to have about my husband have evaporated in the space of time, and there's nothing left but Eric. The man who instantly comes to his senses and realizes how much he loves and cherishes me has never shown his face in this house. The one who gets up early in the morning and brings me breakfast in bed, kissing my cheeks and hands, making love to me in the tender way he never did, was nothing more than a figment of my imagination. The man who sees for the first time how beautiful I am, then apologizes profusely for ever hurting me, lives in another house somewhere else. The Eric who takes me out dancing, treats me like a princess and is the prince whose sole purpose in life is to protect me and make sure I live happily ever after, stood me up years ago.

It's been a gradual awakening, coming with every ugly moment with him. Yeah, it was an awakening that usually followed a slap or a barrage of hideous words escaping from his nasty mouth, aimed at destroying my self-esteem. Fourteen years have dripped through my fingers like water and I'll never get any of it back. It's all been such a waste. I've lived with his ass coming in and out of my life like it's a revolving door, constantly on guard, anxiously anticipating his temper and unwarranted, undeserved demands on my body. For what, to keep the peace and exercise this bruised muscle of my pathetic existence? Basically.

Over the years, his absences from home have left all sorts of ideas running rampant through my mind. Divorce. Skipping town. Suicide. Murder. I've thought a lot about killing him. Arsenic was my first choice, but for it to look like death from natural causes, it takes too long. I've considered shooting him, but I might miss and I wouldn't want to take that chance. I thought about burning the bed with him in it, but he's a light sleeper and might wake up before I got a good fire going. So I've decided to try a more radical approach, like reasoning with him and asking him to leave.

That dirty shirt lying on the floor is the first greeting I get from Eric when I walk in. He's home all right. This is how it's always been, though. With him walking around the house like royalty leaving a trail of shit behind him and me crawling around on my hands and knees picking up after him because he likes a *"clean crib 'case comp'ny comes by."* His grand entrance from the shower turns my stomach, and my knees feel so weak I've either got to sit down or fall. "Hey, Baby," he sings out, then walks over to me and kisses me on top of my head. "They gotchu workin' late again? I tell you, them lawyers don't know how good they got it witchu workin' for 'em." Condescending is not an attractive feature on Eric.

I hate him. I hate all of him with all of me, and a mental image of him filling up with toxic gases and exploding right there in the living room makes me feel just a little bit better. I know even before I open my mouth that I'll regret tonight. I know I'm going to wake the demons, disturb the sensitive molecular structure of this man's universe and set all hell loose up in this house tonight. But I'm blinded by my determination to stop the madness and put an end to this ridiculous circus called our marriage once and for all.

"Where have you been, Eric?" Not that I really care, but it seems to be the logical first question to ask on the "HCLCLDUHATBGD" (How to Confront Lying, Cheating, Low-Down, Unfaithful Husbands After They've Been Gone for Days) list.

"Oh, Baby...you know me." He grins.

"Yes, I do. However, that doesn't answer my question," I say coolly. I'm not upset that he's been gone. I'm upset that he's back.

"Well, uh...Leroy had some business he had to take care of in West Palm." I stare at him watching that rusty wheel of pitiful excuses turn inside his head. Sometimes, if I really pay attention, I can hear torturous creaking noises coming from his brain and out of his mouth while he's talking. I call them lies. "And uh...he wanted me to ride out with him...you know...I had to help him out, 'cause his car ain't workin."

"What did you do? Give Leroy a piggyback ride to West Palm? Because I could've sworn, I saw your car parked outside some apartment building on the South side just yesterday, as a matter of fact."

He ignores me. "I know I should've called, Baby, but...anyway. The line was busy, and...we was runnin' 'round so much I didn't get a chance to..."

"Eric...please. Please don't do this any more." Lord all I wanted was to not have to deal with this tonight. Some jazz would've been nice, a hot soak in the tub and some tea. Some damn tea. I don't ask for much. Just tea.

"Do what, Baby? Whatchu talkin' 'bout?" Eric strolls over to me, kneels down and attempts to put his arms around the waist he complains is larger than he would like.

I quickly pull away, "Stop making up these stupid excuses. You didn't go to West Palm Beach. Who'd you spend the week with this time, Eric? One of your regular ho's or a new ho?"

"Ruthie, now you know..."

"No, Eric...you know. You know I'm right. But you know what else? I don't even care any more. I don't. It's been years since I've cared about who you've been fucking."

"Baby, I'm tellin' you the truth."

"The truth?" I laugh because Eric and the truth are like oil and water. The two just don't mix. "You want to know what truth is, Eric? Truth is our marriage ain't never been worth a damn and I think you've known that better than either one of us."

"Ruth...now I know we got our problems, Baby, but..."

"It's over, Eric. You and me...we're over and I don't want you here any more. I can't keep doing this. I've wasted way too many years of my life on you and I'm tired. I'm just tired, Eric." There I've said it, like I've said it so many times before, but this time is not like all those other times. This time I mean it, like I've meant it all those other times before but this time I really mean it.

"Ruth...look. I know you pissed off 'bout me bein' gone and I know I shoulda called but...you need to chill the hell out, Baby. You need to calm down."

Is he talking to me, Ruth Ashton, the epitome of chill and calm? He's the drama queen, not me. "I am calm, Eric. I've been calm the whole time you've been gone." Damn, forget the tea.

Instead, I pour myself a glass of lukewarm wine, finish it in one gulp, then fill my glass again and gulp that down too. Being drunk right about now might not be such a bad idea. "If you want to fuck around, I can't stop you. I've never been able to stop you, but I can stop you from running back to my bed while you wait for some other heffa to change the sheets! I don't need you here, Eric. I never have."

The condescending Eric decides to leave the house, replacing him with the real Eric. The mean one. "Oh, you need me, Bitch! You definitely need my ass!"

There was a time when words like that would've hurt my feelings, but not lately. Between this wine I'm guzzling and my new found attitude, I'm feeling pretty brave, or maybe it's stupidity I'm feeling. Sometimes it's hard to tell the difference.

"For what? What the hell do I need you for, Eric? Can you tell me that? Please do, because I can't come up with one good reason on my own. I've been racking my brain trying to come up with just...one, and I can't do it. Why don't you help me out? Come on. I'm listening." The callousness of my argument pierces his heart and hurts his feelings though he'll never admit it. Fat ass, black ass, Ruth Ashton has the nerve to stand up to and throw some of her own insults at Eric, player-dawg extraordinaire, and even hits a nerve. I fill my glass again,

"You don't know either?" He's off balance. I can see it in his face and I feel mean. Real mean. Eric mean. "Look, why are we bothering discussing this? You don't want me; I don't want you; so what's the issue?"

"The issue?"

"The issue, Eric! What's the damn point? You haven't wanted me in years."

"You pushin', Ruth, and I ain't in the mood for this shit." he growled.

"So? Leave...just get out! Why the hell do you keep coming back here?"

"You ain't makin' me do shit, Ruth! This is my motha' fuckin' house too, and..."

"And? Since when have you contributed anything to this

household, Eric? When was the last time you got up off some money for the mortgage?" *Enough Ruth.* "When have you bought furniture or paid just one bill?" *Stop now, Ruth. Enough.* "The only contribution you've ever made to this household is sucking up any excess oxygen and space not being utilized by anything important." *Too late.*

Eric's green eyes throw daggers in my direction. Only I'm protected by my impenetrable armor of anger and they bounce right off me. Hell, I'm not even afraid of the inevitable this time. "Who the fuck you think you talkin' to?"

"The only other person in this room. I'm talking to you, Eric. I'm finally talking to you. I'm telling you how I feel. I'm telling you what I think...about you...about us! I'm finally getting all this shit off my chest because I've been wanting to say it for years!"

Eric takes a step towards me. "Oh, and yo' black ass is sayin' it now, huh?"

"Yes! My black ass is, Eric. And you know what? It feels good to say it. And I'm going to keep on saying it until you finally get it through your thick head. I don't want you in my life! I don't want you in my house! I want you gone!"

"I'm happy for you. I'm glad you gettin' such a kick outta this. You keep on, Bitch!"

"Here we go," I say smartly. "Threats, Eric? We can't talk about this like grown people? You gotta come back with threats?"

"Check yo' fuckin' mouth, Ruth! You know better than to piss me off! You know better, but I know you upset 'cause I've been gone some days and yeah, I've been fuckin' 'round. You know I have. Damn right I have!"

"I know you have. I'm not dumb."

"No, you might not be dumb, but you sure as hell can't fuck worth a damn!"

"Thank you."

"If you could, I wouldn't have to step out. I wouldn't have to get satisfaction from those so-called "hos" as you put it."

"Like I care where you get your satisfaction. I'm through being the fool, Eric. I'm through with watching my husband waltz in and out like he's a single man, fucking everything remotely female and I'm tired of letting you bring your sorry ass home when your little girlfriends discover how much of a loser you really are. I'm tired of being fucked by you and I'm tired of you putting your hands on me. Now get your shit and get out!" I yell, picking up the dirty shirt he's left on the floor, throwing it at him.

"I said," Eric throws it back, "I ain't goin' no damn where, Bitch! Now you back the fuck off before I...!"

"Before you what...Eric?" Like I don't already know. In the pit of my stomach I know what he's capable of, but I've got to finish this. It's too late to change my mind now. I've said too much and he's been pushed too far. Even if I were to say I'm sorry, it wouldn't be enough. So, why bother?

"Don't go there, Ruth," he threatens. "Yo' black ass 'bout to cross the line, Bitch! Yo' black ass 'bout to get yo' ass whooped!" That's it. That's my warning, my out. All I have to do is take it and back down like I've done so many times before. But heeding these warnings is also the reason I've been married to this fool all these years. Of course, by not backing off, I'm looking fate dead in his angry green eyes and accepting whatever consequence he hands me.

"I'll tell you what; you don't even have to pack." I hurry into the bedroom and pull a piece of luggage from underneath the bed. "I'll do it for you, Eric. That make it easier for you? I'll pack all of your shit for you!" I grab his clothes hanging in the closet and begin throwing them in the suitcase.

"Ruth! Leave my shit alone! Ruth..." Eric grabs the suitcase from the bed and throws it into the wall just missing my head.

"You will get out of my house, Eric! I want you gone!"

Eric's fist comes out of nowhere, fast, like a missile, two quick, hard punches to my face but after that, it's all a blur. His attack is relentless and cuss words melt into kicks that melt into pain that all melt into me. "You fuckin'...Bitch! I don't hear yo' fat ass mouth now...! Who the fuck you goin' put out? Huh Bitch? You puttin' my ass..."

"Eric!" I scream, "Umph! No...umph!"

Stop...Eric...stop...*umph!* Please...Oh God! No..."

"I told you...shut yo' big ass mouth! Ruthie...I told you...yo' black ass always got somethin' to say! Always...who the fuck you puttin' out, Bitch? I don't see yo' ass tryin' to put me out now!"
***

The house is quiet now that he's gone. Sitting on the lid of the toilet I lean over the basin and stare into the crimson water wondering why. "Why'd you have to go there, Ruth?" I ask myself. Why couldn't I have just kept my big mouth shut and let that man do what he's always done? He'd have poured some sweet part of himself all over me for a good 48 hours apologizing again and again for disappearing like that. He'd remind me of how special a woman I am for being so understanding and patient. Everything would be "baby this" and "baby that" until he noticed I'd put on some weight or until I questioned him one more time about where he'd really been and with who. We've danced this dance so long, we've got it down pact. This time, the pain is too excruciating to wrap in an ace bandage, put ice on or take a couple of aspirin, so I drive myself to the hospital and end up spending the night. Eric's broken my nose again, cracked two of my ribs and left me with a bruised kidney to remember him by.

They give me some really potent sedatives, but not potent enough to keep me from dreaming. I dream about Momma. I dream she's young and pretty just like she was before she died. I dream that she's sitting on the edge of my bed smoothing down my hair promising me, *"It's going to be all right, Ruthie. Just you wait a minute. You'll see."* Her smile is better than any medicine and I feel the warmth of her breath against my cheek as she leans down to kiss me. I force open my eyes because with all my heart, hoping it isn't a dream. I want her here so badly that I feel her soft hand on mine. But it isn't Momma. It's Clara, a hospital Counselor. She's an older woman with a pretty face, soft and round, the color of cinnamon. Except for touches of gray around her hairline she looks like a young girl.

"Hello there," she whispers, smiling as tenderly as anyone's smiled at me in ages. "I guess they drugged you up pretty good, huh?"

"Not enough," I mumble through swollen lips.

"Well...I think they're gonna let you leave tomorrow. Anyway, you'll get more rest at home than you would in this old hospital. That's all you need, Dear...a little rest. Do you have a safe place to stay for a while? I can find you a place if..."

"No...thank you."

"Do you want to file charges, Ruth? There's an officer down the hall and I can..."

"No," I whisper.

"I think you should, Dear. In the long run..." I shake my head no. Just give me a big eraser so I can make all this disappear and I'll be fine, I think to myself. Like so many other times, I can't talk to anybody about what's happened between my husband and me, not the police or even sweet Clara. It's a piece of time that doesn't warrant any more attention than it's already been given. Besides, it's not like talking about it will change what's happened. I'm still laying here feeling like a fool. Talking about it won't change that. My body aches, but I'm used to it. It's as much a part of my routine as washing the dishes or brushing my teeth. The physical wounds have always healed quickly. It's the mess inside that doctors, counselors or policemen can't fix. I doubt it can ever be fixed. I expect her to put up more of an argument and I'm thankful that she doesn't.

"If you ever want to talk..."

"No. Thank you."

***

I call the office as soon as I get home to let them know about the terrible car accident I was in and yes I'm fine and no it wasn't my fault and no my car isn't totaled. As a matter of fact, it should be fixed in a few days and oh yeah...I bumped my face on the steering wheel which explains why I look like Apollo Creed after he's gone a few rounds with Rocky but no...I don't have airbags.

There's no excuse for this. I push and push until he pushes back. But don't I always? I know what I'm supposed to do and what I'm not supposed to do. I know which tone in my voice soothes him and which words endear him to me, even temporarily. I know how to smile at him when I don't feel like smiling and even though I can't remember the last time I looked into his eyes, I know how to make him think I'm looking into his soul. I know my place, and when I step out of line, this is the result.

People with healthy ribs tend to take two things for granted, inhaling and exhaling. Hovering over the cup of hot tea, I give in to the steam caressing my bruised and battered face. Then I remember my mother, who believed every ailment known to women could be cured by a cup of hot tea. Headaches, cramps, colds, botched abortions, miscarriages, broken ribs, crushed noses, 14 years of hell with the likes of Eric. Tea doesn't heal. It just feels good going down.

I remember making her a cup of lemon tea the day she died. It was her favorite. She was the kind of woman you wanted to put in a glass jar like preserves, maybe spread a little of her on a slice of warm, buttered toast every now and then. I wonder what she'd say to me now? What would she think of her Baby Ruth who's just gotten her ass kicked for the umpteenth time by that bastard. Not that it matters. What do I care what she'd think of me when she never even thought much of herself? I'm not 13 years old any more and that woman definitely had issues despite what I'd like to believe. Shit, she was about as screwed up as I am and I know for a fact that the apple never really does fall far from the tree. We'd both been so wrong about life. Karen had been guilty of her willingness to settle for any asshole who came into her life out of her fear of not having a man. She put up with so much bullshit to the point that it killed her. My crime is weakness. I've been too weak to fight back, too weak to leave him and too weak to do what I've wanted to do for all these years. Put a bullet through that son-of-a-bitch's head. The tea feels really good going down and I sure miss her.

Two

Eric was my first everything. My first boyfriend, my first kiss, my first lover. He convinced me that I was a woman even before I felt like one. What did I have to offer someone like him? He was 10 years older than me, had his own credit cards, car and an ex-wife. I was 18, barely out of school and my Grandmother's basement. I worked for minimum wage as a Receptionist at a law firm and lived in the ugliest studio apartment on the planet. All my life I'd been too black, too fat and even ugly to boys, but not to him. He liked my wide hips and thought my big breasts were heaven. My dark chocolate skin made his mouth water and reminded him of the homemade frosting his Grandmother used to make. To him, I was a desirable woman who needed a real man around to take care of her. He became my protector and my teacher, my dictator.

"Sometime it take awhile for virgins to like fuckin', Ruthie. But you wait, baby girl. Pretty soon you goin' to like fuckin' much as I do."

I never did. Sex left me feeling nasty and used, while it left him feeling like a superhero. My faith in him in the beginning surpassed understanding. I believed that when he called me "baby", he was really saying, "I love you," and I believed that he meant he was sorry every time he said it. There were times I believed he was sorry even when he didn't say it. Growing up is hard and growing up in a loveless, abusive marriage is harder. The conditioning that takes place over the years replaces a woman's character and becomes her personality. Ducking and dodging cuss words and fists and shoes thrown across the room aimed at your head is second nature, and living on the defense becomes a way of life. I learned never to let my guard down, because when I did, I paid dearly for it. Every utterance from my mouth, glance in his direction, every movement, was open for interpretation that depended on his mood. No meant yes and yes meant "Whatever the fuck you want, Eric. Whatever the fuck you say, Eric." I learned quickly never to raise my voice even to make a point and never to raise my eyes even to plead my case.

Silently I listened to other black women talk about "gettin' into it" with their men.

"If he ever hit me, he better make sure he kill me, 'cause I'm goin' try to beat the hell outta his ass! He might kick my ass, but he got a fight on his hand 'cause ain't no man goin' to get away with hittin' on me! I gotta daddy and he ain't it!"

I wanted so much to be brave like that. I struggled to find that kind of courage inside myself but never could. So what kind of black woman was I anyway? What was wrong with me? I took my ass whoopings like a coward instead of like the strong black woman I was supposed to be, fighting back with angry words and fists of my own, daring this fool to hit me again, knowing wholeheartedly that he wouldn't because he knew better. Not only didn't my man have respect for me, neither did my sisters. And neither did I.

I realized a long time ago that Eric never loved me. After a few months of marriage he stopped saying it and I stopped listening for it. Soon the "I'm sorrys" stopped too. They turned into the "Look what you made me dos." So why would fate put us together? Or was it God? Or both? Or maybe it was neither. Maybe it was me being more like Karen than I ever wanted to be. Maybe I needed a man in my life too, no matter what the cost.
***
Momma was very flirtatious. Growing up, I watched different men come in and out of our lives, one dissolving into another, and each time, I'd hope this one would be *the* one. The

one who loved her, married her, made babies with her because that's what she hoped for. Over the years the ritual she performed every time she was about to tell me she had someone new in her life became all too common. She'd make me a bowl of ice cream and we'd sit down in the kitchen smiling at each other and giggling like sisters. She'd prop her elbows up on the table cradling her lovely face in her hands staring at me while I inhaled that big bowl of ice cream.

"That good, Baby Ruth?" My mouth would be so full of French Vanilla that all I could do was nod. She never ate any because she thought it would make her fat, but she enjoyed watching me finish mine, moaning and licking her lips like she was eating some herself. I loved those moments when it was just the two of us and she was happy. She stared into my eyes and rubbed her hand down my cheek, "Slow down, Baby." She'd laugh. "You don't have to eat so fast, Ruthie. That ice cream ain't goin' nowhere." Karen's southern drawl seemed out of place in Denver, Colorado. As out of place as she did. She'd taken the girl out of the country but there was still plenty of country in the girl.

She'd left Jacksonville, Florida before I was born, following after my father who was in the Air Force at the time. They met in Florida while he was stationed here, but eventually he was transferred to Colorado. By the time she found out she was pregnant with me, he'd been long gone. Needless to say, Grandmother Johnson, Karen's mother, was not happy about the situation. The Set Aside, Sanctified, Holified Servant of the Lord, Holy Ghost filled woman was so ashamed of her sinful daughter that she literally told Karen to get out. Momma was only 16 at the time. Karen had managed to save up some money from a part-time job and decided to leave Florida on a bus headed for Colorado to find the man she loved. When she did find him, it broke her heart. He was married and had two perfectly good kids of his own, so he didn't have any use for either one of us I suppose. She didn't have enough money to get home, but it didn't matter because I don't think Grandmother Johnson would've let her come home anyway. She ended up settling in Denver, and that's where I was born.

"You know what?" she'd ask as I guzzled down my ice cream. "Momma's met somebody, Ruthie. Somebody nice." She always thought they were nice, and in the beginning, I guess they always were.

"His name's Walter."

"His name's Glen."

"His name's Bruce."

"His name's Cedric."

Walter turned out to be a junkie, stealing what little we had and taking the last of her money to buy whatever it was he was shooting up in his arm. Glen turned out to be married and left Momma to go home to his wife each and every time the woman summoned him back. Eventually, he never came back, so I assumed Mrs. Glen had decided to let him stay. Bruce couldn't keep a job and decided to sit at home, drink all day long and let Karen be the family breadwinner. One day, she happened to mention that she had a problem with this little arrangement and he threw a full can of beer at her, and slapped her upside the head a couple of times just in case she didn't get the message. He left, but came back, though. Had to. How many women do you know are going to put up with a sorry bastard like that? Not many. He came back quite a few times before she finally got tired of the drama and called it quits. Then there was Cedric. Good old Cedric. Out of all of them, he seemed to have had the most potential. He had a good job, didn't do drugs except to smoke a little reefer every now and then. Sometimes I even liked him. It wasn't perfect. I mean, sometimes they argued. He'd hit her, but she'd hit back because she swore she'd never let another man treat her like Bruce did and get away with it. Sometimes they'd fight right in front of me and once, when I tried coming to her rescue, they both yelled at me, to "Get back in that goddamned room and shut the motha' fuckin' door!" So I did. They always made up, though. And when they did, peace reigned in the valley, or in this case, our apartment on the Five Points, and we were the epitome of the All American Family on public assistance. Cedric would be in such a good mood he'd take us to the amusement park or out to eat and Momma hugged, squeezed and kissed all over him and me too until the next time. When she told him she was pregnant, they didn't fight, but he gave her an ultimatum, "Get rid of it, Karen! I don't want no more fuckin' kids and if you don't do something about it...I'm gone!" Rather than lose him, she did something about it but she was the one gone.

She looked tired when she came home from her doctor's appointment that day and all she wanted was to rest. I made her some hot lemon tea and sat next to her while she cradled the cup in both hands and sipped on the tea slowly, letting it work its magic. She didn't say much and I didn't learn the truth about that doctor's visit until much later. Anyway, she wanted to take a little nap before dinner, but she never woke up again. I went in to check on her a few hours later. Her rich, golden skin was cold and gray and I remember staring at her a long time before trying to wake her. The body doesn't look like itself without the soul. Her dress and bed were drenched in blood and I heard a scream but I've never really been certain whether it came from me or if it was the sound of my world crashing down around me. It wasn't the sight of all that blood that terrified me, but what scared me most was knowing that she was gone forever, and I was completely alone. I'll never forget that day as long as I live.

The only relative I had left was Grandmother Johnson and I was sent back to Florida to live with her. I'd never so much as laid eyes on the woman and was sorry when I did. She despised my ass simply for being because I was the result of her daughter's sinful behavior and since Karen was gone it was my right to inherit the curse of her crime. Besides, it was only a matter of time before my true colors came through and everybody would see I was a slut just like my momma. I'd end up pregnant like she did and be left to my own devices raising my 10 kids alone and on welfare until I died of some "nasty woman's" disease. God have mercy on my filthy soul. I lived with her evil glares and harsh words until I graduated high school. Two days later I had a full time job and two weeks after that, I moved out.

***

The day after the beating is always worse than the beating itself. The adrenaline is gone; the drugs have worn off; and the pain refuses to let you forget what happened despite your best efforts to do just that. Eric never tried to hide the hate he feels for me. I've seen it in his eyes, tasted it in his venomous tongue and absorbed the sting of his words through my pores. With everything he's done to me, I think the words have cut the deepest. They've been branded into my soul because they've always been his most accessible weapons and the hardest for me to dodge. He's kicked me hard enough to leave an imprint of his shoe on my thigh and called me "stupid". He's busted my lip a hundred times and called me a "lousy bitch" (as opposed to a good bitch?). He's broken all of my fingers at least once and called me a "good for nothing piece of shit". The bruises go away. The bones mend and the swelling eventually goes down. But the words linger, piling up inside me like garbage, and when he's not around to pile on some more, I can usually regurgitate them to remind myself of who I really am. A "stupid, lousy bitch who's a good for nothing piece of shit". That pretty much explains how I feel right now.

Three

I guess if I've got a best friend, Bernie's it. We work together at the law firm and ever since I first laid eyes on that woman I knew what I wanted to be when I grew up. Her. She's comfortable with who she is and as proud as a peacock. Her vibrant personality is reflected in her style of dress rich with bright yellows, daring reds, and hideous fuchsias. But on her it works. She's got nails a mile long that have been painted every color known to man and even some colors man didn't know existed. But on her it looks good. What you see is what you get with Bernie Watson. If you ever want her opinion all you have to do is ask but she's the type that will volunteer it anyway, whether you want it or not. She'd heard about my "accident" and came right over to check on me. Bless her heart. Bernie doesn't pull any punches, which most of the time is cool. This isn't one of those times.

"A car wreck, huh?" I could tell from the look on her face that she knew I was lying the moment she saw me.

"Yeah, but I'm okay."

"I don't know why the hell you put up with his ass this long, Ruth." Bernie had taken the liberty of warming me up a bowl of chicken noodle soup. "Is he gone?"

"Yes," I said, staring down at my soup.

"For good this time?"

"I hope it's for good."

"Well...then, why don't you make sure it is?" Bernie question is laced with sarcasm.

"I know, Bernie. I know...I should."

"He ain't a whole fool. At least he didn't sleep here. If a man got any sense at all he ain't going to sleep in the same house with the woman he just beat on. Shiiiit. I'm from the old school and I know what I would've done. I'd have poured some hot grits on his nuts. I'd have waited for that son-of-a-bitch to close his eyes and poured them scalding grits right there on his dick. That's what you should've done a long time ago."

"Right, and he'd have killed me before the water even finished boiling."

"He wouldn't have killed you, Baby."

"You don't know that, Bernie. But I do. I know he would've killed me. At least tried to."

"No," she smiles, "because he'd have been too busy trying to cool off them boiling nuts, and I guarantee you he wouldn't have put his hands on you again. I know that for a fact." Okay, so the idea of Eric's balls boiling did bring a slight smile to my face. Even a little one. "So what are you going to do now, Ruth?"

The only answer I've got is to shrug my shoulders and whisper a weak, "I don't know."

"I know you've been living with this for a long time, Honey. I kept hoping you would talk to me about it, but..."

"I couldn't, Bernie. I really didn't know how to talk about it."

"You open up your mouth and say, 'My man's beating on me. I need your help.' Even if you don't want to talk to me, you can talk to a counselor or somebody."

"No. Right now I just want to... Now's not a good time. You know what I mean? It's hard to talk about something like this. Especially now."

"I understand. But when you're ready, you know I'm here."

"I know and thank you."

"Not a problem, Baby. Now, let's get down to real reason I came by here. Did this 'accident' finally bring you to the good sense, I know God gave you, and make you realize it's time for you to take control of your own life now, Ruth? Eric's been doing it long enough and I say you got to draw the line someplace, sometime. Might as well be here and now."

"Bernie, I'm not in the mood for a lecture...please."

"Please nothing. Of course you're going to get a lecture. Why else do you think I brought my ass all the way over here?"

"To comfort and console me?"

"Hell naw! To knock some sense into your head."

"Eric already did that."

"No, Eric knocked all the sense out of your head. That's obvious. Ain't no man got a right to put his hands on you, Ruth. I don't care who he is."

"I know, Bernie."

"You know?" Bernie curls up the corners of her mouth like she always does when she thinks someone's said something stupid. "How many years he been beating on you, Ruth?"

"Bernie..."

"When was the first time? Before you married him? After?" Of course I can't answer that. I've worked so hard to hide the bruises over the years and the last thing I want to hear is the truth of what she's about to tell me. "I got news for you, Baby. I ain't blind. We've been working together...how long? And in all those years, you really think I didn't notice. Hell, everybody noticed."

Hearing that hurt almost as bad as the bruises on my body. Of course everybody knows. How stupid am I to think a little makeup can cover up a black eye or a busted lip? How many times can I explain away ace bandages? How many damn accidents can a woman have in one lifetime, in one year...one month...one week? I've been an idiot for so damn long the only person who thinks I'm intelligent is me. What a fucking joke. "I...I guess I just... I don't know what I'm going to do. I haven't thought much about it."

"Well, we're going to think about it now together," Bernie moved her chair closer to mine and put her arm around my shoulder. "I don't know how long you've been putting up with this mess but you've got to end it and you've got to end it right now,

Ruth. You're the one that's got to decide...enough. No more. I've seen this before. Women getting themselves into relationships with men beating them and treating them like shit, excusing these sorry ass motha' fucka's because they ain't man enough to *not* hit a woman."

"I started it this time, Bernie. I should've kept my mouth shut, and..."

"And nothing. I don't care what you said, Ruth. He had no right to do this to you, but I do blame you for one thing, Baby, and it's that you stayed with his sorry ass all these years. All you had to do was leave him, walk away...divorce him."

"I tried." Tears roll down my cheeks into my soup. "Sometimes I...I tried, Bernie. He'd come after me. You don't know how many times I left." Not enough. Not nearly enough times, and never far enough, never fast enough.

"Well, he ain't coming after you this time. Tomorrow, me and you...we're going to get you a restraining order. Won't take long. His ass come back up in here, call the cops and they'll take his ass to jail. Which is where he needs to be. You file charges?"

I shake my head, "I'm tired of this...of him. I don't want to go through any police reports, or trials..."

Bernie smiled, "I can understand that, Baby. But how else is he going to know he can't get away with this?"

"He did get away with it, Bernie! He's always gotten away with it!"

"Then stop him! File charges, Ruth."

"What the hell for? Look at me," I cried. "So he goes to jail a few months? A few years? It won't fix what he's broken, Bernie! It won't fix me. I'll heal on the outside, I always do. But inside, I'm all torn up and nothing or no one can fix that."

"You can, Baby."

"I don't know how. And don't tell me that telling a room full of strangers in some courtroom about him whooping my ass all these years is going to help me. I don't want to talk about it. Can't you understand that? I don't want to talk to a judge, to you, to some counselor..."

"You need to talk about it, Ruth. You think by ignoring it

you can make it go away? Come on, Girl. Be real. It's not going to disappear because you don't want to talk about it. That motha' fucka' beat on you. You can't close your eyes and pretend it didn't happen. You're sitting here talking about being broken on the inside; well you're the one that let that happen, Ruth."

"I already know this!"

"Stop telling me what you know and do something about it, dammit! Stop feeling sorry for yourself all the time and stop being the victim! It's time to stand up for yourself!"

"I did that! I wanted his ass gone so I told him to leave. This is what he left me with, Bernie!" I point to my swollen face. "I am the fuckin' victim!" For the first time since I've known her, Bernie is speechless for more than 30 seconds and is so uncomfortable about it I almost feel sorry for her. "I did the right thing this time, Bernie. I told him to get out. I told him to go. This is what he did to me. The same thing he's done all these years when I did the wrong thing. Which was whatever...whatever I could do to keep him from treating me like this. I finally stood up to him this time and he still did it."

Bernie stares at me at a loss for answers and full of questions, I'm sure. She slowly stirs my soup because it's the only response she has to give me. I can read it on her face. The struggle going on inside her to try and understand all this. But that's impossible for her to do. "Eat your soup, Baby."

"I don't want it."

"I don't give a damn. I made it, so you eat it."

"I'm not hungry."

Bernie glares at me. "Girl, if you don't eat that damn soup!"

"I don't want the damn soup, Bernie!"

"Ruth! You need to eat something. Now eat the damn soup!"

"And if I don't? What are you going to do?" I ask defiantly, looking for another fight even if it has to be with my best friend over something as silly as soup. Maybe she'll finish what he started and beat my ass into a coma. But Bernie's better at this game than I am and she counters with the best weapon she has in her arsenal.

"Then, I'll talk your ass to death, Ruth. I'll stay here all night long talking nonstop telling you everything you don't want to hear. I even talk in my sleep, Girlfriend. I will talk and talk and talk until I lose my voice and you lose your hearing. Now eat the damn soup!" Her argument wins this battle. So reluctantly, I eat the damn soup.

***

The worse thing about throwing a pity party for yourself is that no one you invite ever shows up, not even God.

Four

I feel him watching me, and his energy is so strong, it stirs my dreams and wakes me up. Eric's standing in the doorway of the bedroom. I don't know how long he's been there but I'm not surprised. He doesn't say a word for a long time. Just stares at me. I can't bring myself to look back at him because I know what's in his eyes. Contempt. Never regret, not any more, not in years. The look in his eyes says, *"You did it again, Ruthie. Look what you made me do."* I can't bear to see that.

Eric sits on the side of the bed and sighs deeply. He looks disheveled like he hasn't slept, then inhales on his cigarette, letting the smoke escape through his nostrils. I know this ritual well. He's contemplating what he's going to say to me, because of course he can't let this whole thing go and not say something. I've had my ass whooped, now I need to understand why he had to do what he obviously felt he had to do so I'll learn from my mistake and not repeat it.

"I'm tired, Ruthie. I can't keep goin' on like this."

So stop it, I want to say. But I don't. I never say anything.

"This shit's gettin' old. Hell...we gettin' old. Been goin' at this too damned long."

Yes. We have, I want to say. But I don't.

"I told you, back off. Didn't I?" He stares at me. "Didn't I?"

"Yes, Eric."

Eric rolls his eyes. "Smart ass mouth you got...," he mumbles then takes another drag on his cigarette. "We been together...how long? Damn near 15 years, and..."

And that's way too long. I want to say. But I don't.

"Yeah, I got me somebody. You know that. Hell, where you think I am when I ain't home? I got me another woman and that's where I want to be. Not here. Not witchu."

So go, I want to say, but...

"You know...I'm cool 'til you start trippin'. We been together long enough for you to know me by now, Ruthie. You know me, goddamn it! You know how I get. So why you fuck with me? So you can end up lookin' like this? Sittin' here lookin' like shit. I'm a grown ass man. Don't nobody talk to me like that. Nobody. Me and you...we ain't doin' nothin' up in here anyway and I do what I got to do. I come and go when I please 'cause you ain't givin' me shit to make me want to be home."

I'm sorry, I want to say, but...

"I got needs, Ruthie and if a man don't get what he need at home he goin' to get it someplace else. She know how to treat a man like a man. You never did. Never did. Feel like I'm raisin' somebody's damn kid. Why you think I never wanted no kids witchu? Had my hands full with yo' sorry ass. You hear what I'm sayin'?"

I always do, I want to say, but...don't.

"You right 'bout one thing. I do want out. I been wantin' out, but I didn't want to..."

Hurt me like that? I want to ask, but I don't.

"You want to end this? So do I. But you didn't have to come at me with attitude, Ruthie. You didn't have to piss me off like that. All this mess could've been avoided. I don't know how many times I told you 'bout that attitude you got."

Too many, I want to...say.

"Shit, this marriage been over, Ruth. It's been over for some years now. We both know that. But how you goin' tell me to get out of my own house? Who the fuck made yo' ass king of this motha' fuckin' castle? This is as much my shit as it is yours. My house, my furniture..."

My prison, I want to say.

"But...it ain't worth it. Not anymore." Eric reaches over to the nightstand next to me and puts out his cigarette. He brushes up against me and that's when I realize I'm crying. He's close enough to kiss and I turn my head away from him. Eric speaks softly into my ear, "You want me gone, Ruthie? I'm outta here, 'cause ain't shit up in this house worth a damn to me anymore." He kisses my cheek.

Eric packs the suitcase I'd tried packing for him the other night. Is he really leaving? Or is this another one of his ploys to get me to perform according to his script? What am I supposed to do? Should I tell him how sorry I am and ask him not to leave me? Because that's what he's doing. He's leaving me. While watching him pack, it feels as if my heart is slowly sinking down into my stomach. What's this I'm feeling? Remorse? No. Relief? Is that what this is? I'm relieved he's leaving? Probably. Yes. Definitely. *You want to go? Then go, you son-of-a-bitch! Get the hell out of my life! And don't ever come back!* Of course I never open my mouth to say any of this, just sit motionless on the bed avoiding his glaring eyes. Praying this is the last time I'll ever have to see him. I'm afraid his leaving isn't real and I'm afraid it is. He's never packed before. He's never left before. I've always been the one contemplating escape. Not him. He finishes quickly and stands inside the bedroom door suitcase in hand, "It wasn't always bad, Baby. I mean that."

It was worse, I want to say, but...I don't.

Eric closes the door behind him but not before leaving the key on the nightstand. I hurry out of bed to lock the door behind him.

***

It's not like I want to die, but I'm tired of living. Life hovers over my head like a big, black cloud and this storm is getting old. In all, I count 30 pills and I've lined them up in two perfect rows of 15. I can't come up with one good reason not to do this. No babies depending on me and no family member will miss me. Eric used to say, *"Ruth! Your black ass ain't shit without me!"* And I think he must've been right because I've never been able to find a purpose for myself. Right now, I'd do anything for just a little piece of purpose. I need a reason for being or else I shouldn't be here. Eric's been my purpose. I've been his wife, his maid, his cook, his second income. I've been the object of his frustration. Whenever he needed a place to plant his anger, he had me and if that's all I've been good for then what the hell am I hanging on to?

Slap! "Where's my food, Bitch?" *Slap! Slap!* "Shut the fuck up!" I cry and I cry because it all hurts all the time and I just want it to stop. *Take the pills, Ruth. Take the pills, Girl.* Just one purpose, one reason for me being on the planet. Damn! Just one reason not to swallow 30 fucking pills and disappear without a legacy, or something...anything to show the world that I ever was. God! Isn't there something? Anything? Think, Ruth. Think. Think. "Nothing. Not one fucking thing! Not one goddamned..." A dining room chair flies across the room and crashes into my glass coffee table, shattering it into a million pieces. Had I thrown it? The pain cuts into my rib cage like a knife and I collapse on the floor, "Oh God! Oh God! What the... I need... I can't...do this! I can't do this anymore!"

There has to be more to me than this. Didn't I ever dream of being...doing something besides worrying about Eric, pleasing Eric, ducking from Eric, crying over Eric, or crying because of Eric? Was there ever a morning when Eric wasn't the first thing on my mind when I opened my eyes or the last thing on my mind when I closed them to sleep? All these years have I been completely driven by this man to the point that I don't have the fuel or the desire to drive my damn self?

There's a place in the bottom of your soul that's dark and far away from anything you can ever know. And when there's no other place to go, it becomes a closet to hide in. In this place it's all right to feel small and insignificant and blend into the blackness. I've come here quite a few times so I know it well. All my life I've had choices, but for whatever reason, I've perfected the art of fucking up and no matter how hard I try, I can't help but make fucked up choices. Have I simply been too hasty? Maybe naive? I can go left or right, backwards or forwards, up or down. But in this moment, I simply choose to stand still.

It's just that all these years he's been my excuse for not being the woman I wanted to be. For not being happy, for not feeling safe, or being thin, or successful, or brave, or fun, or pretty, for not knowing love. I hate him because everything I could've been he's taken from me and all he's left behind is my big messy ass curled up on this floor using every ounce of brain power I've got left to wish myself away. I hate me because I let him. That's important and I can't ever forget that I gave Eric permission to treat me like shit by ever making it clear that treating me like shit was totally unacceptable.

The phone rings but I don't answer it. It's probably Bernie. I don't clean up the glass, or pick up the chair. I lay here struggling to keep everything perfectly still...my body, my thoughts, my memories.

Hours pass before an invisible force lifts me up off that floor because I don't have the strength to do it myself. I don't have the strength to do anything, not even commit suicide. I take a painkiller, just one, and put the rest of the pills back into the bottle. Then I take my shower and climb into bed. In the morning I'll start again and try to make it through one more day.

Five

According to this piece of paper, Eric's got to stay at least 1000 feet from me at all times. Or else. Or else, I call the police and they come to my rescue. Right? Okay. If it's that easy why didn't I think of doing this before? Why'd I have to wait for Bernie's boss to call in some favors to get this restraining order when I could've gotten one myself years ago? Because I know for a fact that if Eric wants to come after me again, this piece of paper isn't going to stop him. That's why. The only thing I've got going for me now is the fact that he's got another woman in his life. He's not interested in coming home because some petite little hoochie is rocking his world in a way I never could. Bernie calls this my insurance policy. My "just in case he starts tripping again" policy. I know it's a piece of paper. That's all.

"Your life would've been a whole lot easier if you'd done this years ago, Ruth."

"I should have done a lot of things years ago, Bernie."

"You were young, and you didn't know better." she shrugs.

"I haven't been young in years. So, what kind of excuse is that?"

"Ruth."

"Bernie, you know I'm right. I've been an idiot when it's come to Eric, but I don't expect you to understand that."

"Me either, but...try me."

"If I told you that Eric is all I had. That there were times I believed he did care for me so much that I was convinced he hit me for my own good. That I believed God would answer my prayer and make him the man I dreamed he'd be was enough to keep me there, would any of that make sense to you?" Bernie stares at me like I've lost my mind. She's been doing that a lot lately.

"You're right. I can't relate."

"Of course not, which is cool. I'm glad you can't. I wish I couldn't. But at the time it made sense. All of it."

"When did it stop making sense?"

"Honestly? I'm not so sure it still doesn't. He's not perfect but then neither am I. It takes two people to make a marriage and it takes the same two to mess one up. I'm not blameless in all this, Bernie. I know how he is and I'm not going to lie. Sometimes I pushed way too hard." There she goes again, curling up that lip. "But this time I had to ask myself what's worse? Living like this with Eric or living some other way without him."

"Took you this long to ask yourself that question?"

"I guess so. I used to be able to excuse it. All of it— the cheating the fighting. I used to blame myself for not being the woman he needed. I don't know. How do you make sense of something senseless? Sometimes the answers are as clear as day and other times I wonder what the hell have I been thinking? That's the hardest part. Trying to justify my actions. Never mind his."

"Maybe none of it can be justified, Ruth. Maybe there's not an answer for everything."

"He'd hit me, then beg me to forgive him, and for the longest time I did. And he'd be sweet to me for days, sometimes weeks. I think that after awhile, I grew accustomed to that pattern. It became the norm for us. Until I realized that other couples weren't living like that. Isn't that crazy? I actually used to think everybody else was living like we were. When I found out different, it pissed me off and I knew he was playing me for a fool, and that's what I've been all these years. A fool."

"You were young, Ruth, and Eric took advantage of you.

Hell! He practically raised you."

"I had to believe in him because the truth was ugly. Too ugly. I had no friends. No family. He was it, Bernie. How could I face the fact that the only person in my world of any significance hated me? I didn't have anything else. All I could do was hope that this time he really meant he was sorry and I couldn't face the truth about him until I faced the truth about myself."

"Which is?"

"It's my own damn fault, Bernie. All of it. I can't blame Eric or anybody else. I did this."

"That's bullshit."

"Is it?"

"You know better than that, Ruth."

"No Bernie. I'm not sure I do."

"But what difference would it make? Whether or not it was his fault, or yours, why stay? He was wrong for what he did, Ruth, and you were wrong for staying. Maybe you just didn't know how to leave, but...I'll never understand it."

"He's my husband."

"And he beats your ass."

"I needed him and he would change or I'd change. Hell, somebody would change. After all this time, we're still the same people dealing with the same shit. The last time I left him was seven years ago. When he found me, I was staying in a motel across town. I was leaving him, Bernie. I really was. It was right after my miscarriage. My baby would be here right now if it hadn't been for him. A month after I found out I was pregnant I found out he was having an affair and I confronted him about it. What the hell did I do that for? I lost my baby and left him and had no intention of ever going back to that man. He'd followed me from my job one day and dragged me home by my hair. He kept me up all night long."

"Doing what?"

"Teaching me a lesson. As long as I live, I'll never forget that night." Images have a way of being too clear sometimes. Images of him spitting in my face and daring me to wipe it off. Images of Eric pulling off his belt slapping it against my legs, carving out welts and bruises. Listening to him grunt out orgasms while he pounded inside my behind. When he was finished, I showered and he gently dried me off, helped me on with my nightgown, tucked me into bed and kissed me goodnight. *"Don't make me have to do this again, Ruthie. You know I don't like actin' like this."*

"I had to learn my place once and for all and I did, and I didn't leave again. I learned how not to make waves. I kept my mouth shut and I let him do whatever he wanted to do. I kept his clothes cleaned, food on the table whenever his ass was home, and he could spend his quality time with all the women he wanted. What the hell would a restraining order do for me? What's it going to do for me now? I know if he wanted to come back here again, he could. This...," I wave the paper in the air, "how's this going to stop him?"

"So why'd I go through the trouble of getting it if it doesn't mean shit, Ruth?"

"I'm sorry, Bernie. It's not that I don't appreciate it, because I do."

"But you think it's a worthless piece of paper."

"It's too easy. Things have never been that easy with Eric."

"It'll help. If he wants to act a fool."

"By the time the cops get here, Eric's got plenty of time to act plenty of fool."

I've got more questions about my life than answers. Before he moved out, Eric said all our time together hadn't been bad. Not all of it was. But those brief moments that come to mind quickly dissolve in the mix of all the arguments, battles and lies and ultimately don't mean shit.

***

My phone's been ringing off the hook all day and most of the night. I know it's him and I know he's pissed.

"Hello?" I finally answer.

"What the hell is this shit, Ruth?"

"Eric...you're not supposed to be calling here."

"Bitch! That's still my motha' fuckin' house and my

motha' fuckin' phone and I'll call when I damn well..."

"You're violating the restraining order by calling me. You're..."

"You know what? I don't give a shit about yo' damn restrainin' order, Ruth! But I'm goin' to tell you right now, this don't mean shit to me! And it can't stop me from puttin' my foot up yo' black ass either! Why you gotta be fuckin' with a brotha all the damn time?"

"You come near me again and..."

"And what? What the fuck you goin' do, Ruthie? Huh? Whatchu think yo' sorry ass goin' do to me?"

"I'll call the police," I whisper so quietly I hardly hear myself.

"What? Whatchu say?"

"I said...I'll call the police, Eric. If you come near me...I'll call the police and you'll go to jail."

"Before or after I kick yo' ass, Ruthie?" *Yeah, Ruthie.* "I already told you I don't want to be bothered with you anymore. You didn't need to get no restrainin' order 'cause I'm through with your fat ass anyway. I'm the one that left, Girl. I'm the one that got tired of you a long time ago, and now...I'm through. I'm comin' by tomorrow to get the rest of my shit."

"Good."

"Yeah...it's all good. You make sure you ain't there." He hangs up.

He picked up the rest of his things the next day while I was at work and I've taken Bernie's advice, changed all the locks, my phone number and put the gun she gave me in the drawer of my nightstand. I can't ever see myself using it, but it seems to make her feel better knowing it's there.

***

Peace is quiet and addictive. Lord knows it doesn't get much better than this. Most of the time I don't turn on anything, the television, the stereo, the lights. I've been indulging myself lately, settling into a calm that's not natural for me. I know I won't give this up ever again. Not without a fight anyway. I'm sitting here cradling my tea, so immersed in this vibe that the rest of the world seems far enough away not to be an issue anymore. How can anybody survive without this? I have to wonder how I ever did. Even when he was gone, the anticipation of him was enough to keep me in hell and I couldn't enjoy being alone. I remember not being able to sit still, checking the refrigerator to make sure it had everything in it he'd want. I'd check and double-check on his laundry, making sure it was folded and put away the way he liked. My mind was constantly filled with the challenge of keeping everything perfect and not giving him a reason to fuss. There was no peace or quiet in that. Bernie's always telling me to relax and I'm learning how to do just that. Sometimes it's not easy, though. I've become conditioned over the years to always be prepared for a fight, and sometimes I still expect him to come through that door mad as hell and ready to wage all out war on my ass. What surprises me most is that he hasn't. Whoever she is, she's doing one hell of a job taking care of that man and she's got him so wrapped up in her that he's not interested in me. I wish I could bottle peace and quiet. I'd spray a little on my wrists, behind my knees, between my breasts, like perfume, and inhale the sweet aroma of the undramatic.

***

I turn off my computer and look up just in time to see Bernie making her way over to my cubicle for her customary end of the day visit. She pretends it's a social call but I know what she's up to. What she really wants to do is look into my eyes and try to read my mind. And I know what she's wondering. "Is this fool still thinking about killing herself?" But what she actually says is, "What's up tonight, Girlfriend?"

I smile, "After the day I've had, nothing. I'm going home, sit in my favorite chair, sip on some wine and listen to Anita Baker sing all that crazy shit about lovin' and apologizin' and baby this, baby that. You know how she is."

"That sistah know a thing or two about love."

"She thinks she does. I'm not convinced, but she sounds good."

"I've got a better idea. Let's go to Jim's Place and get a drink. C'mon, it's ladies' night. Two for one. Get us a big ol' mess of hot wings. You don't even have to change clothes."

"No thanks, Bernie. You know I'm not into clubbing. Besides, I'm on a diet and hot wings aren't on the menu. I wouldn't be very good company anyway."

"Since when have you ever been good company? You ever heard me accuse you of being good..." Bernie looks around the room and says loud enough for anybody to hear, "Anybody around here ever hear me say Ruth Ashton was good company?" Thank goodness everybody was gone for the day. "That ain't never stopped me from hanging out with your boring ass. So let's go."

"You go and have enough fun for both of us. I'm really tired."

"Oh, Girl...fun is all I know how to have, but you wait. By the time I'm through with you, you're going to know how to have a good time for your damn self."

"Reading, now that's a good time for me. You ought to try it. A good book, a quiet evening..."

"Some warm milk and crackers, then a nap. Sounds thrilling, Dear." Bernie's ulterior motives can't help but surface. She just wants me out so she can keep an eye on me and make sure I don't slit my wrists. "Seriously, Baby...you all right? You taking care of yourself?"

"Yeah, I'm okay. Really. I'm just working on getting myself together. It's not easy you know. I've got a lot of baggage," I laugh, "and it weighs a ton sometimes."

"Sure it does and it can take awhile to unpack all that shit and put it away. But you be patient with yourself. You've been through a lot."

"I spend a lot of time crying, but it feels good. Like I'm purging myself. Let's see," I count on my fingers, "anger...guilt...shame...confusion...lack of both self-esteem and confidence... Did I forget anything?"

"No, I think you got all of them." Bernie smiles.

"Well, I don't want them. But they've been mine for so long it's hard to let go."

"Bernie shakes her head, "No, it ain't hard. You got a bad habit of holding on to them, but that's all it is. A bad habit. No woman in her right mind wants to hold on to no mess like that."

"Well there you go. Who said I was in my right mind?"

"Me. Ruth, believe it or not you are more in your right mind now than you've been since I've known you."

"I'm trying," I say smiling. "A lot of prayer, some good books, no drama. It's all I need right now."

"You just promise me one thing."

"Anything."

"When you're finished mending those wounds and that broken spirit of yours, we're going to get together and go to Jim's Place for some Margaritas and hot wings."

"Definitely, Girl."

"Your treat?"

"Absolutely. I owe you."

"No, Ruth. You owe yourself."

Six

The Duval County Courthouse. The place where Eric and I were married and the tomb that's imprisoned my joy for all these years when I condemned myself with those two little words, "I do." Today I'm here to get back what he tricked me out of when I was that naive, 18 year old girl. Freedom.

Sheila, Eric's new love interest is in attendance, dressed to the hilt for the occasion. Go on girl with yo' bad self! I think to myself. She's wearing a red leather skirt and a white blouse with a ruffled collar and cuffs. She accessorizes the ensemble with red pantyhose, red pumps with three inch high heels and a gold-plated chain belt hanging loosely around her petite waist. Her hair is molded into a mound of loops, curls and waves that add at least a foot to her short stature. A silver front tooth completes her fashion statement.

The girl looks young enough to be his daughter. My guess is she's maybe 20 years old. She's an attractive young woman, and for the life of me I can't figure out what she sees in his old ass. For that matter, what did I ever see in him? A woman could ponder that question for an eternity and never come up with an answer that makes sense. She's the one he was seeing when we split up. Bringing her to his divorce is rather tacky in my opinion, but then it really isn't any of my business. I'm just glad he showed up. Eric and Sheila do a lot of whispering while we wait for the judge to call on us, whispering, giggling and looking a lot in my direction.

"That her, Eric?"

"Yeah, Baby. That's her."

"Damn! She is big. Whatchu do with a big woman like that?"

"Shiiit! I made sure I got on top. " There he goes again. Reminding me of how insignificant my feelings are in his little world, while they snicker like children at my expense. But I don't care, because this day belongs to me.

It's been months since I've seen him and I'm not sure what to feel. My husband is sitting across from me with his woman at our divorce and very soon my marriage to him will be over. As if it never happened? Hardly. Remnants of him will always be part of me. I can't wash away the scent of my past with this man no matter how hard I try, and I've tried. The best I can hope for is that time will gradually fade the pungent order of my marriage and soon the memories will become so faint I'll hardly remember his name. I'm the one who filed for this divorce but sometimes I still feel as if I'm spiraling down out of control. Like everybody's pulling on the strings but me, because I'm the puppet. Bernie's the one who convinced me to get that restraining order against Eric and she's the one who talked me into going through with this.

"I know you don't plan on staying married to that fool for the rest of your life, Ruth."

"No, Bernie. But I've got to get my head together before I..."

"Divorcing Eric doesn't have a damn thing to do with your head, Girlfriend. You wanted him gone, now do the right thing and get rid of him." So I filed because I didn't want to hear her mouth and because it made sense. Of course it did. I wanted him gone and this time, unlike all those other times, I had to follow through to the end severing the ties for the sake of my sanity.

I'm seeing him for what he really is now. A 43-year-old man desperately needing to be important. Sitting next to that child, his arrogance is screaming for her attention, because if she doesn't give it to him, no one else in this room will give a shit about Eric. Lord, how come I couldn't see this before? He's not handsome or even remotely intelligent which is why he has to meet all of his girlfriends on their way home from grade school. No grown woman, no mature woman who knows anything about something will give his sorry ass the time of day, and now I see the truth. The truth of why I grew tired of living with him and the truth of why his pathetic ploys of winning me back or threatening me into submission in the past failed to work anymore. I've grown up.

We've waited nearly an hour for our names to be called to come before the judge. Of course that seems like an eternity, but soon it'll all be over with. Any ties I have to Eric will be severed completely, and as soon as this is over, I'm going to get my maiden name back, because I let him take that too.

I spent all night praying and begging God to make sure Eric showed up here today. "Heavenly Father...I know I brought this shit on myself. I know I made a mistake by marrying this asshole. But I was just a stupid kid and stupid kids make stupid mistakes. Please...please don't make me have to pay for this one forever. Get Eric's dumb ass to the courthouse, Lord. I don't care if it takes thunder, lightning, plagues...please. Just do whatever it takes. I don't mind." And he did, which brings tears to my eyes. A little faith can indeed move mountains.

Standing in front of the judge I wait impatiently while he decrees our divorce final. I don't contest and cross my fingers, close my eyes and pray in silence that he won't either. He doesn't. It's over. My marriage is finally over. "Thanks God." Both the judge and Eric look at me. Oops! I didn't mean to say that out loud.

On my way out of the courtroom, I see Sheila, Eric's girlfriend. She's very young, very pretty and if she wants Eric, the girl's an idiot. I almost feel sorry for her until she glares back at me as if I'm the enemy. I want to tell her that the enemy is the man standing next to her, but I don't. Let the little heffa find out on her own.

"Ruthie..." he says as I pass him to leave. I look him in the eyes hopefully for the last time. He's not my husband anymore and I'm relieved, regretful, remorseful. And by the way, did I say relieved?

"Goodbye, Eric," I say floating out of that courthouse. I gaze out over the river and realize for the first time what a beautiful view it is. "Free at last. Free at last. Thank God Almighty. I'm free at last." Maybe this is a good day to meet Bernie at Jim's Place for those Margarita's and hot wings. To hell with the diet!

Seven

I love mornings, especially now. Daylight creeps through the window blinds and etches shadows and sunshine onto my skin. These days feeling good is becoming a regular occurrence for me because I'm starting over. I sold my house and escaped from those dingy walls saturated with our fighting and that dirty brown carpet that sucked up my blood, sweat and tears like a thirsty sponge. This place is so small I have to go outside to change my mind and I like it that way. There's just enough room for me, which is how it should be. The couple who bought the house are moving down from Georgia to be closer to their family. They'll never know the secrets held inside those walls and I hope they can be happier there than I was. I don't know what secrets are held here in my new little apartment, but a fresh coat of paint and shiny hard wood floors greeted me when I moved in and any secrets lurking around here are really none of my business.

Eric gave me a hard time when I told him I was selling. After all, *"It's my goddamned house too!"*. Yeah, his name was on it, but he never did shit for it. I cleaned it, mowed the lawn, fixed whatever was broken. He just ruled it, which I guess, in his eyes, was a valuable contribution. Instead of buying him, out I promised him half of what I got from the sale minus any repairs or damage we were responsible for. He was cool with that. We bought the house for $36,000.00, sold it for $75,000.00 and I gave him

$10,000. You do the math. By the way, I didn't have to pay for any repairs.

I took my part of the money and bought all new furniture. I found a pretty love seat covered in butter-soft suede the color of sand and an antique ivory arm chair. Both with big, fluffy pillows that cradle me like a baby every time I sit down. Then some dummy at a garage sale practically gave away a beautiful antique oak coffee table. Yeah! I grabbed it. Looks good in here too.

The idea of leaving everything behind, filling my car with some extra panties, tampons, and Oreos and driving off into the sunset has been a fantasy of mine for years. But I don't have the courage for all that. Sure wish I did, though. I'd throw caution to the wind and let the road take me to wherever it wanted me to go and when I got there, I'd stop long enough to pee, then get back in the car and drive off to some other sunset in some other town. Maybe one day I'll take myself up on that dream, but until that time comes, this place will do just fine. I feel renewed here because my new home is filled with my energy and no one else's. It's become my haven and sanctuary. Everything here belongs to me and my spirit resides here. That's cool because my spirit is pleasant and easy to get along with.

***

I discovered this little park across from my apartment building early one morning when sleep disappeared a little too early and my mind was flooded with the dreaded disease of thought. Too much of it, like anything, can be hazardous to your health and I needed to get away from it so I went outside to clear my head and I stumbled onto this place. When I first showed up, the ducks in the pond looked at me like I was crazy. How dare I come out here, sit on their park bench and not bring breakfast. Of course now I know better. Pinky, Stinky, Dinky, and Jamal eat good when I'm here...popcorn, bread, leftover pizza.

I see her all the time and she always says hello when she passes me. She's fast, I think to myself. I don't know how many laps she does around the park before I get here, but she does at least five or six more after I sit down. She looks good too, but of course, I try not to stare. She's in shape. I'm not. And she's thin too. I used to be, but that was so long ago I don't remember how it feels to wear anything smaller than a size 18. I'd say she wears about an eight...maybe even a six. A little too skinny in my opinion. Before I got married, I wore about a size 10, which was perfect for me. I'm 5'3" and with the way I'm built, anything less than a 10 makes me look sick. Like weighing nearly 200 pounds now doesn't make me look bad? Here she comes again.

"Mornin'," she says as she speeds by in her spandex shorts and half top.

"Mornin'," I say back while she's still in ear shot. She's pretty. Was my ass ever that tight? Maybe when I was her age. No. My behind kind of went out in search of adventure long before I hit 25. She looks to be about that age give or take a year.

"Damn ducks," I mumble. "Get away from me. It's all gone." They know when it's time for me to leave. They know if I sit here much longer I'm going to be late for work so they rush me out of here every morning about this time. It's cool having pets.

***

My pet ducks have just finished the last of the corn flakes and it's Saturday morning. Miss Speed Walker comes switching through here as usual at her speed of light pace. "Mornin'," she says, only this time she stops and sits down next to me.

"Mornin," I say back. What in the world does she want?

"I'm May," she says, out of breath.

"Hi...May. I'm Ruth."

"You doin' all right?"

"Yeah. I'm okay. And you?"

She smiles, "I'm feelin' pretty good. I see you sittin' out here jus' 'bout every mornin'."

"Well, I live in that building across the street and I like coming out here before going to work."

"You ever thought 'bout walkin'?"

"Walking? Like you?"

"Yeah." She smiles. "I do it every mornin' and I love it."

"Well I've... I don't think I have that much time. You know, with having to go to work so early."

"What time do you have to be at work?"

"Nine."

"Oh, Girl, you got plenty of time to get a good workout in. I have to be at my job at 8:30, and I work downtown. Where do you work?"

"I work...downtown."

"You got sneakers?"

I look down at my feet. "I've got these."

She looks down at my feet and crinkles her nose, "Those the only ones you got?"

"Well...," I think I'm offended.

"You'll need somethin' with more support than that. There's a discount shoe store on Wells Road called Sports Way Shoes. You can get a good pair of walkin' sneakers there for less than $50."

Who is this woman and what is she talking about? And why do I need sneakers to sit out here and feed some ducks? "Thanks. I'll keep that in mind."

"Good," she says getting up. "I'll meet you here on Monday. But you got to be here at 6:30. Okay?"

Whatever, Lady, "Okay," I say, smiling. She's out of her freakin' mind and rude too. Who says I even want to walk with her skinny ass? I'll just have to find me another park with some new ducks to feed.

***

"Hey, Girl!" She beams. "I see you got you some new sneaks."

"Yeah." Of course I only decided to do this because I've been promising myself I'd do something to get rid of all this weight and it is hard working out alone. Having a partner will be nice and give me the motivation and encouragement I need. That's all.

"How they feel?"

"Pretty good."

"Good. You stretch yet?"

"Sure," I say, lying. Who needs to stretch to walk? I mean, how hard can it be?

"Okay. You ready?"

I know one thing, May's ass is a little too perky for my own good. "Whenever you are."

I hate this. My big ass next to her little ass walking around in circles and Lord knows, after this first lap I'm through. But instead of doing the smart thing and sitting down, I feel compelled to haul my cramping legs around that park one more time until tears fill the brims of my eyes and I'm one step away from having to crawl home. May finishes all 10 laps, hardly breaking a sweat then, sits down next to me when she's done.

"You did good, Ruth."

"Please. It was all I could do to finish that second lap."

"But you finished it and that's what counts. It'll get easier over time." May smiles. "Do you know I used to weigh almost 250 pounds?"

Of course I'm shocked. "You?"

"Yep. It's taken 'bout a year for me to get it off. I do this almost every day 'cause I have to, and I cut out all the fried chicken and sweet potato pie too." She looks at me like it's something I should consider doing. But what she doesn't know is...I don't eat a lot. Really I don't. Really. "You'll start to feel better about yo'self too."

"I don't really feel bad about myself, May."

"I'm just sayin', carryin' 'round all that extra weight ain't good for you. You and me 'bout the same height and I know what kind of problems it can cause in the long run. We probably 'round the same age too. How old are you, Ruth? If you don't mind me askin'?"

"Oh, I'm almost 34."

"I'm 36," she says, smiling. Thirty-six! This heffa don't look a day over 25. How the hell is she going to sit here and tell me she's 36?

"I'd have never guessed, May. You don't look your age at all."

"You say that like bein' 36 is old, Girl."

"I'm sorry. I..."

"Don't be. I think when a woman feels good she's automatically goin' to look good. I like tellin' folks my age 'cause I know I look good. And I ain't bein' conceited either. But I take care of myself and that makes me feel good 'bout myself." I see what she's saying to me better than I'm hearing it. I know I look older than what I am. I feel older than what I am. If I could turn back the clock, I would, but I have no idea how to do that. Just as soon as I begin to wonder what her secret is, she tells me. "It's all 'bout takin' care of you on the inside, Ruth. I know we don't know each other well enough for me to be sayin' all this to you, but I've been where you are or close to it. I know you probably thinkin' you don't have control over most things in your life, but you do have control over this and you should do somethin' bout it if for no other reason than your health. Now...I better get goin' or I'm goin' to be late. See you in the mornin', same time?"

"Sure, May. I'll be here."

Damn. She psychic? Or do I have, "My life has been hell since the day I was born", written on my forehead?

Eight

I've never been one to make friends easily. Even with Bernie, she initiated our friendship and it seems May's doing the same thing. She knows my stamina isn't what hers is and she's got one good lap to give me the scoop about who she is and how she got there.

"Jeff is my second husband. My first husband, Frank...was killed in a car accident."

"Oh...," I say huffing and puffing like a whale. I wish she wouldn't make conversation that demanded a response from me. I'm too busy trying to breathe. "I'm sorry."

"Yeah, I was too. So sorry, in fact, that I nearly gave up on my life completely. Girl, I was a mess. 'Cause he was my everything like the song says." She smiles. May's southern accent is as thick as molasses and listening to her takes a lot of patience. Especially since talking seems to be a favorite pastime of hers. "Of course, we had our share of problems. Most couples do. Money mostly. But I loved me some Frank. He was my first love and as far as I was concerned...the only man in the world for me. You ever felt like that 'bout anybody?"

"No."

"Well, when you do...and I know you will 'cause God never meant for us to be by ourselves; I don't care what nobody says. When you find you somebody you goin' to know what I'm talkin' 'bout. Anyway, after he died, I felt like he took a part of me with him so I wasn't good for anything."

"What about...your kids?"

"What about 'em? If it wasn't for my momma I don't know what I would've done, Ruth. My poor babies lost both their daddy and their momma at the same time, only they didn't understand it 'cause I was still here. But I might as well have been dead too. My whole world was wrapped up in that man and I didn't even know it 'til he was gone. All of a sudden I realized I didn't have a damn thing. Oh, I had the insurance money and my kids, but I didn't have anything 'bout myself that knew how to make a life without him. You know how that feels?"

"Yes."

"That's a hard thing for a woman to face 'bout herself. Thinkin' she ain't nothin' without a man in her life. But I found myself sinkin' down into this hole...this big, black hole, and you know what scared me?"

"What?"

"Sinkin' so far down off in that hole that I wouldn't be able to get out. All I did was sit 'round eatin' and sleepin'. I had enough money where I didn't have to work, so I didn't. My kids stayed at Momma's all the time and no matter what anybody said to me or how much folks fussed at me 'bout gettin' myself together... I wasn't even tryin' to hear 'em. Girlfriend, I was pit-i-ful."

"So...what happened?" I ask, gasping for air.

"God. I mean it wasn't like some kind of beautiful spiritual awakenin' like you see in the movies or read in books. Girl, if you ever *want* to know the truth 'bout yo'self, ask God. If you ever *need* to know the truth 'bout yo'self he goin' tell you whether you want him to or not. God put his big ol' foot smack dab in my ass and said, "May! What the hell you think you doin'?" That's what he asked me."

"God...didn't...say that."

"If I'm lyin', I'm dyin'."

"God...cusses?"

"Girl, he God. He can cuss if he wants to and I was bein' hardheaded. He had to cuss me 'cause nothin' else was gettin' my attention."

"How do you know...it was God?"

"'Cause it got my attention. Just like that. What the hell did I think I was doin'? Other people had asked me that same question but I jus' ignored 'em. But let God ask you somethin' like that. How you goin' to ignore God? Even if you try ignorin' him, he's just goin' to keep on askin' 'til you finally answer 'cause you goin' to get tired before he does."

"So...what happened?"

"I started seein' what I was doin' to myself...my children. And you know what?"

"What?"

"I got even more depressed than I already was." She laughs. "And I ate more and slept more..."

"I thought...you said...God said he would...fix it."

"No. God didn't say he was fixin' nothin'. He jus' asked me what the hell was I doin' 'cause it wasn't up to him to fix it. It was up to me."

"Well...what made you want to fix it?"

"I'd been thinkin' all along that with Frank gone I didn't have a damn thing to live for."

"But your kids?"

"Exactly. My kids, my babies. And me. Frank wasn't a perfect man, but he was a good man and he knew how to live. Whatever he chose to do, he worked real hard at it. Always talkin' 'bout, "Don't do nothin' half-assed, May. And don't let them kids do nothin' half-assed either." Frank never did nothin' half-assed whether he was workin' or playin' or takin' care of us. The last thing he'd want was for me to be sittin' 'round like I was, doin' nothin'. He'd always taken a lot of pride in us. Always thought I was so pretty and his kids so well-behaved and I'd managed to let it all fall apart. Everything he and I'd worked so hard for was fallin' apart. So...what the hell was I doin'?"

"And you got over it? Just like that?"

"Hell no! It took awhile. When God asks you a question like that you can't get away with bullshittin' him. He wants the truth. I danced around the truth for months tryin' to blame everybody else but me. "It's all Frank's fault, Lord. He's the one who made me need him so." Then I tried blamin' God, "Why'd you have to take him from us when you knew how much we needed that man?"

"What did he say?"

"He didn't say a word. 'Cause he knew I knew better. Wasn't nobody to blame but myself. Not Frank, not God. May was the one layin' sprawled out on that bed eatin' them pork chops and mashed potatoes. Not Frank. Not God. May was the one lettin' another woman raise her children. Not Frank. Not God. May was the one feelin' sorry for herself all the damn time. Not Frank...

"Not God?"

"Course not. Eventually, I got my fat ass up out of that house and discovered that the world hadn't stopped turnin' simply 'cause I wanted it to. Life goes on, Ruth."

"And on...and on."

"You can't stop 'cause it ain't goin' to stop. So why not make the most of it?"

"I'm cramping. How many laps is this?"

"Four. We're comin' up on your bench. You did good, Girl. Why don't you rest."

"I'm going to go one more; then I'll rest."

"Good for you."

Nine

"Ruth, you had such beautiful hair, Girl," Bernie said turning up her nose, "the kind of hair I pay good money for at the beauty shop. Why, Child? Why in the world would you let anybody put a razor to that head?"

"It wasn't a razor, Bernie. It was clipper with the number two guard and an edge up. Don't look so disgusted. It's only hair; my hair and it'll grow back."

"You think it will grow back, Ruth. It'll never be the same, Darlin'. You mark my words."

"I've been a slave for the majority of my life, to my marriage and those tired ass relaxers; and now I'm liberated from both of them. I like it like that," I say, crossing my arms over my chest, daring that woman to say another word.

Bernie rolls her eyes, "Whatever."

So I roll mine back, "Didn't you promise to make us some Daiquiris?"

"You get the strawberries?"

"In the fridge."

I'm Ruth Johnson again. Yep. Got my maiden name back. Only when I looked in the mirror, I still saw Ruth Ashton and she was fat and she looked ten years older than she was and she really needed to do something with that hair. So far, I've lost nearly 15 pounds and I'm starting to feel pretty good. I've got another zillion or so to lose and then I'm going shopping.

Misery loves company, but it also loves donuts, pizza and ice cream. My gradual and consistent weight gain was often the butt of Eric's cruel insults. "Why don't you take yo' fat ass outside and run around the block or something?" Or, "You too fat for my own good, Ruth." And the classic, "Don't no man want a bone, but he ain't lookin' for Shamu neither." Maybe it's just a coincidence that I started to lose weight after I got divorced, but I've concluded that there's a connection and all that excess weight belonged to him anyway.

For dinner I've made a Chicken Caesar Salad and some Italian garlic bread that's so delicious even "Crab Eating, Send Me To the Grave With A Babyback Rib In One Hand And a Bucket of Fried Chicken In the Other" Bernie likes it.

"I signed up for some classes at JU the other day. Some business classes. I start next semester."

"That's good. You decide on a major yet?"

I shake my head, "Not yet. I think I'm going to take a few different things here and there until I decide what I want to do."

"Ain't nothing wrong with that."

"It's going to take me forever to get a degree though, working full time and taking classes part time."

"Well what's wrong with going to school full time?"

"I thought about it but... I don't know."

"Why not? It's just you, Ruth. It ain't like you got a house full of hungry kids to feed."

"That's true. But don't you think that's kind of drastic? I mean, I've worked for as long as I can remember, Bernie. And just to quit like that..."

"Sure it is. But look at it this way, Ruth. You could have your degree in four years instead of 10. Shoot, if you ask me, it's worth sacrificing a few dollars for now. And you know you can't stand that job anyway. By the way...I like your hair."

"Do you? I mean, really?"

"I mean it. Looks good, Girl."

"I'm still trying to get used to it. It's weird not having hair. I haven't seen my face in years."

"Well, you can sure see it now. All of it."

Bernie and I laugh, "I wonder if that's good or bad?"

"It's good, Ruth. I always said you had a pretty face."

"Yeah, and I always hated hearing it."

"Why?"

"That's one of the few compliments people are willing to give a big woman. She got a pretty face but..."

"See. There you go. You ain't fooling me, though. I see you trying to get skinny. You still walking with what's her name?"

"Her name's May, and yes. We're still walking every morning."

"You know I don't like her."

"You don't even know her."

"I still don't like her."

"Why not?"

"She sounds a little too good to be true, if you ask me. Got the perfect figure, the perfect husband, the perfect kids. Something's got to be wrong with her."

"I never said she was perfect. May's nice. She goes a little overboard sometimes with this fitness thing, but she's cool. I think you'd like her. I told her all about you and she seems to think you're fascinating."

"Don't go there."

"Bernie, if I didn't know better, I'd think you were jealous."

"Damn right I am. I've invested a lot of time and effort into you and our friendship. I'll be damned if some other heffa comes up in here and move in on my best friend."

"That's not going to happen and you know that. Stop feeling so insecure. You and I are more like sisters and nobody even comes close to replacing you."

"You remember that."

"How can I forget it with you hanging around all the time reminding me?"

Bernie gave me my housewarming gift just before she left, and to be honest, I've never been so embarrassed in my whole life. "Here, Girl. You need something to take the edge off. And read the directions first so you don't hurt yourself."

"What's this?" I ask, because I've never actually seen one of these up close and personal before.

"It's a vibrator, Ruth. A sex toy?" Bernie grins back at me like she always does when she knows she's caught me off guard, "Don't worry, Girl. You'll figure it out."

After she leaves, I put that thing back in the box and close it up in my closet. What in the world am I supposed to do with that? I know one thing. She's crazy if she thinks I'm ever going to get freaky and mess around with a vibrator. Me, of all people. I can't even wipe my ass without feeling embarrassed.

There are times when nature takes control and certain urges can compel a woman to examine aspects of herself she wouldn't otherwise consider examining. Masturbation has been the best sex I've ever had, but even great masturbated sex can get a little monotonous. Some urges are so strong they force a woman to look deep inside herself and dare to be honest about her desires. Her needs. That's when curiosity becomes a woman's playmate and suddenly, her vibrator becomes her best friend. I've named my new friend Maxwell, and Maxwell is a hell of a lot more pleasant to deal with than Eric ever was. Whoever thought orgasms came with a set instructions and a warning label?

Ten

The serenity of candlelight fills my apartment and the aroma of peppermint tea saturates my nostrils. I'm wading into this post-education thing instead of jumping in with both feet like Bernie suggested. The idea of going to school full time is cool, but for now I'm enjoying my two little classes part-time, just fine. Of course, I had to take me a psychology class in the hopes of figuring myself out. I keep expecting to see my picture in this book, smiling and looking like the perfect clinical scientific example of a paranoid schizophrenic, post traumatic stress syndrome, manic depressive something-or-other. Introduction to Business Management is the other course I'm taking and it's my favorite. The thing is, I'm really good at school. This stuff isn't as hard as it would've been when I was 18, probably because I know what it is to work for a living and school, in comparison, is a breeze. Besides, I like homework.

Bernie thinks I'm modeling myself after May. Like that's a bad thing? So we never miss our morning walks together. It's productive, not to mention enlightening. I feel the pounds melting off me and even though May talks a lot, she's got some interesting philosophies about life. So I cut off all my hair. Not because she wears hers short, but because I like the way it looks on her and she suggested shorter hair might look good on me too. She was right. I look younger in short hair. I don't idolize May, but

I respect her and I can relate to her. May's been where I've been, buried beneath the weight of her circumstances. She's had to rescue herself and I admire her determination and strength. What's wrong with me choosing to walk in her footsteps? She's already carved out a path to resurrection and I see no reason to reinvent the wheel. When May talks to me, I can hear in her voice that she understands, even though she doesn't know the whole story. It's like she doesn't have to.

Bernie's always been a strong woman and independence flows through her veins like blood. Sometimes I wonder if she even has problems. Every challenge that crosses her path is in some serious trouble because Bernie's kicking ass and taking names. She faces every issue head on and never so much as bats an eyelash in apprehension or anxiety. Sure, I admire that about her, but I can't relate to her the way I relate to May. Bernie can't see things from my perspective because she's never been in my position, and vice versa. May's got herself together the hard way and she knows this and she's proud of this. Someday I want to know it. I want to know Ruth has finally got her shit together.

I know one thing. I'm getting tired of both those heffas butting in on my man situation, or lack thereof. Like having a man in my life is the missing ingredient to my missing happiness. I'm not saying it wouldn't be nice to be in love with someone. Someday. Just not today. Let me have the pleasure of savoring my peppermint tea, candle lit room and quiet home all by myself for a while. Neither of them seem to understand how important this is for me right now. Winding down from a 14-year long tornado isn't easy, but it never fails. I'm always having to defend myself to one of them.

"I'm not ready to be in love, May."

"Girl, love don't come when you ready. It comes when it's ready."

"Well, I'm not ready for it to come."

"Well, you ain't got a damn thing to say 'bout it, Ruth. Personally, I'm on love's side, and I've got tons of brothas I can introduce you to that are jus' dyin' to meet a nice, pretty woman like you and settle down."

Then there's Bernie's argument. "Ruth, you need to get out there and get you some."

"Some what?"

"Some peanut butter to mix with your jelly," she says grinning.

"No, thank you. I'll pass."

"You're going to pass all right. Going to pass right out from lack of male injection. That's protein, Girl!"

"Why do you have to be so crude all the time, Bernie."

"There's nothing crude about fuckin', Ruth. If you'd get you some every now and then you'd know that."

"From what I hear, you're getting plenty for both of us."

Bernie smiles. "Stop making excuses."

"I'm not excusing anything."

"And you're not getting anything either, which explains this snippy ass attitude of yours right about now."

"Whatever."

Maybe one day I'll get there. To that place inside myself that says, "All right, Ruth. Time to gird up those loins, smile, bat those eyelashes, switch those hips, stick out that chest and get you a man. Someday. Just not today.

Eleven

Jazz. Need I say more? I haven't missed a jazz festival here in nine years and I'll be damned if I miss even one second of this one. October in Jacksonville, Florida means I'm not going to melt like butter in a hot skillet if I'm not inside impaled to an air conditioner before noon. This is the time of year I like living in Florida. It's those unsympathetic and relentless summers that make me long for Colorado. Sprawled out underneath an enormous oak tree, I can enjoy the music, avoid the crowds, read my new book and enjoy a thermos of hot cocoa in the privacy of my own dimension. A light-skinned sister scats on the microphone and the sweet, fall breeze licks lightly against my skin as if to say, "Ruth Johnson...girl, you're a delicious woman."

The smooth melodies dance in the air, lulling me into oblivion, and I dare anyone or anything to try and bring me back to reality, even for a second. My eyes are closed, but my ears are wide open, soaking the music deep into my soul.

I have no idea how long he's been standing here or how many times he's said, "Excuse me", but when I open my eyes, they're greeted by the most handsome man I've ever seen and I just know I've fallen asleep and he's simply a character in my dream.

His smile looks tantalizing enough to eat. Then, to my

surprise, he raises a camera to his face, points it at me and snaps my picture. "Oh yeah." He grins. "That's nice."

"Who are you?" And why the hell did you take my picture? I'm thinking this to myself loud enough for him to hear, I'm sure.

"Beautiful woman enjoying some beautiful music on a beautiful fall day...it's a picture I had to take." This man is the color of milk chocolate. His coal black eyes are safely tucked beneath heavy, sculptured brows. That beautiful mouth of his is framed nicely behind a perfectly manicured goatee. He's as tall as this tree I'm sitting under and his shoulders rival the wingspan of a 747. He kneels down in front of me and without even warning a sistah, looks deep into my eyes and hypnotizes me in an instant, "I saw you when you came in." He extends his hand for me to shake. "My name's Adrian."

He's magnificent and I have to make a mental note to close my mouth and stop staring, "I'm Ruth," I say, shaking his hand, which is huge. I wonder...never mind. "You're a photographer?"

"Strictly amateur. It's a hobby."

"So you go around taking pictures of strange women whenever the mood strikes you?"

He smiles. "You don't look so strange to me. And no, I usually don't make a habit of it. But you looked like you were holding on to something real special there for a moment. I was just hoping to get a piece of it. That's all." Oh yeah. Like he can have a piece of just about anything I've got. "What's your name?"

My name? My name is...close your mouth, Ruth. "Ruth. My name's Ruth." I've never believed in all that love at first sight crap. Not until now.

"They've got a good lineup this year," he says. You ever been to one of these before?"

"Sure. Yeah. I come every year."

"Me too. This one's better than the last one, though."

"I think so...too." Okay, Girl, just relax, take deep breaths and don't panic. Oh yes. He is handsome. Handsome is good. And he seems to be really nice. Maybe he is. As hard as I try, I can't think of one interesting thing to say and first chance I get I'm going to kick my own self in my own behind. I was perfectly fine before he came over here. Now, I'm a mental wreck and scrambled eggs inside.

He moves over near me and stretches out his legs, "Mind if I sit down?" Reluctantly, I move over to give him room on the blanket. Yes, this man has my heart palpitating. No, I have no idea what to do with him and it takes every ounce of self-control I have not to hyperventilate.

"You here alone?" It's lame, but it's the best I can come up with.

"No...", he points across the lawn, "I'm here with friends. What about you? You expecting anybody?"

"No. No. I'm not." Damn I wish Bernie hadn't canceled on me. She's much better at this than I am. Batting eyelashes, throaty giggles and putting a warm, friendly hand on an unsuspecting arm, just so. You know? Flirting.

"I hate this part," he says.

"I beg your pardon?"

Adrian shrugs. "Small talk. It's a waste of time, if you ask me. It would be a whole lot easier if people would just get right to the point. Know what I mean?" He looks almost as uncomfortable as I feel right now and that's a relief.

"That would certainly keep things interesting."

"More interesting than talking about the weather or jobs. Know what point I'd like to make right now?"

"No. What?" I ask nervously.

"The point I'd like to make is...that I think you've got it going on. You're very attractive."

Did he say I was attractive to him or attracted to him? "Thank you," quietly escapes from my mouth and my heart is beating so hard and fast I swear he's got to be able to hear it. I can feel him looking at me, but Lord knows I don't have the strength to look into those black eyes and retain my composure, so I won't even try.

"You're not married are you?" he asks, looking at my hands.

I shake my head, "No. Divorced. What about you?"

"No. If I were married, I wouldn't be sitting here trying to talk to you."

"Is that what you're doing? Trying to talk to me?"

"You mind?" Adrian flashes a movie star grin.

"Of course not," I say much too eagerly. "I just..."

"Well, all right then. We've got an understanding?"

"Yes. I guess we do."

Adrian bobs his handsome head to a contagious melody and I can see he loves this as much as I do. "Who's your favorite musician, Adrian?".

"Hard to say. I like the contemporary sound all right, but nobody moves me like Trane."

"You like Monk?"

"Yeah...and Davis. Most of the classic stuff."

"Me too, but I like Klugh a lot. And Benson. I've got a crush on Benson."

Adrian smiles and stares into my eyes. "He's a lucky man."

Wow. Did Adonis ever look this good? And would he have sat down and spent his afternoon having a conversation with me? I'm more surprised at myself than anything. Surprised that I'm not stuttering, spitting or getting my words all mixed up. What in the world did I put in this cocoa?

"You have a beautiful smile, Ruth." Am I smiling?

"Thank you. I like yours too."

Maybe it's the magic of the music or the afternoon. Then again, maybe it's just him. I like him and not because he's breathtakingly gorgeous or a jazz lover, intelligent, funny and doesn't seem to mind me finishing his sentences. He's just a nice guy, that's all. Adrian's a Network Engineer, whatever that is, something to do with computers. He's originally from Ohio, but moved to Jacksonville to take advantage of a career opportunity. He's never been married, has no children and is surprised when he finds out that after 14 years of marriage, I don't either. We share my cocoa, his beer, sandwiches, some fine music and a lovely afternoon in the park. God, could it get any better than this? I hope not. I don't think I could handle it.

Surprisingly, the extraordinary can be undeniably subtle

and comfortable. I like his company and I've gotten over that nervous feeling I had when he first sat down. Adrian's not trying to force any issues and he's not better at this conversation thing than I am.

Time flies and much too soon it's time for me to leave. Adrian insists on walking me to my car despite my very weak and halfhearted protests, "You really didn't have to do this, Adrian. It's a long walk back to the park."

"Not a problem, Ms. Johnson."

"Well...I appreciate it and this was fun. I had a good time."

"Enough of a good time to give me your number?" Adrian's hands are buried deep in his pockets and he rocks back and forth on his heels and toes like a little boy asking out his first date.

I want to give him my number, but my old buddy, Apprehension, decides to rush me like an entire defensive line causing me to panic and throw an interception, "I don't think so." Dammit Ruth!

"I thought you said you had a good time?"

"I did," I say, smiling. "But..." But my ass needs to go home and choke on a bone.

"But I'm not your type. Is that it? What? I'm too short? Too tall? I'm ugly."

I laugh. "Don't even go there, Adrian. You're every woman's type."

He shrugs. "I don't know about all that, but...why don't you let me call you, Ruth."

"So call me Ruth," I tease.

He smiles. "I'm serious. I had a good time too. The conversation was cool and...well, I'd like to see you again. Maybe dinner?"

"I don't think that's a...I'm just...," an emotional wreck with a lot of baggage? I can't tell him that even if it is true. "I haven't dated in years, Adrian and I'm kind of out of practice." I opt to say.

"Years?"

"Literally. Not since my divorce. Shoot! Before my divorce. Before my marriage."

"Damn! That long?"

"Yeah, so..."

"So that means I'm not getting those digits? That's cool. I'm not going to push it. The last thing a brotha needs to be accused of is being pushy."

"I had a nice time talking with you. You're a nice guy."

"A nice guy who can take a hint."

"Thanks again for walking me to my car, Adrian," I get inside and start up the engine. "Take care." From my rearview mirror I see him walking back toward the park looking every bit as gorgeous as he has all afternoon. My mouth is watering. It would've been nice having a man like him in my life. Wouldn't it? I'd like to think so anyway. But this is cool. This way, I'll never know how bad it could've been.

I'm amazed when men find me attractive. Especially attractive men. Although, I don't think I've ever met one as attractive as Adrian. As much as I liked spending the afternoon with him, I'm not ready for a relationship right now. That poor man doesn't deserve the kind of garbage I'm carrying. I wonder when that moment will come or even if it ever will. The moment when I'm finally normal. If there is such a thing. May says God doesn't intend for us to be alone, but I'm comfortable being by myself. I have my friends and for now that's plenty. Am I lonely? Sometimes, but the way I see it, it's a trade off. Loneliness for peace of mind. I can't give a man what he needs because I'm too preoccupied with my own needs right now.

I've been divorced nearly two years and Eric's spirit still haunts me. I'm afraid it always will. I have to remind myself that he's not going to walk through my door and make demands on my life. Still. After all this time.

The other day, I drove past the drycleaners where I used to take his shirts, pulled into the parking lot, turned off the car, then remembered. I didn't have to pick up his laundry anymore.

Twelve

I never expected to ever see her again, but there she is, or at least a picture of her in the newspaper. Clara. Clara Robins, the counselor I met in the hospital the night of my last fight with Eric.

Clara's the director of the Ruby Higgins Center for Domestic Violence, which is having some kind of funding problem and is about to be closed down. The article in the paper talks about Ruby Higgins, the lady for whom the center is named. Ruby Higgins worked as a nurse at the same hospital where I met Clara and the two women became good friends. Together, they helped women in abusive relationships get back on their feet. Ruby Higgins, like Clara, donated much of her personal time, driving women to counseling, helping them find safe places to live, even spending her own money to buy clothes and food for the women and their children. Clara and Ruby had obviously been one hell of a team.

One night, according to the article, a husband of one of the women decided he wanted his wife back. The woman had been staying with Ruby while her new apartment was being painted. He found out where she was, broke in on the women late one night and when Ruby tried to stop him, he shot her. She died at the hospital where she worked. Shortly after she died, Clara received a grant to open the center and she named it in honor of her friend. For legal reasons, her new grant request has been denied and the money is almost gone.

I don't remember why I felt so compelled to get dressed and drive over here, but I'm here, knocking on Clara's front door with no idea of what I'm going say. She answers, looking exactly the way she did two years ago, like she's a little girl pretending to be grown. Clara stares at me for a moment, then smiles, "I remember you. After all this time, you finally ready to talk to me?"

I laugh. "That was a long time ago. How can you still remember that?"

"I make it a point to remember all my ladies. Even the stubborn ones like you. Come on in, Baby." Clara leads me down the narrow hallway into a small office. Photographs cover the walls of her office. Pictures of women and children and Clara with her arm draped over every shoulder. "Have a seat." She gestures to a chair in front of her desk. The shelter's an old renovated turn of the century Victorian and it's quiet in here. So quiet that I wonder if everybody's already moved out.

"You look a lot better than the last time I saw you," she says smiling. Right away, I learn Ms. Robins doesn't mind saying exactly what she thinks. But she's got a way with her delivery. It's gentle and laced with smiles and a good-natured spirit. She'd never tell you something you didn't need to hear and she'd never say anything to intentionally hurt your feelings.

"Thank you." I laugh.

"Feeling better?"

"Much."

"That's all that matters. Feeling good's what it's all about. Don't you think?" She smiles and so do I.

"I read about this place in the paper this morning."

"Yeah...I read that too. I didn't care much for that picture of me though. Made me look old." She frowns.

"Impossible," I tell her. "You could never look old."

Clara looks at me like she thinks I'm bullshitting her, but I'm not. "Child, you see all these gray hairs in my head? 'Course I look old. But that's a real nice compliment and I guess I'd better take it since I don't get too many of them."

"You're welcome."

"So, is that why you came down here? 'Cause you saw me in the paper?"

"Has everybody moved out already?"

"No, but they're out looking. Some of them don't even have jobs, let alone another place to stay. The women living here, they ain't strangers to me. They're my friends and I love them. Took a lot of courage for them to come here and ask for help. More courage than many of them even knew they had and now they've got to go out and start all over from starting over. Ain't that a shame?"

"It's a real shame, Clara."

"We helped a lot of them, though," she says proudly. "Ruby and I. We did a damn good job."

"I'll bet you did."

Clara's expression saddens, "I hate that we ever had to open up this place. Always believed that the best day of my life would be closing it down because we wouldn't need so-called "shelters" anymore. But as long as we got people running away from home, we need to at least have a place for them to run to. So they can rest. Life's so much easier on you if you're rested. Don't you think? Can't make much sense of it if you're tired all the time. The women who come here...they're tired when they get here."

"I understand."

"I know you do."

"The sad thing is we do need to keep places like this open. As long as there are women running for their lives in the middle of the night, carrying children on their hips and everything they own in a paper bag, we need places like this to stay open. How can they expect me to close my doors now? They ain't thinking. Ain't even trying to understand. Pisses me off."

"So what are you going to do?"

She leans forward, resting her face in her hands, "Maybe go back to work for Social Services. I never liked that system, but it's a paycheck and I can still help some people."

"Maybe...maybe you can get a lawyer and..."

Clara shakes her head, "No money and no time for all

that, Baby. Legal battles can go on forever and we don't have forever."

"Well...what is the problem, Clara? Why won't they give you the money?"

"One of the women who used to live here got herself a mean mother-in-law with a lot of money. And you know money talks. Can talk real loud if it wants to. Her son is abusive, but she ain't trying to hear that. Wouldn't surprise me if his daddy bopped her on the head every now and then. Anyway, she managed to get his wife to leave here and then the rich heffa filed a lawsuit claiming I was running a prostitution ring in here. I look like a pimp to you?"

"What happened?"

"Oh, they did an investigation, and of course they didn't find a thing to support her accusations."

"So you were cleared? And they still won't give you the money?"

"Grant committees don't like scandals, Baby." She shrugs. "Doesn't matter if I'm guilty or not guilty at this point. I've fallen out of their good graces."

"I've got some money, Clara. Maybe I could..."

"You don't have the kind of money we need here." She smiles. "But thank you. Thank you so much."

"There's got to be something we can do. Someone we can talk to."

"I've talked till I'm blue in the face, Child. I've talked to politicians, appealed the grant committee's decision as far as I could go. I've begged for donations, and no matter what I've done I haven't been able to get the kind of help we need to stay open. There's just nothing else I can do."

"But maybe I can help. Maybe between the two of us..."

"No, now this ain't your problem."

"Sure it is. I could've just as easily ended up here like these other women. I know how it feels to want to be safe. I didn't have sense enough to leave him sooner, but... If I'd have known about this place then, maybe he'd have been out of my life sooner. There's got to be something we can do about this, Clara."

"We? Well now, if you've got some ideas, Baby Girl, I'm listening."

"I don't have any ideas, but that doesn't mean I can't come up with some."

Clara smiles. "Excuse me, then. All right, Miss Thang. I'm not feeling as optimistic as you are right now, but I can appreciate your passion for the cause and all. I've got enough money to keep this place open a few more months, but after that..."

"It's been nearly two years since that night, Clara. I'm still not over it. Sometimes I wonder if I ever will be. I remember how it feels, knowing my life didn't mean shit to anybody, not even me. I remember feeling worthless and having that beat into me and drilled into my head until I had no choice but to believe it. I wanted to leave him so many times, but I didn't know where to go. I just... If I can help, I'd like to. That's all."

"I've never been too proud to turn down help and I don't see any reason to start now. You got my number?"

These small rooms hold entire families crowded into each of them, but I guess living in a crowded room, a safe room, is better than the alternative. There are a lot of children living here. Sullen and withdrawn, most of them have the eyes of children who've seen more of life than they should've. Clara introduces me to Sharon, a tall, tailored brunette who looks a lot like a young Elizabeth Taylor. She rushes in, carrying a briefcase in one hand and a little girl, with big blue eyes like her mother's, in the other. She's found a new apartment and will be moving out soon.

Sharon and I sit in the small room she shares with her daughter talking like we're old friends. Kindred spirits? "I just started my own business," she says proudly. "Catering. Started it about four months ago." She hands me her business card.

Four year old Megan sits on my lap holding on tight to a doll that's apparently her best friend. The little girl is soft and sweet, which her mother assures me is a temporary condition for my benefit. I used to dream of having a little girl of my own, but the possibility of that ever happening is becoming more unlikely by the second and that biological clock ticks so loudly, sometimes it keeps me up at night.

"How long were you married, Sharon?"

"Four years. He's a doctor. A neurologist. We'd been married about six months before he..." She smiles at her daughter, careful not to say too much about her husband in front of Megan. "What about you?"

"Fourteen years. No children."

"How'd you manage that?"

"He didn't want any," is all I said. It's all I need to say because I could see in her eyes that she understands.

"You ever feel like all that stuff happened to somebody else? Like you were watching a movie?" She asks, staring out the window.

"Yeah. A terrible movie. With some bad actors." We laugh.

"He controlled everything, Ruth. He used to tell me how to dress, when to sleep. It even got to the point that if I wasn't home when he called me from work, he'd take the car keys away from me as punishment. How do you let somebody get control over you like that?"

"Gradually? I don't know. Maybe we put a little too much faith in them." I shrug. She looks to me for answers, but I don't have the heart to tell her she's wasting her time, because I just don't have any."

"Well, if a woman can't have faith in her husband..."

"Girl, I don't get it either."

"People ever tell you, you brought it on yourself?"

"They don't have to. I tell myself that all the time. I've been divorced for two years and I still blame myself for what he did to me."

"Maybe it is our own fault."

"Maybe, but I'm tired of taking all the blame, Sharon. Aren't you? You spent all those years listening to him blame you for everything that went wrong in his world and you're still blaming yourself. That gets old, Girl. And I'm tired of it. Know what I think?"

"What?"

"I think it's perfectly fine to pass on some of that

responsibility. I think we owe it to ourselves to do that. Put the blame where it belongs for a change, Sharon."

She looks at me and smiles. "On him?"

"Why not? Neither one of them is around anymore to argue the point. What's wrong with saying it was Eric's fault my life was hell?"

Sharon laughs. "And it was Darren's fault my life was hell! Whew! I feel better already, Ruth."

"All we need now are some eight by tens with their faces on them, and some darts."

"Cheap therapy."

That's the way it is between us. An understanding that transcends our cultural differences. Our histories are so similar we have no choice but to become friends.

I say my good-byes to Sharon and Clara, with a million ideas running through my head. Clara's been so immersed in the problem maybe she needs someone to look at it from another perspective. What harm could it do?

I've been promising to treat Bernie to lunch for ages, so I figure I'll kill two birds with one stone. Feed her and pick her brain for ideas at the same time. "I don't know, Bernie. I need to do something. And I can't explain why, but I can't just walk away without trying."

"Sounds like she's already tried everything, Ruth. I understand that you feel you need to come to her rescue, but sometimes the system's bigger and badder than we are and ain't nothing you can do about it." I'd offered to take the woman to a nice little Caribbean restaurant I've heard so much about, but she decided on Tyrone's Fish and Grits. As long as I've lived in Jacksonville the fish and grits combination just never appealed to me. So I settle for a fish sandwich.

"There's got to be something she hasn't thought about. She said she'd found a few people who were willing to give donations, but not enough. What we need to do is figure out how to get more."

"Too bad she couldn't have a fund-raiser or banquet," Bernie says nonchalantly.

"A what?"

"Folks have them all the time. Big banquets with $200 plates of rubber chicken and plastic mashed potatoes. Raise a lot of money that way if you plan it right. People like dressing up and rubbing elbows, especially if the "right" people show up."

I laugh so hard I nearly fall out of my seat. "Bernie girl! You are a genius! A fund-raiser! Why can't we do that? Why couldn't we just throw a big ass party?"

Bernie stops eating and looks scared all of a sudden, "Ruth...honey. I don't think it's that simple. I'm sure there are all kinds of legal issues to deal with, not to mention the planning. What do you know about putting together something like that? And you could never do it by yourself. All that work, and..."

I smile at this woman, my best friend in all the world, "Do you have any plans for the next couple of months?"

"No! Ruth, don't you even..."

"C'mon, Bernice. Please? I've never asked you for much the whole time we've been friends. You know I haven't. And I wouldn't ask you this except it is a lot for one person to handle and you're so good at things like this. Much better than I am. I wouldn't even know where to start. You know you're the social butterfly in the family."

"Look, I sympathize with the cause and all, but I am not going to commit myself to something like this, Ruth. It's huge and I've got a life."

"I understand that, Honey. I do. But think about those women, Bernie. Look at me. I'm your best friend and I'm one of those women. You helped me when I needed it more than you'll ever know."

"I helped you because I love you, Ruth."

"Then if you love me, help me do this. Please?" I try my best to look as pitiful as I possibly can in the hopes that Bernie will be moved to do the right thing and stand tall for sisterhood and women all over the planet. It works.

Bernie sighs, "Okay. I'll look into some things."

"Yes! Oh bless you, Girl!"

"But that's all I'm doing, Ruth."

I grin so hard my face goes numb, "Thank you, Bernie. And you know I appreciate anything you can do."

"You're a pain in my ass sometimes. You do know this?"

"Yes. But I love you."

"Whatever. Pass the hot sauce."

I call Clara as soon as I get home to tell her about Bernie's idea. She's more excited than I am and we stay on the phone for hours fine tuning our own ideas.

"I'd thought about a fund raiser, but... You really think something like this can work?"

"I have no idea, Clara. But it can't hurt to look into it and that's all we're doing right now. I mean, who knows?"

"All the news I've been getting has been bad news, Ruth. Maybe my luck's about to change."

"Well, it may turn out that we can't do it after all, Clara. So I guess we shouldn't get our hopes up."

I can hear her smiling on the other end, "Let's get our hopes up, Ruth. Just for a minute. Let's get our hopes way, way up."

Thirteen

Not many people know this, but Cinderella is alive and well, living in Jacksonville, Florida. She's also a black woman who's changed her name to May. I don't think it's possible for a life to get much better than May's. In fact, I imagine some idealistic and happy little girl is playing with her doll house and May and her family are the dolls. Everyone seems so perfect, May, her husband, her kids. Daddy comes home from a hard day at the office, kisses Mommy, who's in the kitchen fixin' up some vittles. The kids escape from the confines of homework and tackle him into his favorite easy chair. All of them laughing until their bellies ache from the excitement of seeing each other and being together as a family once again. Honestly, I don't know how she can stand all that bliss and tranquility. She might've suffered through a bout of dysfunctionalism for a minute, but you could never tell by looking at her now.

May's been bugging me for weeks to have dinner at her place and meet her family. Allan, 13, is her oldest, and a music prodigy, who's got first seat in the school orchestra for violin and, is supposedly the Michael Jordan of the next millennium. Her daughter, Shannon, is nine, an aspiring ballerina, and has made the honor roll every year since kindergarten. If you ask me, perfect kids, kids who never give their parents any grief, have closet suicidal tendencies, suffer from low self-esteem and eating disorders, but that's just my opinion.

Her house is immaculate and perfectly perfect like it's been pulled right out of one of those showcase homes magazines. It's huge! My little apartment would fit inside the place a couple of times.

"You home is beautiful, May."

"You think so, Girl? Thank you. We jus' put it on the market. Know anybody who might be interested?" She winks and smiles at me. Yeah right. Like I've really got the kind of money they're asking for this place. Even if I did, it's way too much house for me.

"I'll ask around and get back to you," I say. "By the way, where're the kids? I was hoping to see them."

"Allan's spendin' the night with a friend and Shannon's at my momma's. Tonight's jus' for us grown folk."

Jeff's grand entrance is breathtaking. The man is gorgeous, with skin the color of mahogany, hazel eyes and the most perfect bald head I've ever seen. The only thing is, he's short. Way short. Like no taller than me short. Really. He walks over to me and we stare back at each other, eye to eye. "Hello," he says graciously extending his hand. "I'm Jeff. You must be Ruth."

"Hello, Jeff. It's nice to finally meet you."

"You too. May talks about you incessantly." That's scary.

"Oh, Jeff. I do not." She gives him on of those playful, painless slaps on the arm.

"It's all good though," he reassures me. Only I'm not so reassured. May doesn't know everything about my marriage because I haven't told her all the details. But that doesn't mean she hasn't put two and two together and figured it out. Someday I'll tell her the whole story. She might've fought her way back from the bottomless pit, but I'm still working on it. When I'm a successful business woman, mother of two perfect children of my own, living in a five-bedroom house, married to the most perfectly handsome, successful man in the whole world, I'll tell her.

Jeff pours me a glass of wine and the three of us talk while May finishes preparing dinner, which she insists she needs no help with. Jeff's an architect. They met at one of her son's basketball games. Jeff has a son too, a year younger than Allan and he was playing on the other team. According to Jeff, it was love at first sight.

"How'd you know she wasn't already married?" I asked.

"That's the same thing I asked him, Ruth. This man jus' walks up to me and asks me for my phone number. For all he knew, my husband could've been right there."

"She came in by herself and she wasn't wearing a ring so I just figured it was worth the risk and I took my chances." He grins and kisses May on the side of her neck. "I won." Suddenly, the doorbell rings and May smiles at me. All of a sudden I know something's up. Here we go. First thing that comes to my mind is that Miss May, who's been bragging all this time about how she'd like to introduce me to a few nice men, is following through with her plan to do just that. I turn in time to see Jeff standing in the doorway of the kitchen with my "date" for the evening and I can hardly believe my eyes.

"Adrian Carter, you've already met my wife, May."

"Yes. Hello, May. Nice to see you again."

Close your mouth Ruth! How many times do I have to tell you that? "And this is a friend of ours...Ruth. Ruth Johnson. Ruth...Adrian." Jefferson's smile looks as cheesy as his wife's and right now I'm trying really hard not to look surprised and pissed. You have any idea how hard that is to do.

Adrian smiles. "Ruth."

"Hi." Damn girl! Is that all you can say? I wonder if he remembers me? No. He doesn't look like he remembers me. Dang! Whatever.

Adrian turns back to Jeff and hands him a bottle of wine. "Zinfandel okay?"

May steps in like Joan Cleaver. "Zinfandel's perfect," she says, breezing past me, taking the bottle from him. She gives me the "follow me into the dining room" look on the sly and I excuse myself from this uncomfortable situation as best I know how.

Safely in the confines of her dining room walls, May begins justifying herself before I can cuss her out like I want to. "Ruth, now I know you're mad at me."

"May..."

"But if I told you he was goin' to be here, you wouldn't have come over."

"No. I wouldn't have."

"He's a nice man, Ruth and ain't he fine, Girl? If I wasn't already married..."

"May, I don't care."

"Look, it's jus' dinner, Girl. It's jus' a few hours of yo' time and if you don't like him, you never have to see him again, Ruth. That's a good-looking man out there."

"I just wished you'd have warned me," I say, trying to keep my voice down.

"I would've, but you so shy sometimes and I met him the other night at Jeff's company dinner and..."

"I'm not shy, May. I'm just not interested in dating right now. I'm not ready to..."

"And you'll never be ready if you don't come out from behind that wall you got built up, Honey. Adrian's a nice man and I think he might be wonderful for you. Jus' give tonight a chance. Please?" When is my ass going to get a backbone and learn how to just say no?

May's dinner is absolutely delicious and I've decided to use it as my excuse not to say much while we're eating. She serves baked chicken breasts, steamed vegetables, wild rice and for dessert, strawberry shortcake. Adrian never mentions our meeting at the jazz festival and I'm not going to embarrass myself and mention it either. I'm sort of offended, but not surprised. A man like him probably meets lots of women and I'm sure he can't remember all of us.

After dinner, we take the party into the living room, sip on cognacs and listen to the tale of Jeff's and May's wedding day while I count down the minutes and wait for the little window of opportunity to open up so I can jump out of it and take my behind home. May and Jeff are cuddled up on the love seat. Adrian sits on one end of the beige leather sofa and I sit safely in the armchair by myself.

"I knew the moment I laid eyes on this woman that she was going to be my wife," Jeff exclaims proudly.

May grins and gazes into his eyes. "You knew no such thing."

"I did," he said, kissing the tip of her nose. "And I was absolutely right. I've never been happier than I am right now, Baby." I glance quickly in Adrian's direction to see if he's as uncomfortable with their display of love and affection as I am. He politely smiles back. Yep. That's affirmative.

"I love you, Baby," she whispers.

"I love you too, Darling. You know I do." Earth to Jefferson. Earth to Jefferson. Hello. There is life outside of that woman's eyes. He must've read my mind because all of a sudden his spirit is back in the room and he remembers the rest of us are here. "Have you seen the model of the new house, Adrian?"

"No. I've heard a lot about it, though."

Jeff leads us all to his office and sitting on this big table in the middle of the room is a scaled down model of his wedding gift to her. "It's bein' built in Ponte Vedra as we speak." She beams.

"This is impressive," Adrian says, leaning over it. "You design this, Jeff?"

"Every inch," he says proudly. "I promised May I'd build her the house of her dreams, when we were married, and... Well, barring any major setbacks we should be moving in by Spring."

"Didn't I tell you it was beautiful, Ruth?"

"You certainly did, and it is beautiful, May."

"When it's finished, we're havin' a housewarmin' party. I know you comin', Girl."

"Wouldn't miss it."

She told me once that all she has to do to get her way with him is pout, or in extreme circumstances, do a little crying. I don't know. Sounds kind of childish to me, but I imagine she's the kind of woman who can get away with something like that. I don't think I ever could. Of course, I've never tried pouting. Crying...yes. Begging...sure. Pleading...definitely. But never pouting.

I offer to help May with the dishes but Jeff insists that I'm a guest and it's his duty to help her. I take it this is their way of leaving Adrian and me alone since we've hardly said more than five words to each other all evening. But you know what? I'm not doing it. I'm not playing this game and giving in to these people's schemes. When no one's looking, I step out onto the balcony and practice my goodnight speech. Ummm...I've had a nice time? Wonderful dinner, May, and yes, next time we'll do it at my place.

May and Jeff have a huge backyard and the full moon illuminates it like a stage. I'll bet it's not shining on anyone else's backyard right now. Just this one. They've got a huge flower garden, hibernating its treasure until Spring and I make a mental note to ask her what's planted there the next time we get together for our morning walk. The mystical sound of his voice invades my solitude and sets all those little butterflies free inside my stomach.

"It's a nice night."

I start to turn around, but think better of it. "Yeah...it is."

Adrian comes over and stands next to me and whispers, "Are they getting on your nerves too?"

I laugh. "Yes. They are."

"Good. Then it's not just me. The last thing they need to know is that we've already met. I'm glad you didn't bring it up."

"To be honest, I'd thought you'd forgotten."

He smiles. "No, I remember. Brothas always remember the women that diss' them."

"I didn't diss' you."

"You dissd. me, Ruth."

"No. I just didn't give you my number."

"Exactly."

"But that's not diss'n you."

"My feelings were hurt."

"They were not."

"Sure they were."

"Well, I'm sorry. That wasn't my intention."

"I accept your apology."

"Thank you. Did you know about this tonight?"

"I knew what they were planning. I just didn't know it was you."

"So, why'd you go through with it?"

"'Cause she was giving him a hard time and I empathized with the man. Besides, he begged me to come. Did you know?"

"I didn't have a clue."

"If you'd known, would you have shown up?"

"Probably not."

"What if you knew it was me? Would you have come then?" I smile. "I didn't think so. You know. I'm trying hard not to take this rejection thing too personal."

"It's not personal," I say trying to convince him that this whole idea of me diss'n him is absolutely ludicrous. I'm not capable of diss'n anybody. I'm just insecure.

"So, what have you got against me?"

"I don't have anything against you, Adrian. I told you at the park. I think you're a nice man."

"But you don't want to have anything to do with me? Makes sense."

"Are you always this sarcastic?"

"Not usually, but I'm not sure what's up. You think I'm a nice guy, but I can't have your number. You wouldn't have come to dinner tonight if you'd known I was going to be here. You're real good at giving a brotha a complex, Ruth."

"Then you shouldn't want my number, Adrian."

"I can't help it. You've got it going on." I laugh. "You do," he insists.

"You're funny."

"I'm not trying to be funny. I'm being honest."

"Well, I'm flattered. Coming from someone like you, that's quite a compliment."

"What's that mean? Someone like me?"

"You already know, Adrian. I don't think I have to say it."

"I wish you would."

"Someone like you? Handsome. Successful."

"Thank you. Now I'm the one flattered. And I can call you...when?"

"You're welcome. And it's getting late."

"And?"

"And I'd better be leaving."

"In the nick of time, right?"

"Excuse me?"

"If I ask you for your number now, can I expect a different answer this time? Or are you going to shoot me down again?"

"Why won't you just give up on me? I'm a hopeless cause."

"I like you."

"You barely know me."

"So?"

"So, how can you be so sure you like me?" Adrian looks into my eyes, slips his arms around my waist and before I know it, his warm soft lips are locked onto mine. My legs turn into limp noodles and it's all I can do to keep from fainting. His mouth is absolutely precious and I savor the delicious taste of this man. Oh God. If this is heaven, just let me die right here, right now. Adrian kisses away all my inhibitions, doubts, fears, issues, regrets, mistakes, pain, tears, bad memories and disappointments. He kisses in hope, desire, longing, intimacy, passion and wishes.

"I'm sure."

"I don't have a pen," I say breathlessly.

"Just tell me. I'll remember."

Fourteen

"You had a date?"

"Don't get your panties in a bunch, Bernie. It was just dinner; that's all. And it wasn't a date...exactly."

"Dinner. Dinner's good. It's a beginning."

"A beginning to what?"

"A beginning to cleaning that old dusty pussy of yours."

I laugh. "It's not dusty, Bernie. I prefer the term "preserved."

"Yeah, whatever. So is he fine?"

"Very." I know she wants details, but I'm going to make her sweat a little for them.

"And?"

"And?"

"What's his name, Girl?"

"Adrian."

"And?"

"And?"

"Ruth! You're starting to piss me off. So, what's he like?"

"He's very nice."

"Nice? What the hell is nice?"

"Nice, Bernie. Nice is just...nice."

"You're being a smart ass, Ruth. You do know this?"

I grin. "I know."

"Would I do him?"

"In your dreams."

"Would you do him?"

"I hadn't thought about it."

"Figures."

"What's that supposed to mean?"

"You don't ever think about doing anybody. I swear. Your ass is some kind of secret experiment engineered by the government to implement the extinction of the black race. How can a woman go without fucking for almost two years, Ruth? It just ain't natural."

"I can't help it if I've got self control. I can't just screw anybody, Bernice. I'm sorry, but I just can't. There are too many diseases going around. Too many freaks."

"Ever heard of condoms? Ever heard of mace?"

"Ever heard of abstinence?"

"Not since I was in the seventh grade."

"I'm not the only one who feels this way, Bernie. All kinds of women are choosing abstinence over casual sex these days and I think it's admirable."

"You would, Ruth. You ain't had real sex in years. Don't bother denying it, I already know. And I also know you've got to be missing it more than you let on."

"Nope."

"Nope? Yeah right. You've been divorced how long, and you don't miss having sex?"

"No."

Bernie stares back at me in disbelief. "Stop lying, Ruth. I know Eric was an asshole but... You serious? How can you not miss it? How can any woman in her right mind, with even a semi-healthy libido not miss sex?"

"I don't miss sex. What's the big deal?" She has no idea how endeared I am to Maxwell.

"Sex is the big deal."

"Sex is overrated."

There's this vein over Bernie's left temple that pops out every time she gets upset and all of a sudden, there it is. If she's not careful her head's going to explode, "Overrated! How the hell can you say sex is..."

"Damn, Bernie. Did I hit a nerve?"

"Girl! I know what it is," she says, trying to calm down. She picks up her address book and starts fumbling around in it, letting the business cards and pieces of paper fall as they may, "I've got the number to a good gynecologist. Now, I'm sure this is something he can fix, Baby. Maybe prescribe you some pills or something. Where did I put..."

"Bernie, I don't need to see a doctor. I don't happen to be one of those women who enjoys sex and that's all there is to it."

"Ruth, something's wrong, Honey. But don't you worry. We're going to get you some help, and... Here it is. You want me to call and make the appointment for you? I can go with you if you like. You're not in this alone, Baby." I don't believe it. This woman looks as if she's about to cry.

"Bernie, I'm not sick. I just do not like sex. Pay attention. I'm fine and I don't need to see a doctor."

Bernie stops and stares at me with so much pity in her eyes, I'm starting to feel bad, "You really don't like..."

"Sex. And no. I don't. I never have."

"But, why not, Ruth?" Dammit! It's not like I told her I have a fatal disease. Why is she taking this so hard?

"It just doesn't feel good."

"Ruth..."

"It doesn't, Sweetie. I've never gotten anything out of it. Well, except for a few yeast infections and some other stuff Eric brought home. Anyway, it's not a big deal. Besides, thanks to you, I've got Maxwell now."

Bernie looks confused. "Maxwell? Oh...Maxwell."

"Girl, I like me some Maxwell." I wink.

"Ruth, Maxwell's not meant to be a substitute for the rest of your life. I just gave you that to tide you over until..."

"Until what?"

"Until you meet a nice man, Honey."

I can't help it. I bust out laughing and end up hurting her feelings, "You're sweet, Bernice Watson. And thank you for caring about me and thank you for Maxwell. But right now he and I are fine."

"You know what? I know what it is now. You've never been with anybody but Eric."

"And Maxwell."

"Stop playing, Girl. This is serious."

"For who?"

"Ruth, Eric was all wrong for you."

"Maxwell's perfect."

"And your body knew that, which is why it didn't respond the way it's supposed to."

"I don't know about all that, Bernie."

"Listen. I know what I'm talking about. You find yourself someone nice, Baby. Someone who cares about you...I guarantee you won't think sex is bad at all."

"Bernie, why can't you just accept the fact that I might be frigid? I have."

"No. You're not frigid, Baby. Not the way you and Maxwell go through batteries. Every man isn't Eric, Ruth. There are men out there who are gentle and caring and loving. Maybe this Adrian is one of them."

"I don't know. I don't want to think that far ahead. One day at a time is about all I can handle. Know what I mean?"

"I know, Sweetie.

No, she has no idea. How can she? For a woman like Bernie the world is her playground and the men she meets are her playmates. Sure, she's been in and out of love like most women, but she never lets bitterness hold her prisoner, or regrets bury her deep inside her past. Bernie brags all the time about her sexual exploits and I listen, trying to fathom how she can enjoy herself so much while someone else pounds himself inside her body just so he can "get his". That's something I don't think I'll ever understand. But the flavor of Adrian, the warmth of his lips, the sweetness of his tongue, these things I understand perfectly.

"Did I tell you he kissed me?"

Bernie smiles. "No you didn't. How was it?"

I smile too. "It was wonderful. Best kiss I ever had."

"Like I said, Ruth...it's a beginning and the best kiss you've ever had is a fine place to start."

I'm tripping all over myself
Trying to get to him
Trying not to fall too hard
Or too much in love
Trying not to break my heart
 But to be happy
Just this once

Fifteen

He's left several messages, but I haven't had the courage to return any of his calls. I plan on it. Really. I'm going to call him back. And say what? Hello? That's good. Hello. It's simple and straight to the point. Hello, Adrian. Now that's even better. It's more interactive and personable. I'll say it slowly. Hel-lo A-dri-an. I've got a feeling I'm about to blow this whole thing and all of a sudden it's dawning on me I am not cool when it comes to dating.

I haven't been able to think about anything but him since dinner at May's house. I think about the way he moves. The way he walks. His smile is absolutely mesmerizing and his eyes hypnotic. It's like someone peeked inside my mind, took a sharp pencil and drew my idea of the perfect man. Then listed his perfect man attributes in a column next to his picture. Classy, intelligent, relaxed sense of humor, romantic, great kisser, all around good human being. Hell, I'm not his type. And where do I get off thinking that I am? He can do so much better than me. I know it. He probably knows it and it wouldn't take long for the rest of the world to figure it out either. You know, insecurity has a way of tearing at a woman's self-esteem like a ferocious anima,l leaving nothing behind but shreds of despair dangling off the bones of her pride, raw and bloody. Okay, so maybe that's a little melodramatic and when I feel like this, there's only one thing for me to do. Where's that quart of French Vanilla ice cream?

That man could have any woman he wanted and he probably does. I'll bet there are lots of women sweating him and if he's like most men, he's probably taking advantage of it. I know he is. Who's he trying to fool? Probably some kind of mega-mack-daddy-player-pimp-I'm-gonna-hit-it-and-run-brotha. Oh yeah, I've got him all figured out. He's smooth, though. Almost had me fooled, thinking he was a nice guy with a personality that wouldn't quit, and pretty, white teeth. No...he ain't getting over on me. I am not the one. So he can take his pathetic ass rap and good-looking self somewhere else and play on some other unsuspecting female's heart strings 'cause he ain't pulling on these here!

Twenty minutes later I'm scraping out the last spoonful of ice cream and feeling really guilty. I feel so bad that I go into the bathroom and stick my finger down my throat to throw it up because I don't want to ruin my diet or the common sense, nutritious eating habits I've developed.

Sleep won't come. All I can think about is him and being in love with him. Where in the world did that come from? And why would something like that ever happen to me? And why is it a big deal now when it hasn't been a big deal in years? I know Eric never loved me. When I was younger, knowing that hurt so bad I wanted to die. It's hard living like that. I prayed over and over again for a miracle that one day he'd fall in love with me. He never did. I never fell in love with me either. So why would a man like Adrian fall in love with me?

The phone rings again and it's him, "Look...I know it's late. But, you've been on my mind since we met, and..."

Without even thinking, I pick it up, "Hello?"

"Hey. Did I wake you?"

"No...no. I just got in."

"I'm warning you now, I've left a whole bunch of messages." He laughs.

"I know. I just checked them," I lie.

"Well, it's late and I'm not going to keep you. I just wanted to let you know I was thinking about you."

"You were?" My heart feels like it's about to leap out of my chest.

"Yes."

"I was thinking about you too."

"Oh yeah? What were you thinking?"

That you're a mega-mack-daddy-player..., "That I enjoyed seeing you again the other night at May's and Jeff's."

"I feel the same way, Ruth. I wasn't all that hyped about that blind-date thing, but when I saw you... It turned out to be a good night. I think you're a beautiful woman and...I like the way you taste."

"Like baked chicken and wild rice?" Ruth, you idiot! The man just told you he thinks you're beautiful. Why do you always have to make a joke out of everything?

He laughs. "Like a sweet black woman with a pretty mouth."

"That's about the nicest thing anyone's said to me in a long time. Thank you," I say, blushing. I'm glad nobody's here to see this. "You're very nice."

"So are you."

Am I nice? Am I really nice? Nice and beautiful. Wow. "I don't do much dating, Adrian."

"Yeah, I remember you telling me that it's been awhile. Right?"

"It's been forever. And I'm not really sure what the rules are these days."

"Who is?"

"I'm serious."

"So am I," he says.

"I don't play games with people's feelings and...."

"I don't play games either. Don't have time for them."

"That's good to know. I'll make you a deal. You be honest with me and I'll be honest with you?"

"It's a deal."

"I hope...or if you just think this is just going to be a sex thing, that's not me. You're a great guy and we can be friends, which is fine with me. But I just think it's important for you to know..."

"I'm not a player if that's what you're thinking, Ruth."

That's not what I was thinking. Not really. Okay, so maybe I was thinking it. "The thought never crossed my mind."

"I'm looking forward to seeing you again. I haven't been able to say that about a woman in a long time."

"Really? I'm surprised. I'd think you'd have your choice of women."

"No, it's not like that. I mean, I date. But nothing serious. I haven't met anyone I want to be serious with in awhile."

"Well, I'm not all that sure how serious I'm ready to get right now either."

"And that's fine. Tell you what. I'll make you a promise right now. We can take this thing as easy as you want to take it. I'm in no hurry either. Right now, we're just two people who like each other's company and that's it. You cool with that?"

"Very cool."

"We on for dinner Friday?"

"Sure. Friday's good for me."

"All right, then. I'll uh...let you go." Please don't. I wanted to say. "But I'll give you a call again tomorrow."

"Okay, Adrian."

"Goodnight," he whispers, then hangs up.

I'm grinning so hard my face hurts and I grab my pillow, wrap my arms around it as tight as I possibly can, close my eyes, pretend it's him and sleep like a baby.

Sixteen

"Hi, Adrian." Oh God, can he see my legs wobbling?

"Hello. I'm a little early."

"Oh, that's okay." *I've only been ready for hours.* "I'll be ready in a few minutes."

"Nice place," he says surveying my little apartment.

"Thanks. It's small, but..."

"No, it's cool. Plenty of room for you, right?"

"Plenty. Have a seat. I'll only be a few minutes."

With the bedroom door closed securely between us, I grab a pillow off my bed, run into my closet, shut the door and nearly scream at the top of my lungs, "He is so fine! Oh my goodness! Lord have mercy! Goodness gracious!" Finally, I stop tripping long enough to come out and check my makeup. My palms are sweating. Dang! When's the last time that happened? I can't believe how nervous I am. I like him so much. Maybe too much. C'mon, Ruth. It's just dinner, Girl. What's the big deal? Adrian's the big deal. Probably the biggest deal to happen to me in a long time and he has no idea. Poor man. I'm not telling him what tonight means to me because nobody deserves that kind of pressure. It's funny. Here I am, damn near 35 years old and I feel like this is my first date. I've got butterflies attacking my stomach, spaghetti noodles for legs and I've barely said hello to the man. He's probably wondering what's taking so long. If he only knew.

God, I don't want him to know. Let him think I've got my shit together. Let him think I'm all that. Please. Just for tonight. Let him think I'm the woman he's always dreamed of.

Dinner is nearly painless. Naturally, I say some things I wish I hadn't, accidentally drop a piece of chicken in my lap and I think I use the salad fork when I should've used the dinner fork, but Adrian is gracious enough to pretend not to notice. After dinner, we both agree we need to work off that meal and decide to take a stroll along the Riverwalk. The lights from the Jacksonville Landing reflect off the St. John's River, dancing on the small waves like stars and the gentle breeze encourages Adrian to do the polite thing and put his jacket over my shoulders. "So, Jacksonville isn't your home either?"

"No. I'm originally from Denver."

"Denver? They got black folks in Denver?" he teases.

"Ha. Ha. Ha. You're funny. Anybody ever tell you how funny you are?"

"No. Nobody ever has. So what brought you here?"

"My mother died when I was 13 and I was sent here to live with my Grandmother."

"I'm sorry. That had to be rough. How'd she die? Or am I getting too personal?"

"Complications from surgery."

"That's a hard thing to deal with at 13. Hell, it would be a hard thing to deal with at any age."

"It was hard then and sometimes it still is. Karen was my world, and as far as I was concerned, we were going to be together forever. All my friends were in a hurry to grow up and get as far away from their parents as possible. But not me. My plan was to kidnap Momma so we could spend the rest of our lives together on some deserted island. Just the two of us."

"What about your father?"

"No room for him. He'd have to get his own island." Adrian smiled. "Actually, I never knew him."

"His loss."

"It was. Momma was beautiful."

"You must look a lot like her, then?"

I laugh. "Anybody ever tell you how charming you can be?"

"Sometimes I am charming. Sometimes, like now, I'm straightforward, which gets me into trouble every now and then." He's so full of shit and wonderfully flattering. "All your family here in Florida?"

"The only family I had was my Grandmother, but she died a few years ago. Now, I'm it," I attempt to smile at that, but it's pretty lame and I realize that the closest thing I have to family is Bernie. "What about you? Do you have a big family up there in Cincinnati?"

"Cincinnati. Cleveland. Alabama. Maryland. I've got a big family. Period."

"You like it? Having a big family?"

"It's cool for family reunions and weddings. Other times it can be a pain in the butt."

"Why?"

"All those damn birthdays, anniversaries, graduations..." I laugh. "Brotha gets a job that pays a little money, then everybody finds out, and bug the hell out of your ass reminding you about Carl Jr.'s birthday, or Little Lisa's graduation from Preschool. Wouldn't be so bad if I knew who Carl Jr. or Little Lisa was."

"It shouldn't matter. As long as Carl Jr. and Little Lisa are happy."

We stop walking and Adrian leans back against the wall of the boardwalk, pulling me into his arms. He's been trying to do this all night, look deeply into my eyes and make me forget my own name, but until now I've been able to avoid it. This time though, he's got me, and I'm hypnotized like the proverbial deer in the headlights. Even if I wanted to turn away, I can't.

"Your mother have big, pretty brown eyes like you?"

I smile. "The biggest and the prettiest."

"Then your daddy must've had some ugly eyes."

"He must've. Who do you look like? Mom or Dad?"

"The mailman," he says, smiling.

I laugh. "If I ever meet your mother..."

"I'm kidding."

"Is your dad handsome?"

"He thinks so. Mom thinks so."

"Then he probably is."

Adrian kisses me lightly on my neck, "You know I'm trying to behave myself?"

"Oh...are you?" I can hardly breathe.

"I promised I wouldn't rush things with you. I think I've kept my promise. Don't you?" He nibbles on my ear lobe, pressing it between two very sensuous lips. "I promised I wouldn't make any sudden moves."

"This isn't a move?" He runs his fingers gently across my lower back and holds me so close I don't know where I end and he begins.

"It's...yeah. It's a move. But if you want me to stop, all you've got to do is say the word. I'll back off."

"No. No, this is nice."

"I think it is. Mmmm. You smell good," he whispers.

The warmth of his breath against my neck is absolutely lethal and my little composure is just about gone at this point, "Thank you. It's called... Oh shoot! I don't...remember what it's...called, but...I just bought it the other day and..."

Adrian interrupts my rambling with a kiss, caressing my lips with his, then eases his warm tongue in my mouth. He kisses me for what seems like forever, but it's over much too soon. When he's finished, he holds me in both his arms and I rest my chin on his shoulders, inhaling him, melting into him, memorizing him. I hope this night never ends and I pray silently that he'll hold on to me like this all night, into the next day and the next night and the next day and...anyway, it's Adrian who finally breaks the spell.

He squeezes me gently. "I'd better get you home."

"No, Adrian. Can't we stay here a little longer, just like this?"

He laughs. "I promised I'd take my time, Ruth. And if I don't get you home...to your home, I can't guarantee I'll keep my promise, Baby."

As good as he feels and makes me feel, I know I'm not

ready for more than this. But it's this...this affection that I've been starved for most of my life. The human touch has been known to revive, cure, revitalize, but Eric's touches stick out most in my memory and his possessed no such hidden powers. Adrian and I walk back to his car and he holds my hand. It's amazing how rehabilitating a good handhold can be.

When we get back to my place, he walks me to my door, then bends to kiss me goodnight, "I'll call you tomorrow. Maybe we can get together sometime this weekend."

"I don't have any plans," I say much too anxiously. I have got to learn to play harder to get.

"I've got to go out of town on Monday and I'd like to see you before I leave."

"How long are you going to be gone?"

"A few days. My company is flying me off to San Francisco."

"I hear it's nice there."

"It's all right." He shrugs. "I'm usually in meetings and hotels all day, so I don't get to see much of it."

"That's kind of a waste. Haven't you been to Nob Hill? What about the Golden Gate Bridge? I've always wanted to see China..." Adrian interrupts me again with another kiss, which is cool. He can interrupt me like this anytime he feels like it.

"The Black Arts Festival is here this weekend at the convention center. I was thinking about going on Sunday. You free?"

"Sure. I'd love to go."

"All right. Then I'll call you tomorrow about a time."

"Yeah, that's fine. I'll be home, so Sunday's good for me."

"All right, Baby." He kisses me again. "You get on inside, now. And goodnight."

It's been a very good night and I'm grateful he was kind enough to share it with me. I have a serious crush on Adrian Carter. Yeah, he's fine and a wonderful kisser, but he's also just an awesome man. If he has any ulterior motives, he's really good at hiding them. Whatever his motives are, his methods are bomb!

Seventeen

"It's ugly, Baby. I don't know what else to say." Adrian glares at the sculpture I like so much like it's the worse piece of art he's ever seen. "You really like that?"

"Well...yes. I mean...it's different." Sort of like me. Kind of odd. But it's tougher than it looks. It's made of smooth, black iron and I find that alluring.

"Yeah, it's different all right."

"I just thought it would look nice on my coffee table. It's unique and I like that."

"Let's keep looking. Maybe we can find something else for your coffee table." We've spent all afternoon at the art show and it became obvious very early on that Adrian and I don't have the same appreciation for some things. I'm not as harsh in my opinion of the things he likes, but maybe I should take lessons because he doesn't seem to mind letting me know what he thinks at all.

"Maybe if you just try to use your imagination a little..."

"What about something like this?" He holds up a ceramic sculpture of a man and woman whose bodies look like two snakes mating.

"It's nice. Very... I've seen that somewhere before. You like it?"

"Don't you?"

"Sure." Ruth! Girl you know better than that. "It's

beautiful."

Adrian stares back at me. "You don't like it."

"What? I do. No, it's nice."

He smiles then puts it back on the stand. "You don't like it." Adrian takes my hand and leads me off to some paintings at another display. He's been like this all day, holding my hand, hating my tastes in art, paying attention to me, asking for my honest opinions and I'm enjoying myself tremendously. "Am I getting on your nerves?" he turns to ask.

"A little," I tease.

He smiles. "Just checking."

While we're admiring the paintings, a tall, gorgeous, goddess-type comes up to Adrian and kisses his cheek. She's almost as tall as he is. Her complexion is honey-gold and long, light brown hair hangs down to her shoulders. "Hello, Adrian," she says, glancing briefly in my direction. Immediately I know I'm nothing more than a fly on the wall to this vixen who ignores me as if my average looks are no match for her extraordinary beauty.

If Adrian's the least bit uncomfortable from this attention, he doesn't show it. "Ashley. How've you been?"

She smiles. "I haven't seen much of you lately. Where've you been hiding?"

"Not hiding. Just busy." Okay, so like I've disappeared off the face of the planet and nobody's even noticed. Right? An old flame? Of course she is. Girlfriend is making it obvious that, at least for some time in the not so distant past, she and Mr. Carter had spent some quality time together. She stands close enough to bump heads with the man and subtly eases his hand out of mine. Okay, the awkwardness of this situation is way more than I'm interested in handling. I see the way she's looking at him and the way he's looking at her. Hell, I can almost smell the sparks flying between these two and it doesn't take me but a second to realize this is not my kind of scene. I decide it's time for me to ease out of the intimate circle they've created for themselves, blend into the crowd and disappear from this man's life forever. "By the way," he says, grabbing my hand before I can escape, "this is my... This is Ruth. Ruth...Ashley."

"Hi, Ashley. Nice to meet you," I say, trying to smile.

She glances quickly at the space above my head, makes me vanish again and goes right back to gazing into his eyes, "Adrian...," she pulls a business card from her purse and writes something on the back. "Here's my number in case you lost it. Call me? Maybe we can get together and do something." She winks and demurely walks away.

He tries not to smile as she walks away and he tries not to watch her ass sway to the rhythmic beat only heard by canines and men, but his effort is futile.

After she leaves, Adrian seems strangely silent. Or is it just my imagination? "She was cute." As soon as I say it, I regret it. After all, the man isn't blind. He already knows she's cute...beautiful.

"What? Oh...yes. She is," he says, admiring the paintings.

"She's tall."

"You like this?" Adrian holds up a painting of a meadow filled with wild flowers and a black woman in a bonnet sitting alone looking off into the distance. She looks lonely and I don't particularly care for it.

"Do you?" I ask him.

He looks back at me, "I asked you first."

"It's okay. It's nice."

"I don't like it." Then why the hell did he pick it up? And why the hell did he ask me if I liked it without telling me up front that he didn't like it? You know what? I think I'm trying too hard. I should've just come out and told the man I thought the picture was ugly instead of trying to spare his feelings. He doesn't bother trying to spare mine. Everything I pick up, he hates—the sculpture, the paintings, the Ethiopian vase that I thought would look so good on the mantle over my fireplace. He didn't even bother hiding the fact that he had it bad for Miss America. So what am I doing here? And what am I doing here with him?

"Can we go now?"

He looks at me, "Now? Ruth, we haven't been here that long."

"I know. I'm... I've got a headache."

"A headache? That was sudden." He puts the painting back on the display table.

"It happens like that sometimes and I'd really like to go."

"This is about Ashley, isn't it?"

"Of course not." There I go again lying. "I'm not feeling well. I get migraines and sometimes they come on pretty fast. I just need to go home, Adrian."

"Baby...look," he wads up the business card in his hand and drops it on the ground. "It's not what you think it is. I'm not interested in her."

Not interested in her? How dumb do I look? What man in his right mind wouldn't be interested in a woman like that? Especially if she was in heat for him the way she's in heat for Adrian. Of course he's interested in her.

"I'm really not feeling well, Adrian. That's all." I make a beeline for the exit door without bothering to check and see if he's behind me. If he isn't, I'll take the damn bus home.

We drive all the way back to my place without uttering a sound to each other. I feel so silly. Not just about my reaction to the whole Ashley thing, but because I know I'm not ready for this. Secure, healthy-minded, independent individuals can have boyfriends. Not people like me. I've got issues and I will always have issues and rather than pursue this thing with Adrian anymore, the best thing I can do is continue to work on getting my issues in check so that one day the Ashley's of the world don't bother me. I'm going to get started as soon as I get inside my apartment.

"Thanks, Adrian. I had a nice time." I quickly open the car door to leave.

He reaches over and closes it. "Ruth. You're making a whole lot out of nothing, Baby."

"Maybe I am."

"She and I used to date. That's all. It's never been anything serious between us."

"You don't have to explain anything to me, Adrian. It's not you. It's me."

"Don't even go there. That's bullshit, Ruth. If you've got a problem with me then you need to talk to me. Tell me what it is."

"I don't have a problem. It's not you. Maybe it's best if we..."

"Is that what you want? You want to leave it alone?"

"There's just a lot going on with me, Adrian. And I'm not ready for any type of relationship right now."

"Why don't you tell me what's going on?"

"No."

"Why not?"

"Because. You wouldn't understand."

"How do you know, Ruth? Why don't you give me a chance to understand?"

"It's complicated."

"It usually is."

"Too complicated."

"I'm listening."

"You couldn't possibly understand this, Adrian. Not many people could."

"Ruth..."

"I've got to go. You take care of yourself."

I feel like an idiot. Like a child who's thrown a tantrum. I feel stupid. I overreacted. Even if she does mean something to him, Adrian's not my man. He never said he was and I never said it either. He's free to do what he wants with whoever he wants. So am I. Every time I think I've made progress, something happens to set me back. Eric flirted with everything that had breasts and that's what I expect from men. All men. The residual effects of my marriage seem to be endless and I wonder if I'll ever be free of them. Adrian probably thinks I'm such a fool. I know I do.

***

A cup of hot chamomile tea is tucking me in tonight. I can't sleep, not after the way I acted today. It's not so terrible, though. Sometimes I forget and days like today remind me that all is not well in the psyche of Ruth Johnson. But the good news is that I recognize that fact and I'm in touch enough with reality to face myself and admit I've still got a long way to go. The phone rings, startling me out of my self-revelation, "Hello?"

"Ruth? It's Adrian."

"Adrian? Hello."

"Were you sleeping?"

"No. Not yet."

"I've um... I've got a couple of tickets to the Luther concert next week and I was wondering if you'd like to go with me?"

"I'd love to."

"I was hoping you'd say that."

"I didn't think you'd call."

"I wasn't sure you wanted me to."

"I'm glad you did."

"So am I. Goodnight, Baby."

"Goodnight, Adrian."

Eighteen

Best friends are where you bury your secrets and plant your hopes for safekeeping. I know everything about Bernice Watson. Not many people know she used to be a housewife. She was married to Monte for 17 years before she found out about the affair he'd been having. I think she could've gotten past that, but it was more than she could handle when she found out he had a daughter by the woman. It took a lot of courage for her to leave him. He'd been her high school sweetheart and he took care of her and the boys. She had a nice house, two healthy kids, a couple of cars, but she didn't have respect for him anymore and that was enough for her to leave. She got a job as a receptionist, worked her way through school, became a certified Paralegal and got a position at the law firm where we met. The boys are both grown now. Sean, her oldest is in the military and David has just graduated college.

I know one thing. That woman can shop her behind off. We spent all day in the mall until I'm finally able to convince her that my poor feet couldn't take anymore. I threatened that if she didn't get me some place where I could take off my shoes and sit down, I was going to start crying and embarrass the mess out of her. So she rushed me back to her place, fixed me a White Wine Spritzer and let me pour myself into that big soft couch of hers while the feeling eased back into my toes.

"I've ummm...been calling around town for places to see where we might be able to host the fund-raiser," I say nonchalantly. She hasn't mentioned anything about it since I approached her with the idea and I'm worried she's changed her mind about helping me.

Bernie leans back and rests her head on the back of her chair. Her eyes are closed, but from time to time she sips on her cocktail, "Is that right?"

"Yeah. Renting a place is going to be expensive."

"I'm not surprised." I wait for her to say something encouraging, enlightening, or even smug. But she doesn't. She just lets her head fall to the side, leading me to believe if I don't say something soon I'm going to lose her and she'll spend the rest of the afternoon snoozing in that chair.

"You uh...you still going to help me?"

"I said I would," she says dryly.

"You're not too thrilled about the idea, are you?"

"Not really. It's a lot of work."

"You're right. It is a lot of work, but you know how much I appreciate you even thinking about giving me a hand with this, Bernie."

"I know." She smiles, then lets her head fall to the side again. Maybe I should leave it alone, let her rest and wait until she regains consciousness. I mean, I don't want to be pushy and get on her nerves. She might change her mind for real. Slowly she opens her eyes and looks at me, "I've got a friend over at the Hilton...a manager. He owes me a favor."

"Woman, is there anybody in this town that doesn't owe you a favor?"

"He owes me a big favor."

"How big?"

"Big enough to loan me a banquet room for one night to feed and entertain about 300 of my closest friends."

I sit straight up, "Bernie girl! Are you serious?"

"Don't I look serious?" she asks calmly.

"Are you...is he for real? Really for real?"

"Ruth, now you know I don't play when it comes to

business. Of course he's for real."

I don't know where I've found the strength, but I force myself up off that couch, hobble over to Bernie on my swollen, throbbing feet and hug her. "Bernie, you're terrific! I knew..."

"There's only one problem, though."

"A problem? What...what problem?"

"We have to use it before the end of next month, or he can't do it."

"Next month? That soon?" Needless to say, that's not good. Next month is way too soon to put together a banquet for 300 people.

"He's leaving, Baby. Moving back to Louisiana, and when he's gone..."

"That doesn't give us much time, Bernie."

"A little over a month and a half." Bernie smiles apologetically. "We can still do this, Ruth. If we put our minds to it and work hard, no half-steppin', we can do this."

"We? I thought you were just going to look into a few things? When did this officially become a "we" operation?"

"Since I know how much this means to you. You've come such a long way from where you used to be. And I'm so proud of you," Bernie says, covering my hand with hers. "Of course we have to do this. And we will, too."

With Bernie Watson leading the way and me as her faithful sidekick, of course we can do this. "Well then...I guess we'd better get down to business."

"I've already started." Bernie goes to her bedroom and comes back with a to-do list as long as my arm. "So, we've got the location," she says scratching the line off her list. "And I've started the list of folks we've got to invite if we want this thing to be successful."

Now, I know Bernie Watson has connections, but the names on the list are too impressive to believe, "Bernie, you know all of these people?"

"Of course I do."

I gasp, "You know Councilwoman Douglas? Councilwoman Susan Douglas?"

"Yes, I know the woman, Ruth. What's the big deal?"

"How did you meet her?"

"We go to the same beautician."

"Connie? But Connie specializes in..."

"Weaves," Bernie says matter-of-factly.

"Bernie! Councilwoman Douglas wears a weave?"

"Now I know you didn't think that was that woman's real hair."

"I did."

"Ruth, I've got more hair on my eyebrows that she's got on her head. Don't be so naive."

"You know Carl Johnson? Channel five's Carl Johnson?"

Bernie smiles, "Oh, I know him all right."

"Bernie!"

"Don't ask." She laughs.

"You didn't. You did?"

"I said, don't ask. I promised the man I wouldn't kiss and tell, so...

"You've never kept that promise before. What's he like in person?"

"Anyway, we've got the location and the guest list. If you think of anyone else, let me know now. I'm going to get the invitations printed next week."

"Well, what do you want me to do?"

"You work on the food. And get somebody decent, Girl. I know these people personally, and the last thing I need is for them to go around talking about how bad the food was at my fund raiser."

"What happened to "we"?"

"That's what I said. We'll need some entertainment, too. You can work on that too. Somebody or something impressive, please. No wanna be rappers or amateur actors. I might be able to help you out on that and..."

I'm sitting here in awe of this woman. Damn, she's got it going on. Bernie has herself so together and I'm touched when I realize this really does mean as much to her as it does to me and I hug her again. "This is going to be great. I know it is. I should call Clara."

Bernie smiles. "Why don't you call her now?"

Nineteen

I'm proud to say, keeping up with Super May on our 10 lap trek to good health and good looks is no longer a problem. I swear, that woman works out like she's just not satisfied with that size eight body of hers. I guess that's why she's size eight, because she doesn't ease up and she doesn't let me ease up either. That's a good thing. I know in my heart of hearts it wouldn't be hard for me to lock all the doors and windows of my house, curl up with a box of donuts and a diet soda and lose myself in cable television. May's my motivation. Well, May and Adrian. He tells me he thinks I'm sexy. He wouldn't think that if he saw me inhaling a box of donuts and a diet soda.

"I got the invitation to yo' banquet the other day," she huffs.

"Good," I puff. "You coming?"

"Wouldn't miss it."

"I'm glad. It's going to be really nice. You won't be disappointed."

"Well, for $200 bucks a plate we better not be," she teased.

"It's for a good cause."

"A battered woman's shelter?"

"A shelter for victims of domestic violence," I correct her.

"Same thing."

"It is."

"You ever live there?"

I'm not surprised by her question. As a matter of fact, I expected that invitation to stir her curiosity. I'm glad it has and I'm glad she's my friend. "No."

"He was abusive, though? Yo' ex-husband?"

"He was."

"I had a feelin' it was something like that."

"Why?"

"'Cause you weren't pissed enough for it to have been another woman and you seem unsure of yo'self, 'specially when we first met. I don't know. You jus' seemed tired and a little scared. When I first saw you, you looked like a woman tryin' to erase her past, maybe even herself. I saw it in yo' eyes."

"My eyes."

"The eyes are the windows to the soul. Haven't you ever heard that? It's true. Sometimes you can look into a person's eyes and piece together a whole history of where they been, who they are without them ever tellin' you a thing."

"You saw my history in my eyes?"

"I saw a history that wasn't very pretty."

"No, it never was."

"You ain't the same woman, though."

"Well duh! I've only lost 40 pounds, May."

"That ain't what I mean and you know it. You got more respect for yo'self and it shows. I don't care if you hadn't lost 40 pounds."

"It's hard sometimes."

"Course it is. But so was living like that. Wasn't it?"

"Very hard."

"How come you never told me?"

"I was embarrassed. That's not the kind of thing I want to share with my new friends. Hello, my name is Ruth and I'm a battered woman. Wanna do lunch?"

"That the only reason?"

"I didn't want you to judge me. It's easy for a woman to say she'd never let a man hit her and get away with it. But it's a whole different story when you've got a mad man standing over you breathing fire through his nostrils with his fists balled up, cussing and calling you names you never even heard of. Screaming about how fucked up you are and how sorry your dumb ass is. It's never the actual fight that scares you. It's everything leading up to that. Waiting for the bomb to drop is more terrifying than when it actually hits the ground."

"I wouldn't know, Sweetie. I hope I never do."

"With a man like Jefferson, I don't think you'll ever have to know, May."

"Did you love him?"

"Thought I did in the beginning. Now I know I never did."

"He ever love you?"

"No."

"Doesn't it hurt knowin' that?"

"It used to, but I think it would've hurt more if he had loved me and treated me like that."

"Well, if you didn't love him and he didn't love you..."

"Why stay married?"

"Yeah."

"I think I depended on him. I depended on him to keep me from being totally alone, even if it meant being miserable. I even depended on his lies, I suppose. There were moments when he made me feel important, even wanted. Unfortunately, it was usually after he'd finished beating my ass over something stupid."

"Is Eric as pretty as Adrian?" She smiles.

"No one's as pretty as Adrian."

"I beg to differ. Jefferson is just as pretty, if not prettier."

"That's because Jefferson is your man and you're supposed to think he's prettier."

"Is Adrian yo' man, Ruth?"

"No. He's my friend."

"But he's workin' on bein' yo' man?"

"Will you stop? He and I are just friends and that's all."

"For now," she says smugly. "Bernie goin' to be at this banquet?"

"Yep. She's helping put the whole thing together."

"She sounds like a good friend?"

"The best."

"I'm lookin' forward to meetin' her."

"She's lookin' forward to meeting you too," I lie.

Twenty

Oh my goodness! Somebody's sick or dead or worse. What other reason would have my phone ringing at one-thirty in the morning? "Hello," I say anxiously into the phone. My heart's pounding hard in anticipation of the dreadful news I know I'm about to hear.

"Ruth? Hey, it's Adrian. I know it's late, but I've been in meetings all day, then dinner with business associates tonight. I told you I'd call."

"Adrian, are you back?"

"No, I'm still in San Francisco. You were on my mind and I wanted to say hello."

I'm grinning like the Cheshire Cat. "I've missed you."

"Oh yeah?"

"Yeah. I have."

"You miss me enough to come see me?"

"What?"

"I can have a ticket waiting for you at the airport, Ruth. I've been meaning to take your advice and see more of San Francisco anyway. So why don't you come see it with me?"

"Are you serious?"

"Of course I'm serious," he says, leaving me speechless. "You thinking about it?"

"Can I call you back?"

"No. You can't. You can tell me you're coming, though."

"Adrian, this is such short notice and I know you don't expect me to just hop on a plane to California just like that."

"We're only talking a weekend, Ruth. One weekend. C'mon, Sweetheart. Let's do this." I don't know what to say. The invitation is definitely tempting. "Well..."

"I'll have the ticket waiting for you at the airport. The plane leaves Florida at nine and I'll see you when you get here, Baby."

Adrian hangs up and I know I won't sleep the rest of the night. I'm shocked. He wants me to come to San Francisco to spend the weekend with him. I mean...Adrian wants me to come to San Francisco to spend the weekend with...him. My brain does flip flops wrestling with this until finally, I call Bernie, you know, for some sisterly advice.

"Ruth?" she asks groggily.

"Who's that, Baby?" The male voice asks in the background.

"Bernie, guess what? Adrian just called me. He wants me to fly to California to spend the weekend with him. He's going to have a ticket waiting for me at the airport in the morning."

"Ruth?" she says again.

"I don't know what I should do. I mean...I hardly know this man."

"Ruth?" Why does she keep saying my name over and over again like that?

"Yes. It's me, Bernie. It's Ruth."

"Bruce? Did you say Bruce? You got some other brotha callin' up in here, Bernie?" The male voice asks. "You know I'm not down for drama, Woman. I thought you said you didn't have a man."

"Bernie, what do you think? You think I should go? I don't know. But that's a lot of money he's talking about spending and I'd hate for him to pay for the ticket and I don't show up. Most of these airlines are really stingy about refunds. He'd be out of hundreds of dollars. How much do you think it costs to fly from here to California? I should call and find out, huh? I'll have to pay him back. You know how I am. I couldn't take his money like that. I'm not one to take advantage of anyone's generosity. Yeah, maybe I'll pay him in installments. Something every month until I've paid him back, because I don't want to owe anybody anything. You know what I mean? Bernie? You there?"

"Ruth."

"I don't know what to do, Bernie. I'd like to go, but...I'm scared."

"Of what?"

"What do you mean of what? Of...of...I don't know. I just am."

"Ruth Johnson, you're a grown woman and if you want to go to California then go to California, but don't call me up in the middle of the night to get my permission again, or I'm going to have to cuss you out." Then she hangs up.

Damn. She didn't have to be so rude about it. Of course I'm a grown woman. I know that, but it's not about me being a grown woman. It's about doing the right thing. I've been so good lately at doing the right thing. I can't remember the last time I messed up or made a stupid decision. Ever since I left Eric, doing the right thing is the only thing that matters. Because with him, I did the wrong thing for a long time and I paid dearly for it. And if I keep on doing the right thing, maybe I won't end up in a mess like that ever again. That's what it's about. Not about being a grown woman who desperately wants to go to California and spend the weekend with tall, dark and handsome Adrian and take some chances with her life, maybe even have the time of her life.

"Don't even go there, Ruth. Now's not the time to be impetuous," I say out loud. "I mean, Adrian is a wonderful man and I like him a lot. But even though I really don't have any plans this weekend, flying all the way to the other side of the country just doesn't make sense. And if it doesn't make sense, then it's not for me. It's not what I need." Besides, Adrian will have me alone in a hotel room for two days and I know what that could lead to. Sex. Sex just messes everything up. Adrian and I have a good thing going right now. Why ruin the whole thing by complicating it with sex? I'm not going and that's final.

I crawl back into bed and close my eyes, daring them to open again before morning. Two seconds later I'm staring up at the ceiling and a big grin spreads across my face. "Okay...okay," I say sitting up in bed. "I'm going to San Francisco?" *Am I?* "Yes! I'm going to San Francisco! I am going to San Fran-cis-co!" Next thing I know I'm jumping up and down on my bed like I'm five years old. "I'm going to San Francisco! I'm going to San Francisco!" Forget right or wrong. My grown ass is going to throw caution to the wind and tomorrow I'm flying to San Francisco to spend the weekend alone with my man!

***

What the hell am I doing in San Francisco? I feel downright stupid standing here in the airport looking like I'm supposed to be in Florida, not California. I pray he hasn't forgotten about me, but hope that maybe he has and I can turn around, go home and spend the rest of my life pissed off at him.

"Hey, Baby," he whispers over my shoulder. I turn around and there he is in all his fine-ass glory. "Damn, I'm glad you're here." He bends to kiss me and just that quick. I'm glad I'm here too.

Adrian takes my hand and my bags and loads me into the car. The top is down; we're speeding down the coast and suddenly, my jet lag is cured. I don't think I've ever seen a more beautiful stretch of highway in my life and if it were up to me, we'd just drive for the whole weekend and never stop. He takes a detour off Highway One to Panoramic and we decide to do a little sightseeing. The Giant Redwood trees of Muir Woods absolutely blow my mind and Adrian lets me take about a dozen pictures. God is a trip sometimes. Where does he come up with this stuff? Panoramic eventually runs back into Highway One and we arrive at Stinson Beach where Adrian's reserved a cabin for the weekend.

He pulls me into his arms as soon as we're inside, nuzzling his face in the crook of my neck, creating a winding trail of tiny kisses from the lobe of my ear to the top of my shoulder. I love it when he does this. But I'm not too fond of that! Adrian's hands have slipped down below the sanctity of my waist to my ass and he palms my behind like a basketball squeezing me entirely too close to him. Oh my goodness! Is that his dick I feel? I ease myself away from him calmly enough for him not to notice I'm tripping.

"I'd better put my things away. Where's my room?"

He smiles and points to a door behind me, "The bedroom is right behind you."

"The bedroom? Where's the other one?"

"What other one?"

"Aren't there two bedrooms?"

"One's plenty," he says squeezing me close to him again.

"Is it?"

"You don't think so?"

Before I flew all the way out here, I thought so. While we drove up the coast across the Golden Gate Bridge, I thought so. Standing here in his arms, in this little cabin, with only one bedroom, I don't think so. What in the world is my problem? I want to do this. I want to trade in Maxwell for the real thing, for Adrian, except I've got knots in my stomach just thinking about it and my feet are icy cold.

Adrian takes one look at the expression on my face and the smile he's worn all afternoon disappears. "You take the room. I'll sleep on the couch."

"No, Adrian. I couldn't ask you to do that. I can sleep on the couch. Really, I'd rather."

"No," he said picking up my luggage, "I insist." He takes my things into the bedroom and I feel awful.

Not only have I let him down, but I've let myself down, not to mention I owe Bernie 50 bucks.

"That man's spending $600 to fly your ass across the country, Ruth. The least you could do is give him a little, for your sake as well as his."

"You don't think I will, do you?"

"I know you won't."

"Well, what if I do?"

"If you do I'll give you fifty dollars."

"And if I don't."

"You pay me."

"I'm almost tempted to take you up on your little bet, Bernice Watson."

"Put up or shut up, Girlfriend."

"You don't think I'm brave enough to have sex with Adrian?"

"Honey. You've been through a lot in your life. Wouldn't nobody blame you if you're too chicken to get your groove on with that man. But hell, if he's all that, like you claim he is, I'm wondering what's taking you so long."

"Chicken? You think I'm scared?"

"Bakkk! Bakkk! Bakkk!"

"Fine, Bernie! Fine. You're on. Fifty bucks says I'll have sex with Adrian."

"Don't do it for fifty dollars, Ruth. Do it because you want to."

"Oh. I want to, Miss Thang. I definitely want to and I'm going to."

"How am I going to know you did?"

"Don't you trust me?"

"With my life. Not with my fifty dollars. How am I going to know?"

"Well. I don't know, Bernie. All you can do is take my word for it. Short of showing you pictures, what else can I do?"

"I guess that'll have to do then. But I want the truth when you get back, Ruth Johnson. And I'll know if you're lying."

Of course I want to make love to him. Who wouldn't? Fantasies of rolling around buck-naked with Adrian have crossed my mind and dreams a million times since we first met. But the truth is, I'm exactly what Bernie says I am. A great, big chicken.

We share a romantic dinner on the beach and watch the sun settle down for the night. Adrian's ordered in a picnic basket filled with white wine, fresh strawberries and green grapes, cream cheese, a fresh sourdough loaf, sliced roast beef, turkey and spiced mustard. Later, we stroll down the white sandy beach, holding hands and dipping our toes into the water. He starts it. He splashes me first and I can't let him get away with that, so I splash him back. But my splash is bigger than his splash and you know how men are about things like that. All of them feel like they've got to have the biggest splash. But before I have a chance to run, he catches me, and Lord have mercy! That man picks my big ass up!

"Adrian! Adrian!" I scream, hanging onto him for dear life. If he drops me, I'll die. I know I will. "Please! Adrian! Put me down! Adrian! I'm too heavy!"

"Oh, Baby! My back! My back! Oh...Ruth!" Adrian's bends over like he's in pain. "You're breaking my back, Ruth!"

"I'm serious!"

"Oh! Ow! Damn, Baby! How much you weigh? You don't look like you that big."

"Will you please put me down?"

"All right. All right," he says putting me back on Earth. "Damn! I think I might need some traction."

"Nobody told you to play weight lifter. Serves you right."

"You're not heavy."

"I've been heavy my whole life, Adrian. I know I'm heavy."

"No baby. You're not heavy. You're thick."

"What's the difference?"

"About 50 pounds," he says, then chases me back to the cabin.

Adrian's taken his shower already and has the nerve to come out wearing nothing but the bottom half of his pajamas. I've never seen a chest that broad and pretty in my whole life. It's lovely to say the least, but of course, I'm not one to stare. Not so that it's obvious, anyway. And where'd he get all those biceps and triceps? And why did he keep them hidden all the time?

"The shower's all yours," he says, pecking my cheek as he passes me in the doorway. And who told him he has to smell that good just to go to sleep?

I shower quickly because to be honest, I'm a bit paranoid. What if Adrian's decided he can't wait and comes bursting into the bathroom, takes off his pants and climbs into the shower with me, kissing me passionately, rubbing soap up and down my back, and... Stop it, Ruth! Either do it, or don't. But don't keep teasing your chicken ass. Make up my damn mind! I stopped at the mall before I left and picked up this sexy, little cream colored nightie and matching thong, but I think I'd better sleep in my old worn out football jersey instead. The bleach stains aren't that noticeable and I sewed up that hole so good I can't even tell where it is anymore.

Adrian's taken a pillow and blanket from the bedroom. "Are you sure you don't want the bedroom, Adrian? It doesn't seem fair for me to sleep in here, after all you paid for the place."

He smiles, then kisses me on my cheek, "No, Love. I'm cool. Sweet dreams."

"Goodnight," I whisper. My dreams will only be sweet, if they're of him.

I can't sleep. How can I, knowing he's on the other side of that door? I don't get it. How many times did I lay there and let Eric fuck me? How many times did I fake orgasms and pretend it felt good when it didn't? I learned to operate like a robot, moaning on cue, coming like a madwoman in the hopes he'd get it over with, cum, roll over and go to sleep. How many times did I put up with his drunk ass slobbering all over me, calling me a bitch because I couldn't fuck worth a damn? How many times did he put his nasty dick in my ass, my mouth? Adrian's not Eric. I've weaved scenarios together in my mind of making love to Adrian, but they're unraveling this very second while I lay here wondering what the hell my problem is. I masturbate like crazy with poor Maxwell, who out of nowhere grows arms, legs and Adrian's beautiful face. Hovering over me he whispers over and over again, "I love you, Ruth." He licks, fondles and tastes every inch of me, burying himself as deep inside my body as he can go without giving me an aneurism. I gaze back into his eyes, waiting and watching for the climax of our consummation until finally, I close my eyes and come all over this beautiful man harder than I've ever come in my life. But when I open my eyes, Adrian's gone and all that's left is Maxwell droning on and on lifeless and rigid until I hit the off switch. Definitely pathetic. How come I can't get over it, whatever it is? What is it? What is it I'm scared of?

Adrian taps lightly on the door and peeks in, "You all right?"

I wipe away tears before he sees I'm crying and sit up in bed, "Yes." He starts to leave, "No."

Adrian comes inside and sits down on the bed next to me. His silhouette is as perfect as he is. He puts his hand against my cheek, "What's wrong, Baby?" I don't know what to tell him. Nothing's wrong. Not anymore. Not with him here. Adrian leans close to me, kisses my eyes, then my nose, my lips. Is this it God? Is this my chance? Do it now, or it may never happen? Adrian stops kissing me and pulls down the sheet that covers my legs. He puts his hand on my knee then slides it slowly up my thigh to the hem of my shirt. I slowly raise my arms and he lifts my jersey over my head. I'm not cold, but I'm embarrassed and draw my knees up to my chest, wrapping my arms around them, holding myself together. Adrian stands up and takes off his pants and I see his erection even in the dark. He crawls over me to the other side of the bed and pulls me into his arms, then does something wonderful. He holds me and softly kisses my head. I've never felt so secure, so safe in my whole life. The rhythm of his heartbeat lulls me into calm and even if it's only for tonight, this is where I belong. In his arms, in this bed, in San Francisco.

"That better, Baby?"

I can't answer, but with all my strength, I try to get even closer to him than I already am. He lifts my face to his and fills my mouth with languid kisses. Then he takes my hand, guides it down his body and gently wraps my fingers around his erect penis like he knows my introduction to this part of him needs to take place before we can begin. Adrian rolls me over on my back and raises himself above. He stares at my body and when I try to hide myself, he stops me. "You're a beautiful woman, Ruth."

"I don't think so, Adrian."

"I do," he whispers.

Adrian makes a trail of kisses down my shoulders to my breasts. Carefully cradling them in his hands he takes his time, giving each of them his undivided attention, savoring my poor deprived breasts like they're precious fruit. "Mmmm...," I moan as he grazes his warm, moist tongue across my nipples which instantly erupt into tiny peaks. My legs spread to accommodate him and the sensation of his dick tickling the opening of my pussy is so exciting, I can hardly control myself, "Put it in," I hear myself whisper. "Please, Adrian. Put it in." My hips reach up to catch him inside me, but Adrian's not having it and makes it clear that he's in control.

"Not yet," he whispers. "We've got all night, Ruth. All weekend."

He takes my hand and softly kisses my palm, then wraps his lips around each of my fingers one by one. Adrian decides to make love to my mouth with his, deeply darting his tongue in and out, in and out, in and... Before I realize it, he eases himself inside me slowly, gently and I lift my knees to welcome him.

"Damn...Ruth," he says. "This is good, Baby. So..."

I'm full with this man and I can't believe how wonderful it feels. Adrian doesn't pound himself inside me, or demand I say things I don't want to say. His moves are smooth and sensual and most of all, considerate. My fingers trace a path down his back to the base of his spine and I feel the slow rise and fall of his ass against my palms. Adrian moans when I raise my hips up to meet his. I don't think I've ever been this wet before and nothing's ever felt this good to me. Not even Maxwell.

"Oooooo...Adrian," was that me?

Suddenly, he surprises me and pulls out, moving on to his next agenda, creating a wet path with his tongue down to my naval and planting a kiss there. The sensation sends chills all over me. "Oooh." I giggle. "That tickles." Adrian continues exploring me with his mouth, kissing and sucking down my thighs to my knees, to my shins until he finds...my feet. Lord! Who knew? Never in all my years of living would I have guessed that it would feel so good to have my toes sucked? "Oh my goodness, Adrian!"

He laughs, "Mmmm...You like this, Baby?"

"Yes," I say breathlessly. "Oh...yes...yes..."

"Me too." Adrian finishes with one set of toes then gets started on the other ones.

"No...Adrian," Dang! This feels incredible. Too incredible.

It just ain't right.

"Thought you liked it?"

"I do...no...I mean, I do...but...no," I pull my feet from his hands. Nobody should have that kind of power over another person. Toe sucking should be illegal.

"You want some more of me?" He smiles.

"Oh...yes. Yes," I say pulling him close to me. My mouth is hungry for him and I devour his neck, earlobes and shoulders, like I'm starving and he's the buffet. He thrusts in and out of me slow and deep. It almost hurts, but it feels too good to admit that. Is this making love? Yeah, it's got to be. Because this is lovely and, oh my goodness! I think I'm about to come.

He lies on top of me long after we're finished, still inside me, kissing my eyelids, nose, lips, "You know how long I've been wanting to do that?"

I smile. "Do you know how long I've wanted you to do that?"

"Why were you crying?"

"I don't know."

"Yes you do. Tell me?"

"It's silly."

"Can't be that silly if it made you cry."

"I wanted to be with you."

"That is silly. All you had to do was peek your head outside that door. I'd have come running."

"Is that all I had to do?"

"That's all you ever have to do, Baby. When are you going to figure that out?"

"I don't think I'll ever understand what you see in me."

"I see everything in you, Ruth Johnson. Absolutely everything, but that's all."

So we don't do much sightseeing. But I'm not complaining. We spend most of the weekend naked in the cabin, occasionally taking long walks on the beach and a trip here and there into town, mainly to pick up fresh crab meat and sourdough bread for sandwiches and white wine to wash them down with.

Adrian asks me out on a date and we meet on the porch of the cabin to watch the sunset. He holds me in his arms and I don't think I've ever been more content in my whole life than I am right now. "Why don't we go AWOL and not go back to Jacksonville? We can stay right here and live off crabmeat sandwiches."

"And each other?" he asks, knowing I'm not going to dispute that.

"I like the idea."

He kisses my head. "It's not bad, but I'm starting to get sick of crabmeat sandwiches."

"We can find something else to eat. Know how to fish? We can really live off the land and catch fish right out of our ocean."

"Our ocean?"

"Yes. That little part right there," I say pointing.

"I wish."

"So, we have to go back?" Am I pouting?

"Yeah, but we're going back together."

I know that's right! Unless he tells me otherwise, he's mine. All mine. "How come you've never been married, Adrian?"

"What's the politically correct thing to say? I never found the right woman?"

"That's hard to believe. I would think you'd have found lots of right women. Have you ever been in love?"

"Sure I have."

"Have you broken any hearts?"

"Yes."

"I knew it."

"But I've had mine broken too."

"By what's her name? Ashley?"

"No, not by Ashley."

"Was it just a sex thing?"

"Pretty much."

"Was she good in bed?"

"How many hearts have you broken, Ruth?"

"Me? None."

"C'mon."

"None. Really. I told you. I've been married forever, so..."

"You didn't break his heart?"

"Eric's? No."

"Who left who?"

"I don't know. We sort of left each other."

"After all those years? There had to be more to it than that?"

"There is. There's a lot more to it, but I didn't break his heart."

"Did he break yours?"

"Lots of times."

"You ever going to tell me what really happened between you two?"

"I don't know. Maybe. I don't know."

"I hope you do."

"Why?"

"'Cause I want to know. I want to know you."

"There's not much to know, Adrian. Besides, you're probably more interesting," I say, kissing his neck.

"Well, I'm not full of secrets like some folks 'round here. You want to know something about me, all you've got to do is ask."

"So I'm asking. Why do we have to go back to Florida? Why can't we sell all our stuff, invest in some loin cloths and fishing poles, pay up the rent on this place for another five years and forget about the real world altogether?"

"And then what? Since you're trying to change the subject."

"And then...we can have sex in our spare time. And I'm not trying to change the subject. I'm just trying to talk about something else."

"That's a nice dream."

"We can make it real."

"You've almost got me sold on the idea, Baby. Keep talking." Adrian slips his hand inside my robe, between my things and gently eases one of those long fingers of his inside my body. Then he pulls it out, puts it to his lips and...eeeew! Wow! That's intriguing.

Twenty One

See. This is why I didn't want to come back to reality. My job. More specifically, my boss at my job. Usually I'm numb to Don McGreggor and all his antics, but lately he's starting to wear out his welcome in my little world and it's getting harder to tolerate the man.

"Ruth?" His voice calls out over my intercom.

"Yes, Mr. McGreggor."

"I still haven't seen that Partnership Agreement for Lewis and Haverty? I thought you told me you'd have that finished today."

"I finished it yesterday, Mr. McGreggor."

"Well, why isn't it on my desk?"

"It is on your desk. I put it there this morning," I'm trying not to sound pissed, but I am. I definitely am. How many times does he do this? Lose my work in that black hole called his office, then demand I do it again like it's my fault he's irresponsible.

"I don't see it," he answers back.

"I put it with the Industrial Lease and the LLC Operating Agreement, Mr. McGreggor."

"The Industrial... Oh yes. Here it is." He hangs up with not so much as a "Sorry Ruth", or "Oops, my bad."

"Ruth," he buzzes through again.

"Yes."

"Do you have Shelton's Guarantee Agreement ready?"

"No. You told me you didn't need it until tomorrow's meeting."

"I told you we moved the meeting up a day."

"No, Mr. McGreggor. I don't think you did. I'd have written it on my calendar if..."

"Never mind. The meeting's today, Ruth, at 2:00 and I'll need that agreement on my desk in an hour."

"An hour? But what about..."

"An hour, Ruth." Again he hangs up and I'm so mad I could spit. Why me? I haven't even started on that damn agreement because I've been so busy with all this other crap he's piled on my desk at the last minute. Shit. Now my head hurts. Bernie walks by and notices me rubbing my temples.

"You okay?"

"I'm fine. Just tired. Why's everything got to be an emergency all the damn time? One minute he tells me he doesn't need the documents until tomorrow, then he comes back and all of a sudden he needs them today because he's moved up his damn meeting without telling me and now I've got to jump through hoops." I'm trying to keep my voice down, but it's not easy. "Sometimes, Bernie. Sometimes, I don't know how much more of this I can take."

"I know, Girl," she says sympathetically. "He's an asshole and everybody in the office knows it."

"I don't get it. What have I ever done to him?"

"Ruth, don't sit here trying to figure it out. He's not worth that kind of energy and you know it. It's a paycheck; that's all."

"Yeah, well, sometimes I wonder if that little bit of money is worth it."

"It is until you start school. That's only a few months away, Darlin'. Try and hang in there."

She's right, of course. School starts again soon and rather than do that two nights a week thing, I've decided to take Bernie's suggestion to heart and attend full time, finding a part time job to help keep me afloat financially. I've even qualified for some financial assistance from the government. Which is cool seeing as how I've generously been donating my tax dollars to them over the years. I can't continue to be somebody's whipping girl for the rest of my life. Shoot. Maybe one day, I can have a secretary of my own.

***

As usual, I end up staying late at the office, but the first thing I do when I get home is take off my shoes. The second thing I do is return Adrian's phone call.

"Hi," I say, smiling much too hard.

"Hey, Baby. You just getting home?"

"Yeah and I'm exhausted. How was your day?"

"Busy. I take it yours wasn't so good?"

"Actually it was about how it always is. McGreggor got on my last nerve. Have I ever told you about him?"

"You might've mentioned him once or twice. Let's see, the inconsiderate, unappreciative, slave-driving, bastard?"

I laugh. "Yeah, that's him."

"So why don't you get a new job?"

"That would be nice. Doing what?"

"What do you want to do?"

"That's the problem. I don't know. But I do know I don't want to trade a paycheck for a paycheck because then I'd be in the same boat. Working for some asshole and miserable. Unless..."

"Unless...what?"

"You hiring? I've got some impressive skills."

"Oh, Baby. You do have some serious skills."

"You know what I mean."

"And you know what I mean."

"Actually, I think you're the one with all the talent. I just follow your lead."

"Then I like the way you follow."

"I like the way you lead."

"You too tired for company?"

"Yes. But I'm never too tired for you."

"I'll be there in 20 minutes."

"Better hurry. I've been known to turn into a pumpkin after 10."

"I'm on my way."

Twenty Two

Sharon and I sit on the floor thumbing through magazines and card files looking for recipes of what to serve at the fund raiser. Winona Judd's rich melodies soothe us on the outside and the bottle of red wine we've just about finished soothes our insides pretty good too. We're like little girls playing with dolls with stamina that long outlasts Megan who's sleeping peacefully in her room.

Sharon's decorated her apartment from garage sale and flea market expeditions, but you'd never know from looking at it. Girlfriend has a serious creative touch and there's no doubt in my mind she could make a shoe box look good. "What about a nice Marinated Filet of Beef? Sound good?"

"What is it?" I ask.

"Marinated Filet of...Beef," she answers, like it's a trick question.

"Is it cooked?"

Sharon laughs and shakes her head. "You're so silly?"

"Is it?"

"You like escargots?"

"No. And I know that ain't cooked."

"Have you ever tried escargots, Ruth?"

"Sharon, I don't need to try it to know I don't like it."

"Maybe our guests will."

"I don't think so."

"Ruth, these people are paying $200 a plate. Don't you think we should give them their money's worth?"

"Absolutely not. The budget calls for chicken, Sharon. How many times do I have to tell you that? We serve anything other than chicken, we don't make any money."

"Chicken's so predictable."

"Whatever. Now look for chicken recipes and stay away from all that expensive, exotic stuff."

"Cordon Bleu?"

"Now you're talking."

"Everybody always serves Cordon Bleu."

"Good. We're keeping with tradition, then. You're not going to cook 300 meals by yourself are you?"

"Oh no. I'm going to get me some help and stop worrying. I keep telling you I've got this covered. You just do your part."

"I don't know, Sharon. You've got me worried, Girl. If I left it all up to you, these people would be eating lobster and escargots and we can't afford that."

"I know. I know."

"Do you? I mean, I hope you do because..."

"Let's not argue, Ruth."

"I'm not arguing."

"Let's not go there."

"I'm not going. I'm just saying..."

"And I hear you. Believe me, Honey. I want this to work as much as you do. Maybe more. I used to live there. Remember?"

"I know. I'm just saying..."

"And I know how important this is to you, Clara, everybody."

"I know. I'm just saying..."

"You want chicken? Chicken it is."

"Thank you. That's all I'm saying." That woman's had too much wine because for some unknown reason she finds this whole conversation so funny, she falls over laughing so hard I'm afraid she's going to pee on herself. That's about the time I notice the bottle is empty. I guess I'll be the responsible one and go see if she's got another one in the kitchen.

"There are going to be a lot of big shots at this thing. Politicians, business executives, local celebrities. Rich folks."

"I know," she says trying to compose herself. "And I'm going to take every advantage of this opportunity too, which is why this meal has to be perfect."

I plop down on the floor and fill our glasses again, "Your business could really take off after this, Sharon."

"Oh, Ruth, wouldn't that be something? I could be catering to the stars and I know somebody's going to want my escargots." She rolls her eyes at me. I didn't know white women knew how to do that.

"Knock yourself out on those raw snails, Girlfriend and more power to you or anyone else who'd let one of those things slither down the back of their throat."

"Don't knock it until you've tried it. You'd be surprised how pleasant some things can feel in the back of your throat." She giggles and gulps down a glass full of wine.

"You drink too much."

"Oh right! Like you've only sucked down half a dozen glasses of this stuff. I've been keeping count."

"I sip. I don't guzzle. You guzzle. A related attribute to deep-throating, Sharon?" Now that wasn't nice.

"Have you ever tried it?"

"Not willingly. It's disgusting."

"Oh, it is not."

"Not to you. You're a white woman. Everybody knows white women get off on that kind of mess."

"Black women do too."

"Girl, please. Not anybody I know."

"Then you are all missing out and I feel sorry for you."

"Why? What's so great about having a dick down your throat?"

"Depends on the dick."

"Dick is dick."

"No, dick isn't dick, Ruth."

"What are you? A dick connoisseur?"

"No, but I know a good dick when I taste one."

"Ugh! That is so gross, Sharon!"

"You're such a prude. I can't believe...how old are you?"

"Old enough to know I don't like giving head. So there."

"You don't know what you're missing."

"You keep saying that."

"Mmmmm...sure would be nice to have one right now." She runs her tongue over her lips.

"Sharon..." Suddenly, I feel like maybe I should leave the room or something.

She closes her eyes and holds her hand up in front of her face, pretending there's a penis in it. "I like to lick the sides first, up and down like it's a lollipop. Mmmm...men like that. Then I take my tongue and graze it over the tip, around and over and around..." I don't believe it. This woman is sitting here showing me how she gives head and I'm watching, mesmerized. "Know what really drives them crazy?"

"No. What?"

"Wrapping your warm, moist lips around the head, kissing it like you'd kiss his mouth. I tell you. Ruth. You don't know what you're missing, Girl."

I've inhaled my glass of wine without even realizing it and all of a sudden, I miss Adrian a whole lot.

Sharon still has pictures of Darren. Come to think of it, I've still got a few of Eric too. I wonder why we keep such things? He's handsome. Doesn't look like he'd hurt a fly, but no one ever accused him of hurting flies, just his wife. She still loves him. I can see it in her eyes when she stares at him in the photos. What an awful feeling that must be. To love the man who tormented you.

"He thinks I'm going to fall on my ass and come running back to him. It's been nearly a year and he still thinks that, Ruth."

"How often do you see him?"

"Every other weekend. He comes to pick up Megan."

"He gets visitation?"

"As long as he continues getting counseling, yes. He's a

good father and she's crazy about him. He'd never hurt her. It's just me he had the problem with. Know what I want?"

"A dick?"

"Besides that. I want to be successful. I want this catering business to take off and make me a ton of money. Wouldn't it be amazing if I proved him wrong? I want to show him and everybody else who thought I was crazy for leaving him that I can do this. That I can be something more than just his wife. As long as that's all I was, Ruth, as long as I paid more attention to that than I did to making a better me, it was easy for him to lose respect for me. I should've fought harder for that. Respect. He loved me, still does. But he's never respected me."

"Can't have one without the other. Can you?"

Sharon looks at me, "No. I guess not. I won't ever go back to that. I can't." Tears flow down her face and I think we've had too much wine. I fill her glass one last time.

"Can never have enough I-told-you-so's under your belt. Here's to redemption." We lift our glasses and toast whatever victories we've earned, now and in the future.

"Can we talk about something else?" She laughs.

"Of course we can."

"How's Adrian?" she asks.

"He's wonderful," I say, grinning. He has that effect on me, though. Just the mention of his name, or a fleeting thought of him, or...shit just about anything having to do with him leaves me grinning. "He's coming over tomorrow night for dinner and we might watch a few movies."

Sharon winks at me. "Yeah, watch movies. How was San Francisco?"

How would I know? I hardly even seen San Francisco, but, I clear my throat, gearing up to give her the lowdown on what little I did see outside Adrian's naked booty. "Let's see...we drove up the coast to Muir Woods. I've got pictures and I'll bring them over next time I come. Ummm...we did manage to catch some really good jazz at this club on Nob Hill and I saw Alcatraz from a distance, but I don't know. A prison as a tourist attraction, just doesn't work for me. Then we..."

"Ruth? How was it with Adrian in San Francisco?"

"Oh...well. He was cool, you know. He played tour guide as best he could, considering he doesn't know much about the place either. Very accommodating. Very considerate. Very..."

"Did you two make love?"

"Yes." I grin. "We did. A whole bunch of times."

She laughs, "I knew it! I've been dying to ask you that all night. C'mon on. Tell me all about it."

"Oh Sharon...it was... He was... I had no idea sex could be that good."

"With the right person, it is good."

"He must be right then, because it was all good all the time."

"I take it you didn't give him a blow job though."

"Not this time. But after tonight I'll definitely give it some thought."

"I'm telling you. You don't know..."

"I know. What I'm missing."

"Guess what, Sweetie?"

"What?"

"I met somebody too."

"Sharon...who?"

"His name is Wayne and I met him at the fresh vegetable market on Lee Highway."

"You give him your number?"

"I did and he used it and he asked me out." I know how monumental this is for her. Sharon's as afraid of the possibilities as I am. "I don't know, Ruth. You think it's too soon? I mean, I'm not even officially divorced yet."

"You're asking the wrong person, Girl. I have no idea what I'm doing, Sharon. Adrian's wonderful and I love being with him."

"You still got your guard up too?"

"Couldn't put it down if I wanted to."

"He sounds like a wonderful man."

"He is, but that's not enough. It's not him. It's me. I can't just throw away 14 years like it never happened. Be nice if I could, but I'm still that woman. Bernie says I'm not, but I am. I know I am and I scare myself more than he ever could."

"What are you afraid of, Ruth?"

"Of not paying attention, not listening to myself. I'm afraid of not speaking up when I should. I'm afraid of forgetting about me again. I haven't changed, I've just started paying attention to who I am and I don't want to forget Ruth. Does that make sense?"

"Tons."

Twenty Three

Lord. I must be in love! Why else would I be out here spending my whole paycheck on T-Bone steaks for dinner with Adrian tonight?

"Thought that was you," he whispers into my ear. He barely touches my arm but it burns my skin like acid and the warmth of his breath singes my neck. My body coils like a snake, repulsed by his presence.

"Eric," is all I can say.

He laughs, "Hey, Baby. Whatchu been up to besides lookin' like a million dollars? I almost didn't recognize you, but then I said, that's her. That's my Ruthie." His Ruthie? Not anymore. Not in years. "Now don't give me that look, Girl. How you been, Baby?"

What should I say? I've been healing and happy and cleaning out my spirit of all the trash you left behind. I've been crying and laughing and dancing and pissing out nightmares and memories of you spitting in my face, calling me a bitch, slapping me, punching me, kicking me? "Fine."

"Yeah? You uh...lookin' good, Baby Girl. Lookin' damn good. Finally got rid of some of that weight, I see."

Watch him, Ruth. Pay close attention. Eric is still Eric. I can tell. I can smell it on him. The stench that comes from being evil is unmistakable and makes me nauseous because I haven't smelled it in a long time. "Still workin' for that lawyer? What's his name?"

"I'm still at the law firm."

"They give you a promotion yet? I told you, Baby. You work too hard for they asses down there. You need to go in one day and tell them they need to give you a promotion. You got it comin'."

I maneuver myself around him, preparing for my escape. "Yeah, well...I'm kind of in a hurry, Eric. I've really got to be going and..." As soon as I turn to leave, I drop my basket and everything in it. Shit! Leave it, Ruth. Just, leave it.

Eric bends to help me pick up my things. "You clumsy as ever I see," I glance up in time to see him staring at me, smiling, and it hurts to be this close to Eric. No. No, I'm not clumsy. I've never been clumsy, except when you were around. "These some nice steaks you got here, Baby." He smiles. "Two of 'em? One of these for yo' man?"

"No I...." Stop it! I don't owe him an explanation. Not anymore.

"He's one lucky son-of-a-bitch, whoever he is," Eric says, staring at me. "You a good woman, Ruthie. Always was a damn good woman." I feel him trying to hold my eyes to his like he's done so many times before.

Eric hands me my mushrooms. "Take care, Eric," I whisper, then hurry to the check out counter. Is he coming? Is he watching me, following me? Is he? That would be silly, wouldn't it? I mean, after all this time to think he's still playing those tired games is ridiculous. We've been divorced for two years now and Eric's moved on with his life like I've moved on with mine. There I go tripping again. When am I going to learn? It's over. Been over for years and it's going to stay over.

Out of the corner of my eye, I see Eric walking in my direction. He stops, then stands next to me holding out an onion. "You drop this too?"

I shake my head and look into my basket knowing it never had an onion in it. "No. I don't think..."

"Look again, Sweetheart," Eric stares back at me, "You sure

you didn't drop this, Ruthie?"

I'm sure. I'm positive. "I suppose I did. Thank you, Eric."

"No problem, Baby. You take care of yo'self." He winks.

I hadn't dropped that onion. I had plenty of onions at home so there was no need to buy more. Why'd I tell him it belonged to me? He knew it didn't. I knew it didn't. Why did I say it did?

"Excuse me? Miss? Miss, I can ring you up now. Miss."

I empty my basket onto the conveyer belt. Dear God, what have I just done?

This whole scene's got me so rattled I can't even drive. I sit in my car trying to get a grip when I notice Eric coming out of the store and getting into his car. The woman he brought to the divorce is following behind him along with two small children. "Get in the car," he tells her. She straps the children in the back seat then quickly gets in next to Eric. I recognize her demeanor immediately. She's done something to piss him off and she's walking on eggshells, hoping to avoid the inevitable. I know it won't take much. One of the kids will cry, or she won't get dinner done fast enough. Something will set him off as soon as they get home and he'll take it out on her.

***

"Dinner was delicious."

"Thank you."

"You keep it up you're going to make a brotha fat."

"You'll never be fat, Adrian."

"You haven't seen my baby pictures."

Adrian and I are supposed to be watching these movies he's rented, but he's the one watching them. I haven't been able to get the encounter with Eric off my mind. It's not running into him that's bothering me. It's my reaction to him. It was like it used to be, when he held me in the palm of his hand. He'd tell me to jump and I'd ask how high. He's been out of my life so long, but today I felt the familiar intimidation I used to feel from him and I don't like it because I thought I'd convinced myself that I was over it. But after what happened this afternoon, I'm not so sure anymore.

"You've been quiet all evening. You okay, Baby?"

"I'm okay," I say quietly.

"No, you're not." He picks up the remote and turns off the television, "What's on your mind? Tell Dr. Carter all your problems," he teases.

Adrian doesn't know much about my relationship with Eric. Irreconcilable Differences, is the reason I've given him for my marriage ending and he seems to be okay with that explanation, for now. Bernie's been bugging me to tell him everything, but the timing's never right. Maybe now it is. "I'm listening," he says quietly.

I've rehearsed what I'd say to him. Practicing answers to questions I think he might ask. But I can't make him understand this. All he knows about marriage is what he's seen in his own house, growing up. Listening to him talk about his family is like listening to a fairy tale. Mom and Dad are crazy about each other and all the kids are crazy about Mom and Dad. I need to tell him the truth. Someday I will, but not now. Not after what happened today.

"Shhhhh," I put my fingers to his lips. "You're going to make me miss one."

"One what?"

"One heart beat." I put my ear to his chest, close my eyes and listen to the gentle rhythm inside him.

He sighs, "This another one of those things you don't think I'll understand?"

"It's just been a long day, Adrian."

"There's more to it than that, Ruth. I know something's bothering you, Baby. C'mon now..." he lifts my face to his. "What's up?"

What am I afraid of? That he'll judge me and think I'm an idiot for putting up with Eric all those years? *Yes.* That he'll lose respect for me, or worse, pity me for being a victim? *Yes.* That if he looks into my eyes one more time, I'll break down in tears, sling snot all over the place and cry like a baby? *Yes.*

"Adrian, I just had a bad day, that's all. I don't want to talk about it."

"Just a bad day, huh?"

"That's all."

"One of these days, Ruth...one of these days, you're going to have to give me more than that, Baby."

"What are you talking about?"

"I don't know what it is you're keeping from me, but I know it's something. I figure when you're ready you'll open up. But I just want you to know that I know you got secrets inside you."

I smile. "We've all got secrets, Adrian. I'm sure you have a few of your own."

"None that I can think of off the top of my head, but if I remember any, you'll be the first to know."

"Promise?"

"Cross my heart and hope to..."

"Don't say that."

I squeeze him, burying my face in the crook of his neck. Adrian lifts my mouth to his, kisses me and makes love to me, filling me with promises. We fall asleep on the couch and I feel safe.

Twenty Four

Bernie, Clara and I've agreed to meet at Higgin's House to discuss the last minute details of the fund raiser. Bernie's list of contacts has already proved to be invaluable as donations have been pouring in from women's groups, churches and anonymous donors from all over the state "It's not what you know, but who you know. That's my motto," Bernie brags. I don't blame her. She knows some very influential people and I've learned to stop asking how.

When we arrive, Clara's right in the middle of getting a woman and her children settled in and she asks us to wait in her office. Bernie's never been here before and is amazed by all the photographs of Clara on the wall, "Why does she have all these pictures taken."

"So she won't forget. All of those women have been through here. Some of them have started over and are doing pretty good for themselves, some have gone back and some...some have died."

Bernie looks at me, "Your picture up here?"

"Yeah." I point out my picture with Clara. "We took this last week." I smile.

Clara peeks her head in the door, "Why don't we take this meeting in to the kitchen. I've got some coffee on and one of the ladies has made some cookies for us."

The coffee is good, but the cookies are better. "The invitations are out and the RSVPS are in. Sharon's got a handle on the menu...I think we're just about ready," I say proudly.

"Not so fast, Missy," says Bernie. I look at her like she's lost her damn mind, wondering when the hell I became 'Missy'?

"What now?"

"Entertainment? I believe that's your area."

"Yes, it is."

"And?"

"And? I'm finalizing some things."

"Like what?" Clara asks. "You say that every time we ask you about it." She smiles. "What are you working on, Girl?"

"Don't just sit there grinning. What? Who?" Demands Bernie with her bossy self. I just roll my eyes at her.

I've been trying to keep it a surprise, but I guess these two heffas ain't having it, "Well...for openers, Sonny Micelles."

Bernie looks skeptical, "*The* Sonny Micelles?"

"The one and only," I say smugly.

"How in the world did you get Sonny Micelles to do this?"

"You're not the only one who knows important people, Bernie."

"Like I said, how did you get Sonny Micelles to agree to do this?"

"How do you think?"

"Begging?" Clara asks.

"Exactly. And it worked too." Bernie and Clara bust out laughing, "What? Look, he's coming and that's all that matters. So...laugh. Laugh all you want." I shrug. Sonny Micelles is big time. I own every CD he's ever recorded and when I saw him on the Grammys a few months ago, I figured I had to ask. "He put on the bomb performance at the Jazz festival and so I managed to get in touch with him through the promoters whose names were listed on the back of the brochure I saved. I wrote to him, telling him my whole damn life story, Ruby Higgins' life story, Clara's dedication to the cause, sent him a picture of myself and pleaded with him to call me if he had any sense of decency as a human being and a man. Bless his heart, he called and agreed to perform."

Clara laughs. "Child, you never cease to amaze me."

"Yeah, got my ass pretty amazed too. How you going to keep something like that to yourself? You know we talk every day about this, Ruth. What else you got going on besides Sonny Micelles?" Bernie eyes me suspiciously.

"Well, Miss Watson, if you must know... Have you ever heard of The Mona Harris Dance Company?"

"You didn't?" Bernie's eyes grow as wide as her big head.

"I did."

"Ruth! Mona Harris is bringing her dancers all the way up here from Miami to dance at our little fund raiser? How the hell did you..."

"Begging," Clara says simply.

I smile. "It's powerful. A powerful thing."

This time, Bernie's the one grinning. "I'm through. I ain't asking you nothing else."

"And..."

"And?" Bernie looks like she can't take much more, but I'm going to give it to her anyway. "Miss Cleo Walker will be our finale," I announce proudly.

"Lord have mercy!" Clara collapses back in her chair. "Child...Cleo Walker? You begged her too?"

"Yeah, which was really hard, because her Publicist is a hard ass and Cleo's on tour so she'd have to make a special trip out here, which Ms. Publicist didn't think was a good idea and told me that every time I called, which had to have been at least 50 times. Then one day I got lucky and Ms. Walker was in her Publicist's office, for some reason or another. She overheard the conversation and asked to speak to me, so the Publicist handed her the phone and we talked and talked. She's really down to Earth. I mean, we talked like old friends. Did you know she was from Texas? Anyway, I told her what was up and do you know...she told me she'd been abused, but not by a husband or anything, but when she was a little girl...anyway...I told her I wouldn't tell anybody because she doesn't want it to get out because she's famous and all, but she said...yeah. She'd do it."

Bernie and Clara stare back at me with their mouths

hanging open and I feel magnificent. I haven't worked so hard on anything in my whole life, but this, this means something to me. It's the most important thing I've ever been a part of and I'm determined to work my ass off for it. After all, my friends are depending on me for a change. Usually, it's been the other way around.

On our way out, I see her. She sits on the side of the bed in one of the small rooms of Higgin's House, brushing her oldest son's hair. "Dang, Boy. You need a haircut already." I stop dead in my tracks and stare at her. Her face is bruised and swollen and the elegant, regal mound she'd once worn so proudly on her head, is gone. She stops brushing the boy's hair and stares back at me. "Yes?" she asks meekly.

I'm not sure what I'm going to say, but I walk into her room, sit down next to her and put my hand underneath her chin, turning her bruised face to me. "You all right?" I ask.

Tears fill the rim of her eyes and she looks away, "I'm cool. I just...," she shrugs, "I got tired of it...that's all."

"I did too."

She looks into my eyes. "Do I know you?"

I shake my head. "No," I lie.

"You live here too?"

"No."

"I'm just staying here till I get on my feet. Shouldn't be long...I hope. I need to find a job and a place to live." She looks at her children. "He wasn't their daddy, but he was better than nothing."

"No, he wasn't. You're better than nothing, Baby. Remember that."

She tries to smile, but her swollen lip won't allow it, "You don't look like somebody whose man used to beat on her. I used to look good too. All the time, before I hooked up with him. Then he kept thinking I was messing around on him, but I wasn't. I even stopped fixing myself up so nobody would look at me. Then he just fussed about how bad I looked all the time. I don't think it mattered one way or another, really."

I smile back and hold her hand in mine. "It never does."

I close the door behind me, leaving her alone with her children. Bernie asks, "Who was that?"

"The woman Eric left me for."

Twenty Five

May makes herself at home, taking off her shoes and socks, sitting sprawled out on my living room floor, stretching her legs to keep them from cramping. If I didn't already have a best friend in Bernie I'd definitely see if May wanted the job. Of course, there's nothing that says a woman can't have more than one buddy for life.

"Bernie said planning this fund raiser would be a lot of work, but that was the understatement of the decade."

"Yeah, but you love it."

I laugh. "I do, Girl. And you know what?"

"What?"

"I'm not looking forward to it being over. I mean, I am, but," I shrug. "Then what?"

"I don't know, Ruth. What?"

"I don't know either. School starts in a few weeks. I guess, I'll be up to my eyeballs in homework."

"I don't envy you. I always hated school."

"Honestly. So did I."

"But it's all for a good cause. A college degree will make a big difference. You'll see."

"I know. But shit, May. I'll be damn near 40 years old by the time I'm finished. A 40-year-old college graduate in desperate need of a real job doesn't sound all that exciting. I'd hoped by the time I was that age I'd be in charge, or doing something important."

"You will be doin' something important, Ruth. You'll have a degree."

"In what?"

"You got plenty of time to figure that out. Four, maybe five years."

"Sounds like forever."

"In dog years, it is." May smiled. "Seriously, Girl. It won't seem like that long. You'll be so busy with term papers, final exams and writin' that thesis, time is jus' goin' to fly by."

"Sounds exciting. Doesn't it? Kind of? May?"

"Hmmm?"

"You ever thought about doing your own thing?"

"My own thing?"

"Owning your own business?"

May stops stretching and stares back at me. "Now where on Earth did that come from?"

"I don't know. Where?"

"You been thinkin' 'bout that, Ruth?"

"No. Not really. No. Well, every now and then. But no."

"Yes, you have." She smiles. "Ruth Johnson, you have been thinkin' 'bout it, haven't you?"

"It's just...well, with planning the fund raiser and all... May I've enjoyed helping put this together. I have. I've loved every minute of it, all the planning and organizing and even the headaches and... I never thought I'd be able to do anything like this."

"Never?"

"No. And it's cool, you know. Working my ass off, putting the pieces together and watching them fall into place. That's cool."

"It's cool 'cause it's important to you."

"That's right! It is. It's very important to me and I didn't mind working hard, putting it together. We've gotten together to set up this whole agenda and all of us has worked hard to see it through and it's absolutely lovely. It feels good, calling the shots and making deals. But you know what's most incredible about this whole thing?"

"What, Ruth?"

"I had faith that Bernie could do it. Bernie can do anything she sets her hard head to. I had faith that Sharon could do her part and come up with a mean menu. That woman can cook, Girl. Do you hear me? I knew Clara would hang in there and do whatever it took to see this thing through because that's her house we're trying to save. But I wasn't so sure about me."

"Ruth..." She stares at me sympathetically.

"No, I'm serious, May. I've never stood up for anything in my whole life and I've never worked this hard for anything. I'm surprised at what I've managed to do, my role in this. And you know what? I'm proud."

"Ain't nothin' wrong with bein' proud, Girl. Shoot. You got a lot to be proud of."

"I think I do, May. I finally think I do."

"So you seriously considerin' startin' your own business?"

"The thought's crossed my mind. Sharon loves being her own boss and she's good at it too. Even if I do go to school and get my degree, I'm still going to end up working for somebody else. Don't you get tired of working for somebody else, May? Doing their work, on their schedules, busting your behind to meet their deadlines. Don't you get tired of it?"

"Well...no. But that's 'cause I like my job, Ruth. I wanted to be a Buyer and that's what I do best. But I see yo' point."

"I want to love what I do too. I want to wake up in the mornings and look forward to going to work. I have no idea what that's like."

"So what kind of business you thinkin' 'bout startin'?"

"I don't have a clue," I say, laughing. "I haven't even thought that far ahead. I don't know."

"Well, let's see. You like planning things like this fund raiser. Maybe you could do it professionally. A professional...Events Planner? I think that's what they call it. How 'bout that? Plannin' events?"

"May, we live in Jacksonville, Florida. I don't think they

have that many fund raisers here and I don't know how many people would pay me to plan their parties. Besides, planning parties is Bernie's forte. I don't know."

"I read somewhere that if you wantin' to start up yo' own business, you need to figure out what it is you like doin'. So, what do you like doin'?"

"I like walking with you. But I don't think anybody's going to pay me to be a professional walker."

"No. Probably not."

"I like jazz."

"You play?"

"No. I like Adrian."

"Ruth, ain't nobody goin' pay you to do nothin' with Adrian."

"Adrian might."

"Why buy the milk when you can..."

"All right. All right. I like reading. I love reading."

"What about bein' a...publisher? Or an agent! Agents make good money."

"I wouldn't know. I wonder what an agent does?"

"Beats me. A publisher might be nice."

"Yeah...maybe. Or a book store?"

"A book store?"

"Sure. Book stores are nice. I don't know how much money they make, but..."

"But, you could look into it."

"Of course I can. See how much money I can make, what I'd need to do to get started."

"What about a black book store? With books just about us and by us. You think that would be a good idea?"

"Girl, yes. And I could have authors come in and sign their books. Terry, E. Lynn, Toni. May, I'm getting excited."

"Me too, and this ain't even my dream. But it sounds excitin', Ruth. Real excitin'."

"It does, doesn't it?"

"You got a computer?"

"At work."

"Girl, you don't have one here? You don't have Internet?"

"No. Do I need it?"

"Ruth, you have got to catch up with the times, Girl. Everybody's got Internet access. Where you been?"

"Here."

"And out of touch."

"Not that out of touch, May."

"Get yo' shoes on. We goin' to my house."

"Right now?"

"Yes. Now."

Of course, it doesn't sound like a bad idea. I mean, at this point, it's just a thought and ain't nothing wrong with thinking. May and I spent the rest of the morning doing research on bookstores, especially African American book stores, and what we discovered was discouraging at best. There's not a lot of money being made by book store owners of stores specializing in books by and about African Americans. The money's out there, billions as a matter of fact, but folks aren't buying their books from these stores. They're buying their books at the larger chain stores and surprisingly, online.

"You ever buy anything off the Internet, May?"

"Girl, yes. CDS, art, books."

"Books?"

"Yeah, it's usually cheaper and it's easier."

"How much cheaper and how much easier?" May took me through the process, showing me websites of some of the major players in online book sales. I even buy a book. Right here online. I'm actually nervous about the whole thing, but May assures me I'll have my book in a few days and my credit card won't be any worse for the wear.

"Do they have any sites just for African Americans?"

"I've seen a few. But most of them all link back to one of these folks, or they're just not real impressive."

May and I look at each other and smile. "I'm just thinking. That's all, May."

"I know. Just lookin' into it."

"Yeah, just looking into it, that's all. You think... Never

mind."

"What?"

"How much you think it would cost to start up something like this?"

"Girl, I don't know. I guess it's cheaper than buying an actual store. Can't be much overhead involved."

"How do you suppose they get their inventory?"

"They buy direct from publishers, I think. Publishers. Distributors maybe."

"I'm just thinking about it."

May smiles. "You said that already."

"Do you think..."

"Yes. I think you'd be very good at it, Ruth."

"Thank you, May. But, I'm only..."

"I know. Thinkin' 'bout it."

What in the world would I look like trying to run a business? And what in the world do I know about selling stuff over the Internet? And what in the world do I know about operating a bookstore? It does sound good, though, owning my own business. Oh well...let me stop. Right now, I'm just satisfying my curiosity. But, if a woman was interested in starting up something like this, how would she go about it? How would she process credit cards? How would she put up a website and who could she get to create one? How much would it cost? How much money could she make? Wow! That much?

Twenty Six

"Damn, Ruth! Is that him?"

Adrian walks in the room like he's just stepped out of some fashion magazine wearing an Armani tux better than Armani ever could. "Yep. That's Adrian." I grin. "Isn't he gorgeous, Bernie?"

Bernie stares at me, "Gorgeous ain't the word. If I had a penis, it would be rock hard right about now."

Suddenly I'm worried. "You haven't slept with him, have you Bernie?"

"Ruth, believe me. If I'd slept with that fine bastard, you'd have heard about it."

Oh, Lord. She's got that look in her eyes. Adrian swaggers over in our direction and Bernie's sizing him up, licking her lips like he's the entree. "He's mine, Bernie."

"I know, Ruth. I know."

Adrian smiles and leans down to kiss me, "You look beautiful, Baby. Absolutely beautiful."

"Dammit!" Bernie mutters. I pretend not to hear her.

"So do you. Adrian, this is my best friend, Bernie Watson. Bernie...Adrian."

"Nice to finally meet you, Adrian. Now I see why she's been keeping you all to herself," she says, eyeing him up and down. "I can't say that I blame her."

Adrian looks at me and smiles, then gives Bernie her share

of attention, "I've been looking forward to meeting you too. Ruth told me you were beautiful, but..."

"Don't start, Adrian. This woman's like my sister and that's all that's keeping me from wearing you like a second skin and rocking your world hard enough to make you seasick."

"Bernie!" I exclaim, but I'm not surprised. Not at all.

She winks at me. "You two have a lovely evening." Bernie saunters off, no doubt in search of prey. She's on the prowl and some poor, unsuspecting man is going to be in trouble tonight.

Adrian shakes off that encounter better than I expected. "So, when are you going to explain to me what's up?"

"I promised I'd explain and I will."

"I hope so. I hate monkey suits."

"Well, they love you," I say, adjusting his tie.

"That dress is loving you pretty damn good too. You wearing panties?"

I smile. "No."

"I didn't think so."

"You can tell?"

Adrian casually eases one hand down my waist to my hip, then discreetly slips it around to my butt. He smiles. "Yeah. I can tell."

I show Adrian to his table. Then, a few minutes later, May and Jeff arrive. "That her?" Bernie asks. "I thought you said she was cute."

"Bernice!" Clara fusses.

I feel obligated to defend my new friend against Bernie's savage attack. "She is, Bernie. She's very pretty."

"Girl, you need your eyes checked."

"Why do you have to be like that?"

"Like what? That is not a pretty woman, Ruth."

"Somebody sounds to me." Says Clara.

Bernie looks appalled. "Jealous? Of what? Her?"

"She's been like that ever since I first mentioned May's name, Clara. I think it's childish and petty. Yeah. She's jealous."

Bernie glares at me, tightening up her lips. "Ruth, if you didn't have to give that speech tonight, I'd take you out back and whoop you up good."

"Bernie!"

"Bernie nothing! Don't you ever accuse me of being jealous of any female, Miss Johnson. You either, Clara!"

"Ain't nobody scared of you." Clara mumbles, then rolls her eyes.

"You're serious." I'm hurt. Genuinely hurt.

"Damn right I am. Love you like a sister. But I'll put a whoopin' on you..."

"I'm sorry! Dang!"

"Ya'll crazy," Clara says, then walks away.

I don't know who's sulking harder, Bernie or me. I swear, sometimes I don't understand how this friendship has lasted as long as it has. Bernie Watson and I are two totally different people with nothing in common, and to be honest, I really don't think I like her mean ass. After tonight, I'm never calling her again.

"Your speech ready?" she asks, like she really gives a damn.

"Yes," I mumble.

"You nervous?"

"A little."

"You know I'm proud of you?" She looks at me and smiles.

"I know." I look at her and smile.

"Give me a hug."

"'Kay." Whew! Glad that's over.

She doesn't think anybody notices, but I do. Most of the night she stands off in the shadows somewhere, alone. Her arms are wrapped around herself and occasionally Clara smiles in awe of the magnitude of this event. We believed in the cause and we believed in her. I don't think she feels so alone anymore.

I almost hate to invade her solitary celebration, but it's time to get things started. I put my arm around her shoulder. "Who'da thunk?" I laugh, looking out into the crowd of more than 300 guests.

"Not me. That's for sure," she says, fighting diligently to keep the tears from falling, but I know at any moment, she's going to lose the battle. "You did good, Baby."

"No, Clara. We all did good. I love you. I love you more than you'll ever know." God, if I could ever have another mother, I'd hope she'd be just like Clara Robins. She's the one who convinced me to speak tonight because all I'd planned on doing was fading into the darkness next to Adrian.

"You got to tell them, Baby Girl," she said. "You got to tell them your story."

"What story, Clara? So my husband beat my ass. What's the story in that?"

"The story's not in what he did, Ruth. It's in how you made it through."

Had I made it through? No. That became evident to me the last time I saw Eric. I was nowhere near making it through. Maybe I never would be. But she wanted me to tell them something and I figured that the only thing I can do is just tell the truth.

Standing on stage talking about my experience is not something I ever expected I'd do. I've spent so much energy trying to erase my past. The first time Clara asked me to talk to her about it, I refused to give that bullshit any more attention than it had already been given. Now, here I am, about to make it the focus of 300 strangers, my friends and Adrian. He's been asking to hear my truth since we met, and tonight, he will. Whatever he decides to do with this knowledge is something I'll have to live with. Not as easy as it sounds, but if I am blessed to share a life with this man, he has to know. Besides, I'm getting tired of dodging that bullet.

"I've never been a resident of Higgin's House, but I could've been. My name is Ruth Johnson, and for 14 years my ex-husband beat me. I'm embarrassed standing here telling you this. It's something I never wanted to talk about. Quite frankly, it's humiliating. And it's... People are quick to pass judgment sometimes, and they demand explanations. Why? Why'd you let him do that to you? Why'd you stay so long? The truth is, I don't have the answers to those questions. None of us living in abusive situations have answers that are good enough to satisfy you, or ourselves. None that make sense, anyway. For years I held on to the hope that one day it would simply stop, the beatings, the name calling. It would all stop and my marriage would be everything every woman dreams her marriage could be because I'd finally learn to stop pissing him off. He'd remember that my name was Ruth and not Black-Ass Bitch. But he didn't stop. He never would've, so I had to. I stopped accepting that this man, this kind of life was all I deserved. I stopped being afraid of him and I realized I had nothing in the world to lose. You can't fall off the bottom. Right? I mean, what did I have? Nothing, not even my life was worth a damn to me or anybody else. I didn't matter and we all need to matter, to ourselves, if not to anyone else. I'm learning that. It's still not easy, but I'm learning and I know I will never go back and I won't accept anything less than respect.

The women at Higgin's House...some will go back, but many of them won't. Not as long as they have a haven, a safe place to think, to heal, to make plans and to finally see that they have choices not to live under the threat of lies, or fists. For a short time...enough time, Higgins House is a home where nurturing and guidance are the foundation for lives needing to be rebuilt. Higgin's House is a resting place and sometimes...a little rest is all any of us needs." I wipe away my tears and take a deep breath. That really wasn't as hard as I thought it was going to be and I feel exonerated enough to feel good about me. "Now...we've got some incredible entertainment lined up for you tonight. So, sit back, relax and enjoy. Peace."

Everyone stands up when I walk off the stage. I hope they got something out of what I said. I don't want their pity, or disapproving nods, but I want them to understand that we're all the same. We all make choices in our lives, some right, some wrong and we all deserve the opportunity to take advantage of our God given right to a second chance. As I make my way toward my seat, next to Adrian, I wonder how he feels about me now that he knows. He answers my concerns immediately by putting his arms around my waist, bending down to kiss me and whispering in my ear, "I love you."

"I love you too, Adrian," I mouth back. Oh yes. I love him more than I ever thought I could love any man, and no matter what else happens in my life, this night will be in my heart forever, because tonight he's said the words I've dreamed he'd say to me since the moment I laid eyes on this fine man. He loves me. Me. Ruth Renee Johnson.

***

In the end, we raised nearly $200,000, which is way more than any of us expected. Not only that, but a private donor, gave Higgin's House a trust fund and for the next 10 years Clara Robins can count on getting $75,000.00 a year to run things. Not bad. Not bad at all.

Twenty Seven

After the banquet, Adrian surprises me with the room he's reserved for us in the hotel. We lay naked next to each other, holding hands.

"Not all men are like your ex-husband, Ruth. I'm not like him and...I'd never hurt you like that."

"I know," I whisper.

"I mean...any man who'd hit a woman isn't a man."

"No, he isn't."

"But the last thing I want you to do is think that I'm going to trip like that. You know what I'm saying?"

"I think so."

"I've got a temper. Hell, we all get mad, but I'm not down for shit like that. And you need to know this and you need to trust me."

"I know."

"Because a relationship is built on trust, Baby. Ours is no different."

"It isn't."

"And communication, Ruth. Don't be afraid to open up to me, Baby. You've got something on your mind...no matter what it is, you need to speak up. Because how can I fix it if I don't know it's broken?"

"Okay, Baby."

"I mean, I honestly don't understand what would make a man act like that and I might never fully understand why you did stay, but it'll never be like that between us. You know what I'm saying?"

"Yes."

"I've been in and out of relationships and I've been in love before, but not like this, Ruth. This...what we're building here...this is what I've hoped for my whole life and we don't need tension between us. You don't ever need to be afraid of expressing yourself, or being yourself, or telling my ass where to get off if I'm being a son-of-a-bitch. And I can be a son-of-a-bitch, Ruth."

"Sure."

"Not all the time, but my job is stressful and sometimes I might bring that shit home with me. Sometimes I might...and this isn't all the time, because most of the time, I'm pretty easygoing, but sometimes, I might even lose my temper and say some shit that I really don't mean, but that doesn't mean I don't love you, or want you in my life, and I'll never disrespect you. You understand what I'm saying?"

I smile, then kiss his chin. "Yes, Baby. I understand everything you're saying and I love you for saying it."

"I can't imagine there'd be anything you could do to make me want to..."

"Then don't imagine it, Adrian. Just make love to me one more time before we fall asleep."

He does.

Twenty Eight

"So, tell me more about this idea you've been working so hard on. Whatever it is, it's got you more excited than an ex-con in a whorehouse."

I grimace at her analogy. Crude. "Well, I'm considering starting my own business." I beam. "A book store specializing in books by and about people of color." Okay, so I expect a more boisterous response from my girlfriend who's been so supportive and caring, but that heffa just sits there staring at me like I've lost my mind. "Did you hear me?"

"I heard you," she said.

"Well? What do you think?"

"Where are you going to get the money?"

"Well, I've saved up a little money over the years. Thirty-four hundred dollars, and I've got an appointment to meet with a counselor at the SBA next week to find out what I'd have to do to get a loan."

Bernie leans back in her chair, takes a deep breath and says, "That's the most ridiculous idea I've ever heard."

Boy, talk about hurting a sistah's feelings. "What? Why would you say that?"

"Black bookstores don't make money, Ruth, and if you'd done your homework, you'd know this. Why you want to waste your savings on some mess like that? Starting a business is one thing, but at least start one where you can make some money."

"I have done my homework, Bernice, and I know that black bookstore owners are struggling," I say with attitude.

"So what the hell are you thinking?"

"I'm thinking...Internet!" Bernie's eyes widen. "E-commerce, Baby. It's all the rage."

"What do you know about E-commerce?"

"A lot. I've been researching it for weeks. There are these big bookstores doing business on line, selling everybody's books for as much as 40% off what you'd pay in the stores. How can they do that, you may ask?"

"I'm asking," she says dryly.

"There's no overhead, at least not like the overhead of owning an actual store. I save money...my customer saves money."

"So if everybody else is already doing it..."

"They're doing it for everybody's books, Bernie. I'm going to offer books specific to people of color. Meaning customers won't have to wade through hundreds of thousands of books to find what they're looking for."

Bernie's expression softens and a twinkle of optimism sparkles in her eyes. "So, how much money do you think you can make from this and where are you going to run this business from?"

"Home." I smile. "And I think I can make some damn good money if I plan it right. The publishing industry generates millions, Bernie, and I only need a tiny piece of that pot to make me happy."

"When do you plan on getting started?"

"I kind of already have." Of course by now, I'm bouncing in my chair because the woman seems genuinely interested. "I've got a business plan, sent out letters to distributors, gotten quotes on the cost of building and hosting a website..."

"Wait a minute...hold up. You're moving a little fast, Honey. Don't you think you need to take your time on something like this? I mean, we're talking a major undertaking, Ruth, and you don't want to get in over your head."

"I'm just looking into it, Bernie, and so far it looks like it could be a good opportunity."

"Sounds like you're doing more than looking into it, Ruth. Take your time on something like this, Baby. People are always getting all excited starting up these new businesses; only they end up filing bankruptcy because they thought they had it all figured out too."

"But I know a lot about this business, Bernie. I read any and everything I can get my hands on. There's nothing better to me than a good book. I've got a whole room full of them and I've been doing the research and..."

"So you love books, Sweetie. That doesn't qualify you to run something like this successfully."

"No, it doesn't. But I'm an intelligent woman," I say proudly. "I'm not going to just dive into this thing without looking."

"I hope not."

"But the more I do look into it, the more excited I get about the idea, and if you'd take a look at my business plan, you'd see why."

"I'm just not convinced that running a business off the Internet is a smart thing to do, Ruth. You've got all kinds of crooks and con artists..."

"But it can be safe, Bernie. As long as you take all the right precautions. And crooks and con artists are everywhere. Running a business off the Internet is like running a business anywhere. You've got to be smart and careful about it and I've been doing that."

"You're really serious about this?"

"I'm serious about looking into it. And if what I find out gives me some warm fuzzies, then yes, I'm serious about doing it."

"And what if it doesn't work out?"

"And what if it does?"

"You could lose a lot of money."

"I could make a lot of money."

"You could lose a lot of money, Ruth."

"And so what if I do, Bernie? I don't have anybody but me to take care. So, I might lose some money. So what? Beats not trying and never knowing. I don't think I'm being hasty or unrealistic. Right now, I'm just checking it out. That's all. But if I do decide to pursue this, I'm willing to take my chances."

"Why are you so determined to do this?"

"Because I've got you as my best friend and I see how much you enjoy your life, Bernie. You do shit on a whim and have a good time with it, no matter how it turns out. You live your life to the fullest and I want to live mine like that. So I have to take some chances too. Besides, aren't you the one always telling me how boring I am?"

"Since when do you give a damn about what I say?"

"Since sometimes you're absolutely right."

"Me and my big mouth," Bernie mumbles.

"Yes. You and your wonderfully big mouth. You've never hesitated to tell me about myself and believe it or not, I've listened. I'm not too old to still be something when I grow up and I'm not so broken that I can't still dream. I nearly gave that up, Bernie. I did give it up, for too many years. And now I have it back and I want to take full advantage of it. I want to do things and go places and meet people. If I mess up, then I mess up. But I know how to get up, Bernie. Not many people have had to pull themselves up from where I've been. I've been down and I've been careful. Now I want to be an entrepreneur."

Bernie stares at me, while I quietly climb down off that soapbox. "You mind if I take a look at that business plan of yours? Make sure you didn't miss anything."

I smile. "I was hoping you'd say that." I get up from the table and in less than a minute I'm back with my business plan.

She reads the cover with the name of my new business, "*Pages.*" She smiles. "I like it."

"Me too."

We stay up way late making corrections to my plan and it isn't long before Bernie is a believer in the business and in me.

Twenty Nine

"What about this one, Adrian? It's got an 18-gigabyte hard drive?"

"Ruth, you really think you need an 18-gigabyte hard drive?"

"I don't know. Do I?"

"No, Baby.

"Maybe not now, but later on I might need it."

"With what you're planning? I doubt it."

"What about this one? It's got a 56K modem. That sounds good."

Adrian smiles, "That is good. Check this out. Now this is exactly what you need. Memory, 128 megs, a nine-gig drive, zip drive, speakers, 17 inch monitor and a printer. $1200.00."

"That's all?"

"That's it."

"Is that enough? I mean, won't I need some more RAM or ROM or something?"

"This has got all the RAM and ROM you need."

"Okay. Then I'll take this one."

Out of the corner of my eye, I catch a glimpse of an apparition. Tall and slender, the light skinned frame turns the corner before my eyes can satisfy my nightmare. Was that Eric?

"Ruth? You hear me?"

"What?"

"I said. You've got a rebate coming back to you when you buy this. Damn, I need to get me one of these. You all right, Ruth?"

"Yeah. I just thought I saw someone I knew. I guess I was wrong."

"C'mon. Let's find somebody to get your new computer."

Is my mind playing tricks on me? Was that Eric? No. Couldn't have been. What on Earth would he be doing in an office supply store? Ever since that encounter at the grocery store, I've had Eric on my brain, and everywhere I turn, I keep expecting to see him.

I pay for my new $1200.00 toy and Adrian loads the boxes onto the back of his truck. I happen to look up in time to see a gray sedan slowly drive out of the parking lot . A gray sedan that looks a lot like the one I saw Eric get into a few weeks ago. That couldn't have been him. Could it?

Adrian expertly assembles all those cords into slots and outlets with ease. He has me set up in less than 15 minutes and I watch him in awe of his incredible self while he makes the whole thing look effortless. "You think it's a dumb idea?"

"What? The business?"

"Yeah."

"What do you think?"

"I asked you first."

"No, I don't think it's dumb. New Internet businesses pop up every day and a lot of them are making bank."

"I'm still not sure I'm going to do it. I mean, well...I'm just thinking about trying it and seeing how it works out."

"That's all you can do, Baby."

"I've been calling around to see how much it would cost to get a website designed. It's really expensive."

"Yeah, it can be. But don't worry that. I've already talked to a friend of mine. He'll hook you up. Just let me know when you're ready."

"Really? I could pay him, not a lot, but I could give him

something."

"You could, but you won't have to. He owes me. Come here," Adrian reaches out his hand to me and I take a seat on his lap. "You do know how to work this?"

"I know how to work the word processor and the spreadsheet. And I know a little about databases. The only thing I'm not so sure about is the Internet."

"What don't you know about the Internet?"

"How to navigate my way through it. I've seen May do it, but she knows what she's doing and I got kinda lost. You know. I must be out of my damn mind. Looking into starting a business on the Internet and my stupid ass has no idea how to use the stupid thing."

"Your ass ain't stupid, Baby. As a matter of fact, next to your lips, your eyes, your titties, your pussy and your feet, it's my second favorite part of your body."

I laugh. "You're a trip."

"I might be, but right now, I'm your teacher and we're about to start school, Internet 101. Everything and anything you ever wanted to know about the Internet, you're going to learn this afternoon. Pay attention. There's going to be a test afterwards."

Adrian takes his time, patiently showing me the ins and outs of web surfing, explaining links, search engines, channels, even scrutinizing web pages of my would-be competitors. And he's right. There is a test afterwards, but it has nothing to do with the Internet.

Adrian's sleeping, but I can't. I nuzzle up against his back and drape my arm across him. Even in his sleep, he knows I'm here and pulls me closer. I lied to May. Of course I think about marrying this man. My dreams are filled with him and of sharing a life with him. I know there's nothing I wouldn't do for him. All he'd ever have to do is ask me. It's as if my life has started over from scratch and my second chance includes him. Nothing will tear me away from this man, not if I can help it. I'll be with him for as long as he lets me, and I pray that's forever.

I hated the thought of forever with Eric. Was that him I

saw earlier today? I'm almost positive it was. And if it was, what does that mean? Does that mean, he was simply shopping for office supplies too? Maybe he needed pens, or pads of paper, or envelopes. Or, maybe he was looking for me. But that doesn't make sense. He wouldn't be looking for me because we're divorced and our marriage ended years ago so that's a ridiculous thought. And it couldn't have been him because Eric doesn't buy pens, or pads of paper, or envelopes. It couldn't have been him.

Adrian turns to face me, "What's wrong, Baby? Can't sleep?" He mumbles sleepily.

I put my head against his chest, "No."

"Excited about that new PC you got?"

"Yes," I whisper.

"We'll play some more tomorrow." He kisses my head.

"Go back to sleep, Honey." I kiss his chest. "Goodnight."

Adrian moans, then cocoons me inside him and the last thing I remember before I fall asleep, is how much I love him.

Life is sweet
Then it's bitter
Making me smack my lips
Bringing tears to my eyes
It's hard to tell
The difference between the two
Sometimes
But...I don't care

Thirty

"Hey, you back?"

"No, I'm still in San Francisco."

Seems like lately, he's always in San Francisco."Still?"

"Yeah. I'll be here a few more days."

"So, you won't be back in time for Bernie's dinner party?"

"Sorry."

"Well you know. I could come out there for the weekend. We could overdose on sourdough and sex. Sound like a good idea?"

"Sounds like a wonderful idea, but it's not happening. I'm in meetings and conferences all the damn time and I wouldn't be able to spend any time with you."

"So? Who says you need to spend time with me? Maybe I just need a vacation and want to spend it in San Francisco. Doesn't mean I have to spend time with you, chasing you up and down the beach and fucking you like a wild animal when you're weak with exhaustion. I might just want to do something else."

"Damn. I hope not."

"So, can I come?"

"Nope."

"Adrian..."

"Honey, I've got too much to do here and you'll just be a distraction. I'll be home in a few days and we'll spend some time together then."

"Promise."

"I promise."

"I'm holding you to that."

"I know."

"As long as you know."

***

He's been quiet all evening, trying to hide a solemn demeanor behind forced smiles and conversations. Pretending to listen to me, nodding on cue. But I know he's only going through the motions, watching my lips move and not listening to a word I'm saying. Not that I'm going to shut up. I keep right on talking and laughing at my own jokes, hoping something about me will snap him out of whatever kind of mood he's in. I've never seen this side of him and I don't think I like it because I don't know where it's coming from, or where it's going. He says it's his job and I pray that's all it is. They're working him too hard, always flying him off to California, then back here just long enough to change his underwear. Meanwhile, I catch up with him when and where I can even if it's just to get a glimpse, a whiff, a taste of him. I'm not hard to please. For me, just being in the same room with him is enough for me. He doesn't even have to talk to me. Bernie says I'm whipped. Hell, I can't argue with that.

Sometimes I wonder if I mean as much to him as he does to me and then the truth slaps me right upside my head. The only way he could love me the way I love him is if he's had a big gaping hole in his soul that's just my size and I'm the only one who can fill it. He fills up that part of me that's been missing my whole life. There's nothing in me that wants or needs anything this world has to offer when I'm with Adrian. When he's gone, God knows, I sting like an open wound. My appetite for this man is strong and I'll never get full. I would tell him all this, but I think it'll scare him. Not many sane people want to be a universe to somebody. That's a lot of responsibility.

I've taken the liberty of inviting myself over under the premises of "I'm not staying long, Baby. I've just been missing you like crazy and I'd like to see you". I've packed an extra pair of panties in my purse, just in case my plan works and I get to spend the night. He's relaxed, with his head in my lap and Will Downing crooning in the background. I figure this is a good time to take advantage of the opportunity and find out what's really on his mind.

"You've been quiet all evening, Honey. You okay?"

He's taken off into orbit and the sound of my voice reminds him it's time to come home. "Yeah. I'm just tired. This trip really took a lot out of me. The project's almost finished and we go live in a few weeks. Everybody's tripping, worrying we won't be ready."

"Will you be ready?"

"Damn right we will be. I've worked my ass off to make sure of that. It's my job to make sure that whole division is up and running and ready to take calls, process orders, create records. It's the biggest project I've ever managed, Baby."

"Well, I've got faith, if it's any consolation. I know you can do it."

"I have done it, Ruth. Bottom line. And I've done it in less than two months." I don't understand the edge in his voice and I wonder if it's directed at me, or if I'm just being too sensitive.

"That's wonderful, Adrian, it is, and now I understand why you've been so tired."

Adrian sits up and gulps down his glass of wine. "No. You have no idea," he says smugly.

"Okay, so maybe I don't. But I'm trying to. You've been under a lot of pressure lately and I do understand that. But it'll be over soon and we can take that trip together like we've been talking about."

"We'll see."

"We'll see? I thought..."

"I said, we'll see, Ruth. I'm not sure what's going to happen after this project is completed. I might be assigned to another one real soon."

"But you can take a vacation, Adrian. Surely, your boss can understand that."

Adrian rubs his eyes, signaling that he's tired and doesn't

want to talk about this. "It's getting late. I'm going to turn in." Adrian gets up and puts our glasses in the kitchen.

"You want me to stay?"

"That's up to you, Ruth." He goes into the bedroom, leaving me sitting here. Was that an invitation?

Reluctantly, I follow him into the bedroom, not quite sure if I'm welcomed or not. "Have I done something...or said something? Are you mad at me?"

"No...Ruth. I told you, I'm tired, Baby, that's all." He tries to smile and that's what I've been waiting for all night. An attempt at a smile is better than no smile at all and is enough encouragement for me to interpret it into, yes, he wants me to spend the night.

While Adrian undresses, I sneak up behind him and wrap my arms around his waist. Then I kiss that sensitive spot between his shoulder blades that I know drives him crazy and smile when he squirms. "Well, why don't you let me give you one of my famous massages? I'll run you hot bath, wash your back, suck on your...the body part of your choosing and rub you down with something that smells good. How's that sound?"

"Sounds wonderful. But you know you're going to put me right to sleep with all that."

"That's the idea, Baby. You need some rest."

He keeps his promise and Adrian is asleep as soon as that warm oil hits his back, but I don't mind. I've had a pretty rough week too and getting a good night's sleep isn't a bad idea. I sleep so good when I'm with him. I've gotten used to it because when he's in town, we sleep together almost every night.

Early the next morning, I wake up in time to see Adrian getting dressed. "What time is it, Adrian?"

"Hey, Baby," he leans down and kisses me. "I didn't mean to wake you."

"You didn't, but it's early. Where are you going? I thought we would have breakfast together."

"I've got to go into the office for a few hours and finish up some things. I've got a meeting in the morning, so..."

"Can't you finish it here? I can make breakfast, then leave

right after and I won't bother you. Promise."

"You know better than that. I can't get any work done with you around, Ruth." He smiles.

"But I won't bother you, Adrian and I'll go home right after breakfast. I've missed you. C'mon, Baby," I plead. We've hardly seen each other lately. Don't you miss me too?"

"Every second we're not together, Love." I'm flattered, but still disappointed that he's leaving.

"Can't you stay for coffee? It wouldn't take long for me to..."

"Can't." He picks up his keys and heads for the door, "Lock up when you leave."

Quickly, I jump out of bed, to chase after him, "Will you call me later?"

"You know I will." Adrian kisses me and leaves.

I waited all day, but he never called. So the next day, I call him, several times, but he doesn't answer or return any of my messages.

Thirty One

She said she wanted some company, but from the way she's acting, I'm not sure coming over was a good idea. May's spent all afternoon screaming at the kids, slamming pots and pans around the kitchen and clenching her jaws tight enough grind to her teeth into powder. The new house is magnificent and every time I leave here to go back to my little apartment, I feel really claustrophobic. The ceilings have got to be 100 feet high and you can look down into any room in the house from upstairs. Actually, my whole apartment is about the same size as her kitchen, which looks like a school cafeteria, if you ask me. No, I'm not jealous; it's just that it's huge and everything is silver, the stove, the refrigerator, the dishwasher. It's cool. Not exactly the kind of place I'd imagine having intimate, cozy dinners, but hey...

I don't think she's as happy here as she thought she'd be. It's a big place, and to be honest, I wouldn't blame her if she thought it was a little too big. Big houses scare me because there's plenty of room for the bad guys to hide, not to mention ghosts and demons. Jeff wanted to build her a castle and he's come pretty close, but I get the feeling that the princess was more comfortable in the cottage. Yeah, it was smaller, but she was closer to her family and friends. May likes that sense of security.

"What's wrong, May?" I ask as she slams that hot cup of tea down in front of me.

"Nothing," she grumbles back. I must've asked her that half a dozen times since I've been here and gotten the same response every time. You'd think I'd learn by now to stop asking.

"Allan!" she screams, "get yo' ass in here and take out that trash like I told you, Boy!"

Allan slumps into the kitchen, mumbles something under his breath and gathers up his prize to take to the dumpster. "How many times I got to repeat myself before I get you to do something?" His lip is poked out a mile long and he shrugs his shoulders as he leaves out the back door. "And clean that room when you finish!"

"Momma?" Shannon holds up a book to her mother, "Momma I can't..."

May swishes her out of the room, "Can't you see Momma's tryin' to talk, Baby? I ain't got time for that right now." The little girl's eyes are full of disappointment as May collapses in the chair next to me, only I'm not sure I'm in the mood to talk to her anymore. "Girl, those kids are gettin' on my last nerve. I swear they are."

"Your period coming?"

May stares at me. "No, Ruth. My period ain't comin'." She rolls her eyes so hard at me I expect them to pop out of her head and roll around on that shiny, no wax floor. May sips on her tea and neither of us say anything for what seems like a long time. "How's Adrian?" I know she's trying to avoid talking about what's really on her mind which is fine. I need to talk about Adrian to someone who isn't sick of hearing about him.

"Not sure." I shrug. "I haven't seen much of him lately. He's been busy with work and some new project he's working on."

"He still flyin' back and forth to California?"

"All the time. I don't know, May. His job keeps him busy, it always has, but he's always found time to spend with me. I hope he's not losing interest in me...us."

"That bad?"

"Probably not." I laugh. "I'm probably making a big deal out of nothing. But I'd be the first to admit, I'm paranoid. Especially when it comes to him. I miss him."

"You think he got somebody else?"

Did I say something to imply that, or is she just tripping? "No, I don't think that. I just said he's busy. I don't see him as much as I used to and I miss him." May shrugs and takes another sip of her tea. "I keep wondering if maybe I've said or done something..."

"He ain't said nothin'?"

I shake my head, "No. Just that when things settle down at work, we'll spend some time together."

"Ain't nothin' wrong with that."

"We've been together almost seven months, now. Doesn't seem that long. I don't know what I'd do if he wasn't in my life. I hate not seeing him, but I'm trying not to smother him. Adrian's like those potato chips. Can't eat just one. Gotta eat the whole damn bag. If he were food, I'd be big as a house." I laugh. May doesn't. "You think it would be crazy if I proposed?" She doesn't say a word, just stares off into nothingness with a million thoughts dancing in front of her eyes.

One last time, "What's wrong, May? And don't tell me nothing."

She waits for Allan to finish lining the trash can with a new bag and leave the room before finally answering my question. "You wanna know what's wrong?"

"I wouldn't have spent all day asking if I didn't." Her kids may be scared of her, but I'm not. Hell, May ain't nothing compared to Bernie, who scares the mess out of me. May slumps back in her chair and looks like she's about to cry. That's when I realize how serious this is. "May? Honey, what's wrong?"

Tears fill the brim of her eyes. "That son-of-a-bitch!" She bites down on her bottom lip.

"Who? Who, May?"

"Jefferson."

"Jeff? What's going on? Has he done something to you?" Oh, Lord. Don't tell me he hit her. Please, don't tell me that.

"How can that bastard jus' leave me like this, Ruth? How can he fly off like that and leave me here to take care of these kids and this house? What the fuck kind of man is that?"

"I thought you said he was gone away on business. Oh my goodness, May. Has he...left you?"

"I can't do all this by myself, Ruth. I can't take care of the kids and work. That bastard jus' up and left and..."

"He's not coming back?" May begins to cry harder, "May? Isn't Jeff coming back?"

She attempts to compose herself, "Says he'll be back Sunday night."

"Sunday? Then, he is away on business?"

"I keep tellin' him he don't need no job that keeps him away from his family like this. We need him here, Ruth. His ass don't need to be flyin' off to bum-fucked Egypt every time them bastards tell him to. What the fuck we s'posed to do while he's gone?"

I don't believe this. Jefferson's been gone for less than a week and May's about to lose her damn mind. She's falling apart right in front of my eyes. What happened to that crap she told me about realizing she didn't need a man to make her whole? Maybe I'm missing something. Maybe there's more to it than this. "He's coming back on Sunday, May? That's only a few days away."

"I can't do this 'till Sunday, Ruth! I can't! He needs to be here with us! I don't know what the hell he's doin' out there! How do I know he ain't fuckin' around? He could be laid up with some piece of trash right now! He should be here, Ruth!"

"May," I say, trying to calm her down. "May, now you know better than that. Jeff loves you and the kids more than anything. Of course he's not with another woman. You know he's not. And it's not like he's never coming back. He'll be home in a few days."

"What the fuck do you know?" She snaps at me, then slaps my hand off her arm.

"May, I..."

"How you know he comin' back? Anything could happen, Ruth! Ain't no guarantee he's comin' home!"

"I think you're tripping a little too hard, May."

"Fuck you!" She storms away from the table, then paces the kitchen floor like a lion in a cage. "You ain't got room to tell me I'm trippin', Ruth. Lord knows what the hell Adrian's doin' out there in San Francisco all this time."

"You know, I think I'd better..."

"How the hell you know he ain't fuckin' some bitch while he out there? He ain't been fuckin' you has he? Well? Has he?"

May has lost her mind and I'm not in the mood to sit here arguing with a crazy woman. I pick up my purse to leave when the phone rings. May sprints across the kitchen to answer, "Hello? Jeff? Jeff...baby. I been waitin' on you to call. How come you didn't call me earlier?"

The soft, sweet, honey dipped voice she's using now is a far cry from the shrieking she's done since I've been here. She's so wrapped up in her conversation with him, she doesn't even notice me leaving. On my way out, I see the kids sitting in the living room. The television's on, but neither of them is watching it. I wonder if they go through this every time he goes away on business? If so, I feel sorry for them.

Just because May wasn't in the mood for company doesn't mean I'm not. Bernie answers the door, still wearing her nightgown. "You still sleep? Girl, it's one o'clock in the afternoon."

Bernie grunts out a hello, then leaves me standing in the open door while she pours herself a cup of coffee. I know the signs. For her to be just getting out of bed, someone spent the night here. I peak around the house, on guard in case I see someone run through here naked.

"He's gone," Bernie says. She blows on her cup of coffee. "You want a cup?"

"No. Thank you."

"Where you on your way to this early?"

"It's not early, Bernie, and I've just come from May's."

"How is Miss Queen of Florida and her big house?"

"There you go again."

"You know I'm just kidding."

"She's...tripping."

Bernie's eyes light up, "Really? Like how?"

"I think she just misses Jefferson. He's been out of town on business a lot lately and it's getting to her."

"I'm not surprised. She acts like the type that needs a man around all the time."

"Bernie, you need a man around all the time too."

"For fuckin', Ruth. I like to fuck. Love to fuck, and yes, I need a man in order to do that the way I like it done."

"So, you need one for fucking and May loves Jefferson. You're no different than she is. Shoot, than most of us."

"Us? Wasn't that long ago when you didn't need a man. Perfectly happy without one if I remember correctly."

"That was a long time ago. Before I knew what it was to be with a real man like Adrian."

"Here we go," Bernie says, rolling her eyes. "A real man like Adrian. That brotha must've whipped it on you good, Girl!"

I smile, "You know he did, Bernice and stop laughing."

"Does he eat it, Ruth? 'Cause if a man don't go downtown, he might as well put back on his clothes and get the hell out."

"You are so..."

"Right?"

"Yes. Absolutely, and he's great at downtown."

"Make your eyes roll up in your head?"

"Stop."

"Does he?"

"Yes."

Thirty Two

Lately, my nerves are on edge and there's an uneasiness flowing through my veins. I've been trying to ignore these feelings, but it's hard to do. I sense a shift occurring in my little universe. Adrian seems like he's pulling away from me and I have no idea why. He won't talk to me except to say he's tired, or busy, promising we'll talk later, but later never seems to come. Most of the time I sit here waiting for the phone to ring, hoping it's him and hoping things will be back to normal again. When that doesn't happen, I go to bed trying not to be depressed about us breaking up and trying not to make plans for my life without him in it. But today he surprises me. Today he rings my doorbell and I know things have got to be back on track between us.

"I should've called first," he says, "but I came straight over from the airport. Damn! I've missed you, Baby." He takes my hands in his and puts them against his face, kissing my palms. "I know I haven't been spending much time with you lately. So much has been going on and I've had a lot on my mind," he whispers. "Work's been kicking my ass."

"Oh...Baby. I know you've been busy. I understand." Liar. "Whatever's on your mind you can talk to me about it, Adrian. You can always talk to me."

He shakes his head, "Right now...,"Adrian pulls me to him and holds me close. "...you're on my mind, Ruth." He acts like he's

186

glad to see me. He seems like he's been missing me, but there's something in his eyes, something about his vibe that keeps me from being convinced.

"We'll talk later, Ruth. Right now I just want to...." Adrian undresses me, then himself, and lays me down on the floor. He kisses me tenderly on my face, my neck, my breasts. Then he gently spreads my legs and buries his handsome face between them, making love to me with his tongue. He doesn't hurry and I know he enjoys the taste of me as much as I enjoy the sensation of him. The juices flow from me like a flood and he laps them up like he's so thirsty. I can't help it when my hips swirl against his face. I don't want to help it. He holds my thighs in his hands and I hold his head in mine, "Oooooo...Adrian. That's feels so good, Baby," I whisper. "Don't stop, Adrian. Please...make me come. Make me come all over you."

"Mmmmmm," he moans. How long has it been? Too long. I've missed him so much and I think I'm going to explode right this second.

"Adrian!" I scream, then come like I don't think I ever have before in my life. Adrian hovers over me, smiling, "Damn! You are sweet, Ruth. Taste it, Baby," he leans down to kiss me, "taste how sweet you are." I smell myself on his lips. He eases himself inside me and just lays there, savoring our connection. Adrian kisses me and caresses me, staring deeply into my eyes, reaffirming his love for me and easing any doubts I might've had that something's out of place inside him.

"I love you, Adrian," I whisper. "I love you so...so much." Can he feel it? Oh, he has to be able to feel it emanating from my pores spilling out all over him. I hold him as close to me as I can, wrapping my legs around him, pleading inside myself to God not to take him from me. I can't lose this man. Whatever's bothering him, whatever problems he has I want to be there for him. I want to be his woman and help him work through them. No matter how difficult, or how impossible things might appear to him, I can and will do anything for Adrian Carter. He has to know this.

I make him a drink and Adrian and I curl up on the couch

together. "I don't know, Ruth. If I don't get some time off soon…"

"Whatever happened to Consulting? You said you were looking into it, once. Why can't you do that instead?"

"It's not that easy, Ruth, and it's certainly not a guaranteed salary."

"Wasn't it you who told me that you were the best at what you do? Wasn't that you? Or was that your evil twin?"

He smiles, "I think it was me and I am good, damn good at my job."

"So why are you so insecure about doing your own thing?"

"Same reason you are." Adrian smiles and pecks me on the lips. "I might not be happy with what I'm doing, but right now, it's a sure thing. I know where my paycheck is coming from. Consulting…," he shrugs, "…who knows?"

"Well, don't give up on the idea, Honey. I think it's an option you need to seriously consider."

"Oh you do, huh?"

"Absolutely, and I know you'd be great at it like you are at everything else you do," I laugh, then climb on top of him, because this time…it's my turn to drive.

Thirty Three

It's late and I'm tired. As usual, I'm the last one to leave the office and yeah, this is getting old. I've put off becoming a full time student for another semester. I still want to get my degree and I will. But it's not that easy walking away from a full time, salaried job into the unknown. I haven't worked part time since I was 16 years old and all I can think about is minimum wage and having to wear a sun visor with a big "M" on it.

It's gotten to the point that I feel guilty if I leave work earlier than seven and that's a damn shame. Adrian called and asked if he could stop by tonight. Of course I said yes. I don't know why he even bothers asking. Like, have I ever told him no? I think I'll fry him some catfish when I get home. He loves my fried catfish.

The parking lot's not completely empty, but damn near. As I approach my car, I notice something on the hood. It's a package. Daisies.

"Heh...heh...heh," I turn in time to see Eric getting out of his car. "Hey, Ruthie. I thought you'd get a kick out of this." He walks over to me and the chill running down my spine freezes me where I'm standing. "You remember the first time I gave you daisies? Damn!" He rubs his chin. "You were fresh outta school back then. Weren't you? Fine as I don't know what. Just like now." Eric stares me up and down, then licks his lips. He still sees her inside me. That lonely girl he met all those years ago getting off that bus. I still see him exactly the way he was and still is.

He believes it really is this easy for him. I can tell he does. Has it been? Yes. He's never had to work hard to get me and his confidence is screaming this to the world. He wouldn't be here if he thought it would be hard. Daisies, a smile and a compliment. Mix that with my hope that somebody would love me and you've got the perfect love potion. Deception. "You lookin' a little tired, Baby. Like you been workin' too hard again. How many times I got to tell you all that ain't necessary?" Eric makes himself comfortable, leaning his back against my car.

"What do you want, Eric?" I ask, coldly.

"What do I want?" Eric smiles. "What the hell kinda question is that, Ruthie? What do I want? What do you think I want?" His gaze burns into me like the butt of a cigarette. I've never been able to fully understand Eric, but over the years I learned to anticipate him. His words never matched his actions. He'd say something nice to me, but he'd do something horrible and in the end I was left confused, but obedient.

"I have no idea."

"I jus' wanted to drop you off them flowers, Ruthie. Anything wrong with that? A pretty woman got to have pretty flowers." He picks them up and hands them to me, but I don't dare touch them.

"I don't want your flowers, Eric. It's getting late and I've really got to be going."

Eric stares into my eyes, "I got these for you, Baby. I ain't leavin' 'till I give 'em to you." He holds out the flowers again and this time, I do take them.

Slowly, I unlock my car door. Eric looks annoyed, "Man, can't I even get a thank you?" He leans in close to me putting his ear close to my mouth, "I can't hear you, Ruthie."

"Thank you, Eric," I whisper. There it is again. That control he has over me to perform like a puppet on a string.

He laughs. "You very welcome, Ruthie. You know...we should hook up sometime. Jus' to talk, that's all. I mean, I know you got yo'self a new man these days. Don't you?" Of course he knows I'm seeing someone. Eric always knows. Everything. "Fancy motha' fucka' too. Damn! What kind of car is that he drivin'? A Benz? Always sportin' 'round in them expensive ass suits. He ain't cheap, that's for damn sure." He laughs again. "He treatin' you right? Better be. You a good woman and he better 'preciate it. You was always a good woman, Ruthie. I always thought so." He looks sad for a moment. "But...my dumb ass didn't 'preciate it at the time. I know I was wrong 'bout a lot of things, Ruthie. What they say 'bout hindsight? It's 20/20."He laughs. "That shit's clear as day now, Baby. Believe that. I ain't the man I used to be, Baby Girl. That's for damn sure. Losin' you...hell! Like somebody cut off my arm, Ruth. My world ain't been worth a damn without you in it. So? He good to you?"

Tears rest inside my eyelids threatening to fall at any second. Doesn't this merry-go-round ever stop? Standing here listening to this bullshit, I'm reminded of how many times I've heard it before and how many times it's lured me back into that marriage. Oh, Ruth. How sad a fool you've been and the worse thing is, he sees the fool in you too.

"He's very good to me," I whisper. Now, let me have this, Eric. If you have one thread of sincerity inside you, leave me alone and let this be enough for you to disappear out of my life forever.

"I could be good to you, Ruthie. I know I could, Girl." He looks into my eyes like he always did when he was just about to tell me another lie. "I mean it, Ruthie. Things would be different this time, Baby."

"Eric..."

"No, Baby. Listen to me, Ruthie. Jus' listen to me for one minute."

"I've got to get home, Eric," I say, opening my car door. Eric leans up against it and closes it.

"I know, Baby. But look, we got a lot of years between us, Ruthie. Now, it wasn't good all the time, Baby and that's my fault. I know this now. I know what I did wrong and I know how to fix it. All I'm askin' for is a chance."

"No..."

"A chance to show you how good I can be to you, Ruth.

That's all. I've changed, Baby. I'm not the same man I used to be back then and I can prove it to you, if you jus' give me another chance. Jus' one more..."

"To do what? Kick my ass again?"

"How many times I got to say I'm sorry for that?"

"You never meant those apologies, Eric! Not once did you ever say "I'm sorry, Ruth" and mean it! Not once," I cry.

"So, I'm fo' real this time, Ruthie. I'm sorry, Baby. I'm sorry 'bout all that." Eric looks desperate. Desperate to convince me that he's a changed man and things will be different between us from now on. But I'm desperate too. Desperate to get as far away from him as possible.

"What kind of fool do you think I am? You've said that a million times before, Eric and..."

"And this time I mean it, Ruthie. I lost the most important thing I ever had when I lost you, Girl. Lord knows I did. A man can't help but change when he lose the only thing in his life that ever meant a damn to him." Before I realize what's happening, Eric pulls me to him and presses his lips against mine. Disgust surges through my body like lightning and I yank away from him, slapping him across his face and shoulders with his damn daisies.

"Don't you ever touch me again!" I scream. "Don't put your hands on me, Eric! Don't you..."

"Bitch!" Eric growls and pushes me away from him. "You lost yo' motha' fuckin' mind, Ruth?" He balls his hand into a fist and I hurry to get inside my car. In the distance I hear voices. He hears them too. A group of men are coming out of the building into the parking lot. Eric's fist disappears and glares back at me with eyes all too familiar, filled with contempt and hate and lies. He hurries back to his car and drives off.

It's not over. This isn't the last I'll see of him. Realizing this, I slump into my car, too shaken to drive and sit there until I can stop crying and drive home.

***

The moment I lay eyes on him I wrap my arms around him and hold on to him with all my strength. "I'm glad to see you too,

Baby," he says holding me.

"I've missed you."

"Obviously." He smiles.

Adrian's arms around me are all I need to feel secure again. Of course I have to tell him what happened and of course he'll hate hearing it because Adrian despises drama. But I can't ignore what happened today with Eric and I'm afraid to think about what he'll do next. Adrian has to be prepared, like I have to be prepared. Eric knew too much about him. He knew what kind of car he drove, how he looked. I have to warn him of what Eric's capable of.

"I've got something important to talk to you about, Baby."

"And there are some things I have to tell you too, Adrian."

Adrian takes my hand and I follow him to the couch. His expression is serious and as anxious as I am to tell him about my encounter with Eric, I'm more anxious for him to open up to me and tell me what's really been bothering him. "What's going on, Adrian? Talk to me."

He sighs deeply. "A lot's been going on lately, Ruth."

"With work. I know."

"Among other things."

"What other things, Adrian?"

Adrian leans forward and rests his elbows on his knees. He stares straight ahead and I can see how tired he really is. "You know about the California project and how hard I've been working to get the system up and running."

"You said it's almost finished, though."

"It is, but..." He sits back and drapes his arm over the back of the couch. The monkey he's got riding on his back is taking its toll on him and I know it's more than just his job.

"But what, Baby?"

"I've been asked to relocate, Ruth."

"Relocate? To San Francisco?"

"Yes. The company figures that since I'm the one who designed and set up the system, it only makes sense that I should be the one managing it, and I think they're right. It's been my project from the beginning and I'm not ready to hand it over to somebody else. Not yet."

The knots in my stomach are getting tighter and to say this has been a bad day would be the understatement of the year. "When would they want you to move?"

He hesitates, "Soon. Within the next couple of weeks."

"Do you want to go?"

He shrugs, "There's a big bonus attached to it and like I said, I'm not ready to give it up. It's a huge project and I'd be running things, at least on the technology side of the house."

"It's a promotion?"

"A huge promotion. Director of IS." He smiles.

Is this what's been bothering him all this time? I want to laugh, not at him, but at me. All this time I've been afraid I might be losing this man and this is it? This is nothing. Relocating, moving could be the answer for both of us. He'll get his promotion and I'll be away from Eric once and for all. More important, we'll be together.

"Are you worried about our relationship being long distance? Because if you are, I love San Francisco and I could pack up and move..."

"No, Ruth. I can't ask you to do that."

"You're not asking. I'm volunteering, Adrian. If that's all this is about, moving, I mean, that's nothing, Baby. That's no big deal for me. I just want us to be together and..."

Adrian puts his finger to my lips, "Let me finish, Ruth."

"Finish? There's more?"

He stands up and walks to the other side of the room, burying his hands deep in his pockets. What else could there be? I don't like the look on his face. Whatever else he's about to say isn't good news. "On one of the firsts trips I took to San Francisco, I met someone." Someone? That's not so bad. I'm sure he meets lots of "someones". What's the big deal? And why does he look like he's about to break my heart? "It wasn't serious, but we spent some time together off and on for a few months." He glances at me quickly, then looks away.

Suddenly I feel like I've been kicked in the stomach and I

ask the next logical question, knowing his answer will crush me. "You're in love with her?"

"I didn't say that," he says calmly.

"So...what are you saying? Why are you telling me this?" My heart's beating like bongos in my chest and I pray he says something, anything to set me at ease and reassure me that I'm the only woman in the world who can make him happy.

"We stopped seeing each other not long after you and I met, but recently I found out that...she's pregnant, Ruth. Almost eight months." Adrian stares at me, "Before you even ask, yes...it's mine."

"Pregnant?"

"I found out about the baby a month ago. She called the office and left a message for me to call her back. She said it was important, so I called her and that's when she told me. The baby's due soon and I have to be there. Hell, I want to be there, Ruth."

As soon as he says that the, truth stands naked right in front of my eyes, "Did you ask to relocate, Adrian?" He doesn't answer. Of course he did. "I need to know. Are you in love with this woman?"

"No...I'm not. But I'm in love with this baby. I'm nearly 40 years old, Ruth, and honestly, I was beginning to think..."

"That you wouldn't have children?" That's what this is about, isn't it? Children. Adrian's like most of us, feeling the need to perpetuate his own existence outside of a computer program and boast that he'll live forever in a miniature version of himself. "But I can give you children," I say desperately. "If you wanted a baby, all you had to do was tell me and I can give you a child, Adrian. I'll push out a whole football team for you if that's what you want."

He shakes his head, "Baby, don't do this."

"Do what? Break down because my man is leaving me for another woman? Because she's pregnant?"

"It's not her I'm leaving for, Ruth. Right or wrong, she's not the reason."

"Then, you are moving?"

"I'm doing what I feel I have to do, Ruth. I don't want to

be a voice over the telephone. I can't live like that. I was raised in a family and I want to raise my children that way. With both parents in the picture."

"And what about me, Adrian? What about us? Tell me. Exactly what does this mean for you and me?"

"Put it together, Ruth. What do you think it means?" The end of everything I've held close to my heart since I first laid eyes on him. Hope. Love. Possibilities. "I never meant for you to get hurt in all this, Ruth. You've got to believe that."

The weight of this day is heavy and I'm drained. All I want to do is close my eyes and push back the clock to the last time he held me, made love to me. And that's where I'd stop time. At that moment. "Doesn't matter what I believe, does it? You've made up your mind about what you want to do. What the fuck does it matter what I believe, Adrian?"

"What do you expect me to do, Ruth? Send a check every month and visit on weekends?"

"Yes!"

"That's not me!"

"And you and I are over, just like that? Nice and neat all wrapped up in a little box? 'Sorry Ruth, but I've got me somebody else' and that's all there is to it?"

"That's not all there is to it, Ruth. You ought to know me better than that. I've been wrestling with this for weeks now and it's been tearing me up inside! You know what you mean to me. You know how much I love you."

"Then don't do this to me, Adrian! Please. Don't do this. Not now." Because my maniac is back and he's after me again and if you're gone who can I run to? Who can I hide behind? Who can protect me? Finally. Who can I give myself to simply because I want to?

"There's nothing else I can do, Ruth. Believe me, Honey. If I felt there was another way..."

"There are other ways, Adrian. Lots of other options, and together, we can come up with some, but we can't if you walk away from me like this. Don't walk away from us. Adrian. Please."

"Ruth, I've already made up my mind," he says solemnly.

"I'm not here to discuss my options. I'm here to tell you I'm leaving and that's all there is to it."

"Are you going to marry this woman?" He stares at me, "Adrian?"

"After the baby is born..."

"After the baby is born...what?"

"Yes, we're planning on it."

Blessings are like fragile pieces of hand blown glass. If you squeeze too hard, they shatter into a million, tiny pieces. "You son-of-a... We made love right here not more than a week ago, Adrian! How could you make love to me knowing you were going to leave? Knowing all the time, you were planning to marry somebody else? What the hell is that?"

"This has been the hardest thing I've ever had to do in my life, Ruth! I love you and God knows I want you."

"You can have me!"

"But I can't walk away from this. This is my responsibility, and as a man, I've got to take care of it."

"Then take care of it! But don't let us go in the process. You don't have to do that. It doesn't have to go this far."

"It has gone this far, Ruth. I've got a kid that's going to be here in a month. It's gone that far already. I've got to be there. I can't do anything else." Adrian walks to the front door, "I'm only doing what I feel is right, which isn't always easy. You can believe me, or you don't have to, but I'll love you forever, Baby. That's all there is to that."

He closes the door behind him, and I fall apart.

Thirty Four

Clara's home is as comfortable as her personality. She's lived in her house for nearly 25 years, having shared it with husbands one and two and her daughter Carolyn. Carolyn's married and living in DC with her husband and their two children who absolutely adore their "Nana". I can't say that I blame them.

We sit on her patio looking out into her garden filled with Tulips and Lilies sipping on wine coolers while watching evening blanket the sky. I came here hoping she'd have the answers I need, or maybe the answers I want to hear. Answers reassuring me that Adrian is my soul mate and temporarily insane. Answers telling me that it's as impossible for him to live without me as it is for me to live without him. I don't want to hear that I should just get over it because shit happens and that's the way life is. If I wanted to hear that, I'd be at Bernie's house right now, not Clara's.

"Do you have any idea how much I love him, Clara?"

"'Bout as much as a woman can love a man, I suppose."

"This baby's important to him like all babies are important. But I don't understand how he can let us go so easily."

"You know this wasn't easy for him. He put a lot of thought into this, Ruth. He told you that."

"He told me a lot of things, Clara. None of which mean a

damn, right now."

"You're hurt and there's nothing anybody can tell you that's going to make one bit of difference, Ruth. You're going to believe what you want to believe."

"Why couldn't he have come to me in the beginning? This whole thing isn't just about him; it's about me too, and I think he owed me that. He could've talked to me before making his decision. Adrian made up his mind for all our lives, me, him, that woman. How much you want to bet he talked to her about it? He left my ass in the dark while the two of them decided what my fate would be. You know that shit ain't fair."

"Now, you know you too old for that." Clara looks at me. "Whoever told you life was fair?"

"Okay, but all I'm saying is, we could've come up with another solution. Maybe joint custody, or liberal visitation. He says he doesn't even love this woman. What kind of sense does that make? It's impossible to make a decent life with someone you don't love. I know because I tried and it can't be done. Am I that wrong? Do you think I'm being selfish?"

"Sure you are, but I don't know a woman who wouldn't be."

"He's all I wanted, Clara. Adrian is literally the best thing to ever happen to me. He makes my life worth living. What am I supposed to do now?"

"Making your life worth living was never his job, Ruth. Nobody deserves that kind of responsibility. That's something you're supposed to do for yourself."

"Maybe it's not his job, but that's how it is. Before he came along, I was content with nothing because it was better than being miserable with Eric. He made me feel like I was "all that" every time he looked at me."

"So, now that he's gone, you ain't "all that?""

"You don't understand."

"Oh, I understand all right. I understand you need to feel sorry for yourself now and that's fine. We all have to do that from time to time."

"I love him, Clara."

"I know. You already said that. But loving him isn't going to change what's happened. Adrian's made a decision that unfortunately affects you and there's nothing you can do about it. The only thing you got any control over is you. You have to get on with your life, Ruth. Without him, Baby."

"It's not that easy."

"No. It isn't. But what else can you do?"

"That's like starting over from scratch. From where I left off with Eric."

"No, it's not, Ruth. You've come a long way from being the woman you were then and not just because of Adrian."

"He had a lot to do with it. More than he'll ever know."

"Why the hell does it have to fall on somebody else? Why do you always have to blame every problem you have on a man? First Eric and now Adrian. When are you going to learn, Child? Men don't define who you are? You're supposed to do that."

"I don't know how to do that, Clara! It's either been all good or all bad. With Adrian it was all good and with Eric...my life sucked! So you tell me how I'm supposed to define myself? I wouldn't even know where to start."

"You need to get it in that hard head of yours, Ruth," she puts the tip of her finger against my forehead, "that everything you need to make it in this world is right here. Been here all along and nobody, not Eric, not Adrian got the power to take that away from you unless you let them."

"I'm not talking about..."

"I know what you're talking about, and yes, that bastard broke your heart. Doesn't matter why he did it. He did it. But you're not any less of a woman without him, Ruth. Are you listening to me?"

"Yeah, I'm listening. Basically, you're saying I need to get over it."

"Basically, that's all you can do. It won't be easy and it ain't going to happen tomorrow, but you can either get over it or be miserable for the rest of your life. That's up to you." Clara finishes that wine cooler in one big, long gulp, then wipes her mouth with the back of her hand and burps.

"I always thought that if I ever fell in love, my whole world would suddenly fall into place. My man and I would do what we were supposed to do. Get married, have children, live happily ever after. The end."

"Most folks think love fits nice and neat inside a jar, but it doesn't. It's big, sloppy, messy. Most of the time it doesn't even look like what we think love's supposed to look like. Most of the time, it can be downright ugly."

"Adrian used to tell me he loved me all the time."

"Adrian does love you, but he loves his child, and in his mind, he had to make a choice and he made it. May not be fair, but like I said, very few things in life are fair, which is why ain't nobody ever promised it would be."

"Well, somebody should."

"Nobody can, because everybody's different with different goals, different needs. Everybody's got their own goddamned agenda, which means..."

"There are no guarantees with love."

"There are no guarantees...period."

"I'd have walked on hot coals for him. All he ever had to do was ask. I'd have done anything for that man without hesitation or question. It was that good between us. How am I supposed to pretend it never happened?"

Clara puts her hand on mine, "You're not supposed to erase it, Ruth."

"I wish I could. Be a whole lot easier," I say, wiping the tears from my face. "Here I go again feeling sorry for myself. You'd think I'd be tired of it by now."

"Child, ain't nothing wrong with feeling sorry for yourself. If you don't do it, who else will? Feel sorry for yourself right now, Baby. Everybody's supposed to mourn their losses. The hard part is knowing when it's time to stop mourning and get on with things."

"How will I know when it's time to stop?"

"Don't worry, Dear, when everybody starts telling you they're sick and tired of hearing about it, that's a good sign that it's time for you to move on."

Thirty Five

He's looking for an opportunity. Any opportunity to kick my ass. I've tried telling myself that I'm imagining things. No, Ruth. That's not Eric's car parked outside your apartment again. It just looks like it. Girl, you crazy? Of course he's not sitting across the street from your office building watching you hurry across the parking lot, getting into your car and speeding home. And no, Ruth. That's not him you see in your rearview mirror. But now I know better. He just sits in his car outside my apartment, sometimes for hours, waiting. My heart races as fast as my feet do, hurrying to get inside some place safe. I haven't felt this way in years. Scared. Vulnerable. Helpless.

Why is this so important to him? Me. Why am I so important to Eric? I've asked myself that question a thousand times and I still don't know the answer. He's been with other women, while we were married, while we weren't. His first wife put him out and the woman he left me for walked out on him. Did he do this to them? Did he beg them to forgive him and take him back? Did he threaten to kill them if they didn't? I think I've probably played his game better than the others. When he hit me, I never hit back. I never threw things. I never called him a motha' fucka'. I never called the cops. I took my whoopings and tucked them away someplace safe where only he and I knew how to get to them. Eric's mouth always held the key, "Bitch! Get yo' black ass in here! Yo' dumb ass must want my foot up yo' motha' fuckin' pussy! Sorry ass, motha' fuckin' ho!"

I can't do this anymore. I don't want to live like this, ducking and hiding from Eric. I mean, it's not like he's going to get tired and go away. This is what he does better than anybody else, make my life hell. And he won't stop. I know he won't. Not until he's gotten what he wants, me crawling around on the floor pleading with him to leave me alone.

I've got some money saved up, and lately, I've been thinking a lot about leaving Jacksonville, maybe even moving back home to Denver. I should've moved away a long time ago, as far away from him as I could get. Not just across town. Jacksonville is too small for both of us. If I'm going to move, I need to do it right. I need to get out of Florida altogether. That's the only way I'm ever going to feel safe. Yeah, I think that's a good idea. That's what I should do.

I desperately need to hear his voice and this time I let the phone ring long enough for him to answer, "Adrian? It's me. Are you busy?"

"I was just on my way out. How've you been, Ruth?" Call me baby. Call me sweetheart, like you used to, like you miss me, like you're happy to hear it's me on the other end of the phone.

"I've...I miss you. I've been trying not to call, but...I miss you."

"I've been trying not to call, too."

"Really? So, you thought about it? Calling me? It's okay to call me, Adrian. I mean, if you want to talk, we always were able to..."

"Ruth, I was just on my way out. Can I call you later?"

"Will you call me later? I think that's the question."

"I've been very busy lately, running around trying to get ready to do this move, so... It might not be today." Or ever.

"How about I make you dinner one night before you leave?"

"Ruth."

"I'll make your favorite. Fried catfish? We can just eat and talk..."

"You know that's not a good idea, Ruth. Not now."

"Oh, c'mon, Adrian. What's a little fried catfish between friends? Don't tell me we have to give that up too. Just dinner, that's all." I just want to see you. Please, give me that much.

"I'll think about it."

"Or maybe we can go out. If you feel more comfortable, we can go some place."

"I said, I'll think about it."

"Can I call you back? I know you're busy and you might forget, but I can call you."

Adrian sighs, "That's up to you, but I don't have time to talk right now. Like I said, I was on my way out the door." The irritation in his voice rises and I know I'm wearing out my welcome, but it doesn't matter. At this point, nothing matters.

"There's a lot to discuss, Adrian. I'm having a hard time with this. I'm having a hard time without you."

"Ruth, I know this is hard for you; it's hard for me too and that's why I haven't called."

"I just miss you so much. I don't know how to let go, Adrian."

"You just do."

"And that's what you've done? Just like that?"

"I don't know what else to tell you." Tell me you love me. Tell me you need me too. Tell me you'll die without me. That's all. "My priorities have changed, Ruth. I've got a baby coming that I need to focus on and that comes before me...and you. Like I said, I never meant to hurt you, but life can change on a dime and when it does, sometimes there's nothing you can do about it but change with it."

"I still think there are other options, Adrian. You just haven't looked at them because you decided all on your own without discussing it with me, without considering that there might be something else you can..."

"Discuss what with you? How I'm going to raise my kid? What the hell does that have to do with you, Ruth? What?"

I'm hurt he asks the question when the answer is so obvious. "You said you loved me, Adrian. That has plenty to do with me."

"I made the only decision I could under the circumstances. You might not understand it, but it's not for you to understand. I'm the one who's got to take care of this responsibility, Ruth. Not you."

"I'm not trying to take anything away from your child, Adrian. Believe me, I'm not. And I do understand your obligations, but..."

"I've got to go, Ruth. I'll try and call you back when I get a chance." Adrian hangs up, without even saying goodbye.

***

It's after midnight and Eric's car is still parked outside.

Thirty Six

It was only a matter of time before she caught up with me. Bernie makes herself comfortable in the seat beside my desk, crosses her legs and cradles her cup of coffee between her hands, blowing on it every now and then to help cool it off. She takes a couple of sips before she says anything, which is her way of making the statement that she's not happy about being dissd.

"You can't call a sistah? You can't visit a sistah's cubicle? You can't return a sistah's messages?"

"Adrian left me."

"I know. Clara told me. Question is, why didn't you tell me?" I don't feel like answering, so I shrug my shoulders instead. "When's he leaving?"

"I think he's gone. His phone's been disconnected."

"You going to be all right?"

"Nope."

"I hate it when shit like this happens. Feels like the end of the world. Don't it?" I nod. "Wish I could say something to make you feel better." She smiles.

"I wish you could to."

"Might not seem like it, but you're going to be fine, Sweetie."

Why'd she have to come over here? I've been fighting back the tears all day long and sitting here talking to Bernie isn't helping. "It was like I'd won the prize. You know? Like Adrian was my reward for putting up with Eric's ass all those years."

"Well, maybe for a while, he was."

"I wanted forever, Bernie."

"I know."

"Guess that was asking too much, huh?" Bernie pats my hand.

"There are plenty of other prizes out there, Ruth. He's not the only one."

"Eric's back, Bernie."

Her warm, sympathetic expression disappears, "Back? What do you mean, he's back?"

"Hang out here with me until I go home and you'll see him...sitting in the parking lot. Stop by tonight after work and you'll see him parked outside my apartment. Everywhere I go, there he is. Watching me. Always watching me."

"You call the police?"

"He hasn't done anything, Bernie. There's no law against sitting in a parked car."

"How long's this been going on?"

"Few weeks."

"Why haven't you said anything, Ruth?"

"For what? And who am I going to say anything to, Bernie? Eric does what he wants to do. Always has."

"You can at least get another restraining order."

"Like that's going to do any good. I know how he is. This time, that won't do any good. He's back, Bernie."

"And what the hell are you going to do about it, Ruth? Sit around and wait for that fool to try and kill you next time?"

"Of course not."

"Then what?"

I open my purse and lay an airline itinerary in front of her. "One way. From here to Denver, leaving on Saturday. I can't stay here, Bernie. Not as long as Eric's got breath left in his mean ass."

"Just like that? You're going to pack up and leave, just like that?"

"What choice do I have?"

Bernie stares at me, searching for another answer, but she knows there isn't one. "What are you going to do about your things?"

"I'm taking Friday off. I've got movers coming in to pack up everything. It should all be there when I arrive. I'll just stick it in storage or something until I find a place."

"McGreggor know you're leaving?"

"Not unless you tell him. Personally, I don't think it's any of his business."

"You want to stay with me for a few days?"

"It's bad enough he's running me out of town, Bernie. The least I can do is try and stand my ground for a few more days. Besides, I've got a lot of packing to do. But thanks for the offer."

"You still got the gun?"

"Gun? Oh Bernie...I doubt it'll come to that."

"You still got it?"

"Yes. I have it."

"Good. Make sure it's loaded when you get home."

"Bernie..."

"Promise me, Ruth. Please."

In all the years I've known her, this is the most serious I've ever seen Bernie. "I promise."

Thirty Seven

My face is nuzzled in the crook of his neck and he's so real, I can smell him. Adrian's body is a cocoon around mine and we lay in each other's arms, naked. He whispers over and over again, "I love you, Baby. I'll never let you go."

"But you left me, Adrian. Why did you leave?"

He squeezes me tighter and tighter, until I can't breathe. I can't breathe. I can't... My eyes open to the sound of a knock at the door. I'm gasping for air and the apartment is dark. But it's him knocking. It's Adrian at my door. He's come back. I knew he would. I prayed he would. I stumble through the darkness, hurrying as fast as I can to get to him. To answer the door before he changes his mind and decides to leave. Quickly, I unlock it. Unchain it. Unbolt it. My heart's racing in anticipation of seeing him and holding him. But when I open the door, it's not Adrian standing behind it. It's Eric and Eric's fist.

I don't remember falling, but I remember hearing the door close behind him. Eric stands over me then reaches down and grabs a handful of my hair. He pulls me to my feet. *Whap! Whap!* Am I still dreaming? Has it turned into this, a nightmare? Am I in bed, asleep? Eric pulls back my head and growls in my face, "Who the fuck you think you think yo' sorry ass messin' with, Bitch?"

"Eric...please," I beg. "Don't...don't do..."

"Fuck you, Ruthie! Yo' black ass think you all that! I'm

goin' show yo' ass who the fuck you are! Who you always been! My piece of ass! Mine! Not his!"

He drags over me to the couch by my hair then bends me over the back of the couch and forces himself inside me from behind. The sensation of him burns me like acid and nausea wells up in my stomach. But before I can vomit, he pulls my head back and swears into my ear, "I told you this my ass, Bitch! Didn't I tell you that?" He grunts and growls like an animal, "You miss me, Bitch? Huh? You miss me, Ruthie? Tell me, how much you missed my big, black dick up yo' ass, Bitch!" My mouth moves, but the words don't come. "I can't hear you," he grunts. He rams inside me as far as he can go, torturing me from the inside out and the outside in.

"I miss you," I whisper.

Eric pounds furiously against me, but he won't cum. Not yet. He's too mad to cum. Too angry. I remember. He pulls out, then drags me into the bedroom, throwing me on the bed. His hard dick stares back in my face, angry for release. "Suck it!" He demands, standing over me. Then, pulls back my head and forces his dick inside my mouth. "I said...suck it, Bitch!" He's not expecting pleasure, but this is to punish me for living without him all these years and defying him. Refusing to let him back in my life. Refusing his daisies.

Eric pushes me back down on the bed, then climbs on top of me and pushes himself inside me. "Who's yo' fuckin' daddy, Bitch? Who the hell am I?"

"Daddy," I answer, staring up at the ceiling. Willing myself awake and away from here.

"That's right," he says pushing deep thrusts inside me, forcing groans from my body until finally, he loses himself to the sensation of this catastrophe. His eyes roll back in the sockets and he throws back his head, "Fuck! Fuck you...Ruthie! Oh damn! Shiiii...!" Eric's orgasm explodes and when it does, he relaxes, just for a second, and that's all I need. I reach over to the nightstand grabbing that sculpture Adrian thought was so ugly. With all the strength I have, I slam it into the side of his head. "Oh...motha'...shit! Ruthie!" Eric rolls off me holding on to his head trying to stop the blood from flowing down his face. I to push him off me, crawl out of bed and all I can think about is running. *Run, Ruth. Run as fast, and as far as you can. Don't stop. Don't look back. Don't pass go. Don't collect $200.* "Bitch! I'm goin' to...kill your black ass...Ruth!" I hear him calling behind me as I stumble through the living room heading toward the door. "Don't let me find yo' ass, Ruth! Don't let me..."

Kill my black ass. Kill my black ass? Eric will. He'll kill my black ass. He will. As long as he knows I'm alive, I know he'll kill my black ass. That's when I remember the gun Bernie gave me. It's time to stop running. It's time to stop letting him rule my life. I run back into the bedroom. Eric's rolling around on the bed clutching at the gaping gash on his head. Then I reach into the drawer of the nightstand and pull out the gun. It's time to stop running. I'm tired, goddamn it! I'm too damn tired to run anymore. This maniac has forced himself on me for the last motha' fuckin' time and running away isn't an option anymore. This time, I'll die before I run. Or better yet, I'll kill him.

"Ruth! You fuckin' bitch! You fuckin'..." Eric wipes the blood from his eyes and stares into the barrel of the gun I'm pointing at him. "What the..." He starts to get out of the bed.

"Don't you move, Eric!" Tears run down my cheeks into my mouth, "Don't...if you move...I'm going to kill you!" Slowly, I walk over to the bed with the gun aimed at his head. Blood streams down his face and he raises his hand to wipe it away. "I said, don't move, Motha' Fucka'!" My hands are shaking uncontrollably, but I'm not afraid. For the first time since I've known this man, I'm not afraid of him. Because I know that tonight, someone in this room will die and this will all be over. Might be him, might be me, but either way, I'm better off. The irony here is incredible and I marvel at the fact that this time, I'm in control. I have the power, and I laugh. I laugh so hard, I'm afraid I can't stop. I don't want to stop, because then I'll break. He's been trying to break me since I was 18 years old and he almost did, but I've held myself together. I'm stronger than he is. Always have been because I've put up with, survived and overcome this bullshit. He's hit me, kicked me, cussed me, but I'm still standing. This motha' fuckin' gun's about to go off in his face and it might as well be him pulling the trigger because it's him who drove me to this and I'm the maniac now.

"You...will...never put your fuckin' hands on me again!" Eric doesn't say a word. "Did you hear me? You will never put your fuckin' hands on me again!"

"Ruth...I'll leave, Baby...just...put the gun...put the gun..."

I crawl onto the bed next to him and sit close enough to see beads of sweat form on his forehead. Eric raises his hand with his palm facing me, only this time it isn't to slap my face. It's to stop a bullet. "I told you...I didn't want you, Eric. I've never wanted you, but you never cared about me, or what I wanted. You forced yourself into my life, my pussy, my peace because...why? Why, Eric? Why me? What the fuck did I ever do to you?"

"I can leave, Ruthie. You jus'...put that gun away, or...jus' let me get up out of here and you won't see me...jus' let me get up out of here, Ruthie and I promise..."

"You promise?" The taste of blood pools in my mouth. This time, I spit in his face, "That's what your promise means to me, Eric." I laugh. "How many promises have you given me before? How many have you kept?" The gun feels good in my hand, warm like it's a natural extension of who I am.

I hate him with every ounce of who I am and I've got to be the one who rids the world of his filthy ass. "You wanna shoot me, Ruthie? Huh? You wanna shoot my ass? So shoot! Shoot me, Bitch!"

I put the barrel of the gun on his face, between his eyes, "Shooting you isn't an issue, Asshole! The only issue I have is where I want to put the fuckin' bullet!" Eric raises his hands in surrender, afraid he's pushed me too far, and he has. I'm seconds away from doing what I've dreamed of doing damn near from the moment I met him.

"Ruth!"

"Eric! Right between your fuckin' eyes...yeah," I say, licking the blood and tears from my lips, "this would be a good place to put a bullet. Get rid of all those silly ass ideas you got floating around up there in that empty space where your brain should be. You're a stupid man, Eric...and stupid men, give birth to stupid ideas. Like hitting women."

"You don't want to pull that trigger, Ruthie...I know..."

"You don't know shit, Eric! You don't know shit! You don't know me! You never did! I slowly moved the barrel of the gun down to his chest, "Maybe this is where I should shoot your dumb ass. Maybe this would be good, because...but no...this wouldn't be a good place. A heart's supposed to be there and we both know...ain't shit there! Bullet would just go right through you, huh?" Eric tried to laugh. "What's funny, Eric?" I grind the gun hard into his chest. He grimaces. "You think this is funny? What you've just done to me...is that funny? What about what I'm going to do to you?" Then I move the gun down to his groin. That pathetic lump of dark flesh he's just attacked me with. His lethal weapon. "Is it still funny? Answer me! Is this shit funny now, Eric?"

Eric's eyes grow wide, like saucers, "Oh shit! Ruth...no! Please...please...don't...not...!"

I smile. "Now this...this would be the best place of all. I shoot this off and what would you have left? Hmmm...ain't this your world, Eric? I never liked fuckin' you. Did you know that? Did you know I hated every minute you stuck that piece of shit inside my body? You're the one who's always been all wrapped up in that. Not me." I shrug.

It's not until I look into Eric's bleeding, terrified face that I suddenly realize where I want to plant my bullet. I raise the gun to his mouth. "Open your mouth, Eric."

Eric shakes his head from side to side, "You need to stop...Ruth! You need to jus' let me get my ass up out of here and..."

"I said open your fuckin' mouth!" Before I know it, I've hit Eric in the mouth with the butt of the gun.

He buries his face into one of the pillows, twisting in agony, from the pain. I stare down at him remembering all the times he's put his fist in my mouth and all the nights we stayed up late until I'd learned my lesson and I was a bruised, bloody mess. Was this his lesson? Staring at him I also realize, I've finally lost my damn mind. I can't stop laughing because along with everything else he's taken from me, tonight he's taken that too. I reach for the phone and dial 9-1-1.

"Hello...you have to come and get him," I say quietly. "You have to come and get him now...or I'm afraid I'll have to kill him." I let the phone fall to the side of the bed and watch Eric writhe around in pain, screaming obscenities mixed with my name. "You touch me again, Eric and I'll kill you."

By the time the police and ambulance arrive Eric is lying groaning on the bed and I'm curled up in the corner of the room on the floor across from him with the gun pointed at him, daring him to leave.

I don't remember giving up the gun, or how I ended up at the hospital. But Clara's here and as soon as I see her I feel safe enough to collapse in her arms.

"Shhhh...Baby Girl," she whispers. "It's all right now. It's over, Honey. It's finally over, Baby."

I was examined for evidence of the rape then taken to the police station to make a formal statement. Eric's been charged with assault, battery and rape. Clara's taken me to Bernie's and all I want to do is sleep. Clara and Bernie wait patiently for me to shower, then they tuck me into bed like I'm a child. Did I ever wake up from that dream? Or am I still sleeping? Sometimes it's hard to tell. Maybe everything else was a dream. Maybe I only dreamed Adrian was my man. Maybe I dreamed starting my own business and maybe May and I never really took walks in the mornings. Maybe this has always been my reality and I'm just now waking up.

Momma would've brought me a cup of hot tea. She would've sat down on the bed next to me and rubbed my hair from my face. Then, she'd have kissed my cheek and whispered, *"You go on and cry now, Baby Ruth. A little cryin' never hurt a thing."* But it isn't Momma, it's Clara. She slips off her shoes and crawls into bed next to me, then wraps her arms over me. Clara doesn't have hot tea, or comforting words, but she has a delicious tune that she hums sweetly into my ear, lulling me to sleep.

Thirty Eight

I've taken up shelter in Bernie's spare bedroom. My life has unraveled in my hands once again and I'm scattered and misplaced with no real direction in sight, no real remedy for piecing myself back together. My body aches' my heart's broken; and my spirit...I think that's gone. Because I feel empty. Not afraid or hurt. Not disappointed, sad, or angry. Just empty. Numb. Dead. I sit for hours staring out the window, at what I can't say. Thinking, always thinking, about absolutely nothing. I hear, but I'm not listening. I eat, but there's no flavor. I drink, but can't ever seem to quench my thirst.

Bernie doesn't say much, bless her heart. I know it's killing her because she likes to think she's got answers to everything. Not this time. Honestly, I don't even think she knows the questions. She smiles and puts her arm around me from time to time to let me know she's here. That's plenty.

Sharon's been by. Took one look at me, then broke down crying. Damn. Do I look that bad? But I let her cry until she couldn't anymore. For a moment I thought about crying with her, but what for? Couldn't find a reason for it. Oh well. As long as she had a reason and cried a good cry that's cool. It made her feel better I suppose. I promised her I'd cry later.

The last time I saw May she was saved in the nick of time from having a nervous breakdown by a phone call from Jefferson.

She comes into my room, sits down on the bed patting the spot next to her that she's saved for me. May puts her arm around me and gives me a gentle squeeze.

"You doin' okay, Sweetie?"

"No. No, I don't think I am," I whisper. May looks into my eyes from behind the tears glistening in hers. I see sadness in her soul reaching out to bond with mine. Not many people know how it feels to be this alone. But I think May knows. Her tears become infectious and I feel my own welling up in my eyes for the first time in days.

"You know what my momma used to tell me when I was a little girl? She used to tell me that the hardest part 'bout bein' wounded is the healin'." She laughs, "I had no idea what that woman was talkin' 'bout. Momma's elevator is usually stuck in the basement most of the time, if you know what I mean, so I never put too much stock in too many things she said. But when I grew up, I understood what she was sayin'."

"Adrian's gone."

"I know, Baby," She rests her hand against my cheek.

"I miss him."

She smiles. "Bernie says you're leavin'? Goin' back to Denver?"

"I'm going home. That's where I grew up. I can't stay here. I can't stand it anymore, May. As big as this place is, I feel like it's closing in on me."

"You know anybody back there?"

"Not a soul."

"You sure leavin' is a good idea? 'Specially now."

"I'm suffocating here."

"But all yo' friends are here, Ruth. And we all love you."

"I know and I love you too. But I can't stay."

"Whatchu goin' to do up there all by yo'self?"

"I haven't even thought about it." I shrug.

"You got a place to stay?"

"I'll find one."

"You got money?"

"Some."

May holds my hand between hers, "If you need more...you call me. I still got money left over from Frank's insurance policy. Told Jeff I was savin' it for a rainy day. Gotta be rainin' some damn where," she laughs. "Whatever you need, baby. You call me."

"I will."

***

Standing on the balcony of my hotel room, I gaze down on a city that's like a foreign country to me. Denver, Colorado might as well be Paris, France because as it turns out, I don't know a thing about either one of them.

"I miss you already, Girl," Bernie whispers. I promised I'd call her as soon as the plane landed, but I didn't get a chance because she called first. "Is it like you remember?"

"It's too soon to tell. I hope so."

"If it's not and you get homesick for your best friend, you know you always got a home here."

"I know, Sweetie. And thank you."

I spent the first 13 years of my life in this place, but the place I knew as Denver was a small ghetto neighborhood called the Five Points near downtown. I used to spend my summers swimming at the pool at Curtis Park and Welton Street was my playground. Old Mr. Tony used to sell Pig Eared sandwiches on Welton. I never had one, but they must've been really good because he always had a line outside his store and all he sold was Pig Eared sandwiches, hot peppers and Dr. Pepper. Momma and I would take the city bus to downtown and spend hours looking around in stores we could never afford to shop in. I used to promise her that one day, I'd make thousands of dollars and buy her anything she wanted when I grew up. She always made sure we had a few dollars for hot dogs, though. Now, all that's familiar to me are the Rocky Mountains which are as eternal as time, and I find that comforting.

Thirty Nine

I made it a point to contact a Realtor the minute I got here and within a few days she found me a place and offered me the deal of a lifetime, depending on your perspective, of course. An elderly couple had a summer cabin in Golden that they were looking to rent out during the times they weren't using it, which, according to the Realtor, is pretty much all the time. Well, I fell in love with the place and rented it as soon as I saw it. It's convenient enough to the highway. That way I know I can make a quick getaway in the event of an avalanche or a ferocious, woman-eating bear. And it's secluded enough that I never have to see a traffic jam. Best of all, it's cheap because these people bought the place back in the middle-ages and have no idea what the property value is in this town.

I can't believe how much Denver's grown. The Five Points is going through some kind of weird metamorphosis stuck some place between being the hood and being what many consider to be prime, up-and-coming, downtown real estate. There's Lo-Do, Lower Downtown, which is where a yuppie who's any yuppie hangs out. Shit, I didn't even know there was a Lower Downtown Denver, but somebody sure found one and it must've been big enough too because they've found enough room to throw in a baseball stadium, an amusement park and a big fish tank. Go figure.

***

My favorite time of the day has always been mornings and mornings in a cabin in Golden, Colorado are breathtaking. The months have passed quickly and Fall is settling in getting things ready for winter. Things move slower up here than they do in the city. Slow enough to watch the leaves change from green to red, orange, yellow. Real exciting stuff, but every morning I make myself a cup of coffee, wrap up in my long johns, big ugly robe and thermal socks, sit on my porch and watch the rays of Old Mr. Sun dance through the leaves and come up to kiss me dead on the lips. I don't mind the impending cold, or the long drives to the grocery store. I don't mind the lack of neighbors, or social interaction. Solitude is the best therapy I can have. He doesn't say too much and he's a great listener too. Doesn't have opinions at all and I like that.

"Why the hell you gotta live in the mountains?" Bernie asks with her usual tactfulness.

"I like the mountains, Bernie."

"Only white folks live in the mountains, Ruth. Crazy white folks, who shave their heads and dream of starting race wars."

I laugh. "You're so funny. Sharon said she'd love to live in the mountains."

"She would," she says smartly. "So, when you coming home? I miss your little ass."

"I miss you too. I'll be home next month."

"You said that last month."

"Did I? Well, I meant next month."

"You ain't never coming back, are you?"

"Don't be silly. Of course I'll be back. Next month."

"You coming back for the sentencing?"

"Probably not."

"C'mon, Girl. At least go to see the look on his face when they tell him how long he's going to be locked up."

"I'd rather watch the grass grow, Bernie."

"You different from me, 'cause I'd be there with popcorn, some 3-D glasses and 20 of my closest friends."

"I'm sorry that I can't muster up that same level of

enthusiasm. Besides, he plead guilty and with time served, everybody knows he won't get more than five years."

"Yeah, well..."

"Better than nothing, right?"

"Guess what I'm looking at right now?"

"What?"

"Pages' website. It's beautiful, Girl."

"Thank you."

"I guess you been taking advantage of all that free time you got, huh?"

"Girl, I can design websites with the best of them."

"Business picking up?"

"Yep. More every month."

"So how do I buy a book?"

"Point, double-click and put in your credit card number."

"What about my discount?"

"What about it?"

"How much is it?"

"Ten percent."

"Ten percent? I'm your best friend in the whole wide world and the best you can give me is ten percent?"

"Okay...Fifteen."

"Ruth?"

"Bernie. I'm trying to make a living here."

"Fifteen percent and free shipping."

"Your ass is cheap."

"You just now realizing that?"

Pages has been in business for almost four months now. It started out slow, but it's definitely picking up, enough to keep the bills paid, anyway. I figured I had nothing else left to lose, so why not start the business. I didn't start it because I believed I'd gotten my head together. I didn't start it because I wanted to be a pioneer and my determination was so strong, my drive such a force, that it was my destiny to run this business. On the contrary. I started Pages because I didn't have the stamina to look for a job and I had no desire to be around a bunch of people, asking too many questions, forcing out smiles I didn't feel. I needed a job, money, and this idea has been burned into me for months. That's why I started Pages.

It's too soon to say I've gotten myself together. Honestly, I don't ever see that happening because I'm not really sure what that means. Have I put my past behind me? No, because it's a part of me forever and it's molded me into who I am, so I can't ignore it and I won't. Have I exorcised my demons? Not even close, but I'm learning not to be afraid of them anymore. I'm learning to look them in the face, but they'll always be with me. I still think about Adrian and I still miss him. But like everything else, that'll be easier to deal with in time. That's one thing about living in this place. There's more time than anything else, so whenever I need some, all I've got to do is stick my head out the door and inhale. It's the only thing I know that's free and the supply is endless.

Forty

It's taken Sharon's wedding to bring me back here and do you know what the heffa had the nerve to do? She's made me the maid of honor and didn't bother telling me until today, the day of the wedding. Yes, it pisses me off! But seeing how happy she is and how beautiful she looks it's hard to stay mad at her.

I've missed everybody, especially Clara. As soon as she sees me, she smiles and plants one of her sweet kisses on my cheek, "How you doing, Baby?"

"I'm fine," I say, grinning. "I missed you, though. When are you coming to see me? It's a beautiful place. I know you'd love it."

"Child, you know I don't fly and I don't like too much driving either."

"That mean you're not coming?"

"That means you're welcomed in my home anytime, my love."

"Thank you." I smile.

"How long you staying?"

"Not long. Just a few days. I've got to get back and run a business."

"That all you doing these days? Running businesses?"

"That's all I want to do."

"You're a young woman, Ruth. Don't grow old before your

time, Baby."

"I'm cool, Clara. Really. Stimulation is not something I'm ready for right now."

"A little stimulation never hurt anybody." She winks. "I need me some every now and then myself."

"Clara!"

"What? Even women my age need to get their groove on from time to time, Baby. I ain't dead, you know."

I laugh. "Thank God."

Sharon looks beautiful and Megan, my doll baby, makes a perfect flower girl.

"Hello, Miss Ruth," she screams, jumping up into my arms.

"Hello, Megan, Sweetie." I try hard not to squeeze the life out of the child, but boy am I glad to see her.

She gives me a big, wet kiss, then rubs her little hand down my hair. "You let your hair grow."

"I couldn't help it. It just kinda grew on its own."

"I like it." She smiles. "You don't look like a boy anymore." She's young so I'll let that comment pass without incident. But her momma definitely needs to teach this child some manners.

I gasp, "Megan! What happened to your tooth?"

"The tooth fairy took it," she shrugs. "And she gave me a quarter for it."

"A whole quarter?"

"I wanted a dollar," she says disappointedly. Cheap ass tooth fairy. I'll be talking to her after the wedding.

Sharon smiles apologetically. "I'm glad you're here, Ruth."

"You know I'm mad at you? You could've warned me before I got here, that I was the maid of honor, Sharon. I would've worn a nicer dress."

"Oh...you look beautiful and you could've worn jeans for all I care. I was not going to stand up here and marry this man without my best friend by my side."

"Better not let Bernie hear you talk about that best friend stuff. She thinks she's got dibs on me."

"I'm not scared of Bernie and today is my wedding day. If I want you to be my best friend, then..."

"Then, I'm your best friend, Honey. Forget that old Bernie." I smile.

"I heard that," Bernie shouts, coming out of the house.

The wedding is beautiful, but then, what did I expect? I have to admit, standing here watching Sharon and Wayne exchange vows, I can't help but think of Adrian. How many times have I pushed away fantasies of him and me standing at the altar, reciting vows to each other? Too many. Maybe that's the problem. Instead of pushing those fantasies out of my reality, maybe I should've held on to them. Then maybe he wouldn't have left me. Maybe I'd be Mrs. Adrian Carter and maybe the altitude in Colorado is starting to get to me.

Bernie and I sit back and watch our friend and her new husband dance together. We've both eaten too much cake and downed too much champagne to stand for longer than 60 seconds on our own, so we've decided to be on the safe side, stay in our chairs and chill.

"She's looks so happy," I slur.

Bernie nods. "Yeah, she does."

"Don't you think she looks like a young Elizabeth Taylor?"

"Yeah, she does."

"You think you'll ever get married again?"

"I'm thinking about it."

"Really? Since when?"

"Since...since...hell I don't know. Since today."

I laugh. "You're drunk."

"Yeah, I am."

"I think I like being single. Don't have to answer to anybody, or be responsible to anybody."

"This is true," Bernie agrees.

"I can come and go as I please and nobody can say a damn thing about it."

"That's right."

"I'm thinking about getting...a dog." Bernie and I look at each other and laugh hysterically.

All of a sudden, she gets serious, "I've got something to tell you."

"Don't do that. We're having a good time."

"I wasn't going to tell you because I didn't know how you'd take it."

"Then don't tell me."

"And I definitely didn't want to tell you before you got here because I knew if I told you, you wouldn't come."

"What is it, Bernie?"

"And if you didn't show up that would've broken poor Sharon's heart and ruined her wedding day. You know that heffa thinks you're her best friend? If it wasn't her wedding day, I'd..."

"Bernie? Would you just say whatever it is you've got to say?"

"Adrian's back."

Numbed by the effects of all that champagne, I just sit here trying to make sense out of what she's just said. "Adrian's back? What the hell does that mean?"

"It means...he's back. Moved back from San Francisco because apparently things didn't work out with his baby's momma so...he's back."

I finish my umpteenth glass of champagne and shrug. "So he's back."

"He called me."

"For what?"

"Looking for you."

"What did you tell him?"

"The truth. That you don't live here anymore."

"Good. Good answer." I pour the last of our last bottle of champagne into my glass. I hope she didn't want that.

"And that Eric attacked you."

"Bernie!"

"And that he was a sorry ass bastard for leaving you like he did for that other woman, even if she was pregnant with his baby because you loved him more than you'd ever loved any man and he had no right to break your heart the way he did and how could he have the nerve to call me up looking for you after what he did and..."

"You did not tell him all that? Tell me you didn't?"

"If I told you I didn't, I'd be lying, Ruth."

"Why would you..."

"Because his pretty ass needed to hear it! That's why. He ain't all that...thinking he can just waltz back into town, find you and make everything all right by saying a few fancy words and putting a little comfort between your legs."

"Bernie Watson!"

"Bernie Watson nothing! If his sorry ass would've been here, maybe Eric wouldn't have come at you that night."

"If Eric wanted to get to me bad enough, Bernie, he was going to do it. But you had no right to tell him all that..."

"Damn if I didn't! He called my house, Ruth. That was an invitation to sit and listen to every motha' fuckin' word I had to say and he did too. He sat there and let me say my peace."

"And then what? After you said all your little peace about all my business..."

"He admitted he was wrong and he said he was worried about you and wanted your number so he could check on you."

"You didn't give it to him? Because I'm over him, Bernie. I really am and I like being over him."

"You're not over him."

"I am over him. Maybe not completely, but..."

"I knew you weren't over him."

"You had no right, Bernie. None."

"I know, Girlfriend."

"So you didn't give him my number...did you?"

"Hell no!"

I sit back, relieved that at least she kept her mouth shut about that. "Good."

"I just told him you'd be in town this week."

"Bernie!"

"At least talk to the man, Ruth."

"How could you..."

"He was so sweet about that cussing out I gave him, Ruth. He really thought he was doing the right thing with that woman and he's really upset that he couldn't be there to raise his son. But he realized that raising that boy in a house with two people who couldn't stand each other wasn't fair to the child and he knows that you're the only woman for him and if he can ever make it up to you...even though he knows you might not trust him right away, he'll do it. Whatever it takes."

"Whose side are you on?"

"Yours."

"No, that's not how it sounds to me."

"Ruth, you know you love that man."

"Sure I love him, Bernie. And that was the problem. I loved him and he still left me."

"He was only trying to do what was right."

"Fine. He tried. Obviously he failed. I'm sorry that things didn't work out for him, but I'm not disposable. He said we were finished. We're finished."

"Fine. Then be finished. But just talk to the man, Sweetie."

"What on Earth for?"

"Let him tell you himself, how sorry he is. Just give him the opportunity and yourself the satisfaction of hearing him admit he fucked up."

"I don't need that."

"Yes you do. Every woman needs that. We all need for the men who break our heart to come crawling back on their knees, in tears, telling us how wrong they were for hurting us the way they did."

I laugh. "You speaking from experience?"

"I'm straight up...straight. You know I'm right."

"Whatever."

"You going to talk to him?"

"No, Bernie."

"Think about it? Please. For me?"

"This has nothing to do with you and you know it."

"Just think about it."

"I'll think about thinking about it."

"Good enough." Bernie rests her case.

It's not that I'm holding a grudge against Adrian, but I've

moved on. Time has a way of dulling the pain and helping me to get over him. I've needed big doses of time. I'm sorry things didn't work out the way he'd hoped. In retrospect, I admire him for even wanting to make things right for his child. But it didn't work out. Am I supposed to be here waiting for him just in case? That's not fair. He moved on with his life and despite all the drama. I've moved on with mine.

Forty One

May and I laugh as soon as we lay eyes on each other, "Girl, people are going to accuse us of reading each other's mind. You let yours grow back too?"

"I had to, Girl. Gets cold up there in those mountains and I need all the insulation I can get."

She looks good. Even better than she did when we first met. We're having fish for dinner and this time she insists that I help out with the cooking. "How are things between you and Jeff?" I've never said anything to her about tripping the last time I was here. I try not to judge people who trip because I've tripped pretty hard my damn self on occasion. "Child, please. We're fine. I jus' need to stop bein' so insecure all the time. He ain't travelin' as much as he used to. I guess it was hard on him too, bein' away from us all the time."

"The kids okay?"

Jeff walks in, "The kids are great." He comes over and hugs me, "How you doing, Ruth?"

"I'm fine, Jefferson. How are you?"

He looks over at his wife, "Better than ever," then walks over and gives her a nice, long kiss right there in front of me. "Hey, Baby."

"Jefferson Anderson, now you know you can't be gettin' nothin' started now. We got company." She blushes.

He whispers loud enough for me to hear, "I'll start something later."

"Mmmm...promise me," she purrs.

"Maybe I should leave?" I suggest.

"Don't you dare leave, Girl. Sit down. See what you did, Jeff? You made her uncomfortable."

"I'm sorry." He smiles. "Forgive me, Ruth. The last thing I want to do is make you uncomfortable."

"I'll live," I tease.

May and Jeff lock eyes as he leaves the room. Don't those two ever get enough of each other? "Now," she says, finally coming back into this time zone. "...what 'bout you?"

"What about me?"

"How you doin'? I mean, really?"

"I'm fine." She looks skeptical. "I am, May."

"You datin'?"

"Now, don't start."

"I'm just askin'. You know how I am, always thinkin' love's what makes the world go round. Can't help it. I'm a romantic."

"Then be romantic. Lord knows with the way Jeff is always sucking on you, you have reason to be."

She laughs, "You don't miss havin' somebody suckin' on you?"

"Not yet."

"So you ain't seein' nobody? They got black men in Colorado?"

"A few."

"Adrian's here."

"Yeah, Bernie told me he was back. Can I have a carrot?"

"No, Ruth," May stares at me. "Adrian's...here."

It takes a few minutes for that statement to register, but when it does, all the oxygen in the room seems to disappear. I've dreamed a million times of being in his arms, only to wake up to the truth that somebody else had that privilege. I was addicted to Adrian Carter like he was a drug. His kisses intoxicated me; his touch invigorated me; and purging him from my system has been agonizing, to say the least. I still cry over what I had with him and what I lost, but not as much as I used to. Not nearly as much, and that's how it should be. That's what I've worked for since he left. I can't afford to jeopardize the progress I've made. Seeing him could set me back a lifetime and I'm not going back. Fuck Adrian.

Suddenly, I'm not hungry and I'm not interested in reminiscing anymore either. I leave May's kitchen, in search of my purse. She follows. "Ruth," she calls after me. Her house is huge and it wouldn't be hard to hide a six foot tall, gorgeous, black man if it was absolutely necessary. But I'm pissed and I'm leaving. "Ruth," she grabs hold of my arm. "He wants to talk to you, that's all."

"What about what I want, May? Which is not to talk to him."

"Baby, I think this is important. I think you need to hear what he has to say."

"He said everything he needed to say to me before he left, May. He's said all I ever want to hear."

"Ruth..."

"I'm flying out tomorrow. Tell Jeff I said goodbye. You still coming out next Spring?"

"Ruth." There's no mistaking his voice. It still stirs those damn butterflies hibernating in my stomach and I feel like I'm going to pass out. Jeff comes over, takes May by the hand and they leave the room. I'm afraid to turn around. Afraid I still love him now as much as I did then. I don't want to see Adrian. I don't want to hear what he has to say. I've worked too hard all these months to turn back. I can't afford to do that to myself. I owe me more than that. I don't owe him a damn thing. He walks over to me and I don't have to see him to know this. I can feel him. I can smell him and, oh my God, I can still taste him. He stands in front of me, but I can't bring myself to look at him. "You look beautiful," he says.

"I...have to go, Adrian. I have an early flight tomorrow."

"Don't go. May's making a dinner Jeff swears is the bomb. Can't you stay through dinner?"

"I'd rather not," I say, heading for the door. "I'm sorry. Tell May, I'm sorry." I hurry out to my car, but he follows me. Lord, not this. Not tonight. I'm not in the mood for explanations, or apologies, or the resurgence of old memories, or feelings. I just want to go home, back to my Colorado home. I miss my mountains and my high altitude, my dry skin, my solitude. Have I really run away? Absolutely, and I've never regretted it.

He takes hold of my arm and turns me to him, "Let me buy you a cup of coffee. We can go somewhere and talk."

This time, I look into his face, his eyes and yes, I still love him. "What are we going to talk about, Adrian?"

"Bernie told me what happened. How you doing?"

"I'm fine, but that's not something I want to talk about with you."

Adrian looks hurt and that's not my problem either. "I haven't been able to get you off my mind, Ruth. Things didn't work out in San Francisco. Shit! Turned out that we couldn't stand each other."

"I'm sorry to hear that."

"Are you?"

"Yes, Adrian. I know how much you wanted to be there for your child. And I'm sorry that didn't happen."

"I just wanted to do the right thing, Ruth."

"And you tried and it didn't work. I don't know what you want from me."

"You. Like I've always wanted you. I hurt you and I know that. I wasn't there for you and I know that too. But you can't honestly stand there and tell me you don't still care for me, because I still care for you. It was deep, Ruth. What we had was real deep."

"It was and that's what hurt so much. You were my soul mate, Adrian. And when you left, you took a part of my soul with you."

He smiles. "Don't you want it back?"

"I've learned to live without it."

"You don't mean that, Ruth. How can you just…"

"Just let us go? How could you?" He doesn't have an answer, not that I expect him to. These days, I try not to expect to much of anything. Life just sort of happens, running its own course, doing its own thing. Expectations seem to hinder progress. "Goodbye, Adrian." I climb into my car and drive away. No, I'm not going to regret this. I've given up living with regrets. They nag and complain way too much. Is that my heart I hear breaking again?

Forty Two

"How'd you find out where I was staying?" Let's see, May could've told him, or Bernie, or Sharon, or maybe there's an ad in the newspaper.

"Can we talk, Ruth?"

"Adrian, it's late."

"I know. Can I come in?"

Something inside me won't let me cuss him out and tell him to leave me alone. But I've barely got a hold of it and if he says one stupid, insensitive thing, I'm going off. "I've got an early flight in the morning, so..."

"This won't take long." He stares at me and I wish he wouldn't because he's got laser vision that melts me like butter. "I was hard on you. Too hard and I'm sorry for that."

"Apology accepted," I say quickly. "Is that it?"

"No." He smiles. "My Dad used to say, the only woman in the world worth having is the one you dream about when you're sleeping."

The expression on my face asks the question for me. "I don't get it either." He laughs. "But I do dream about you."

"Adrian..."

"Lana and I..."

"Lana?"

"I wasn't fair to her either, Ruth. I kept looking for you in her and when I realized what I was doing I knew I couldn't live like that. Didn't take her long to realize it either."

"So what am I supposed to do about it, Adrian? Jump back in your arms like it never happened?"

"Yes. That would be wonderful."

"And impossible."

"I know," he says sadly. "I just wanted to explain. That's all."

"And you've done that."

"If I could take it all back, Baby, you know I would."

"Maybe, but you can't. So what does it matter?"

"I never fell out of love with you."

"I loved you too and that's why I can't go back. It still hurts to much."

Adrian sighs and I see tears glistening in his eye through the tears in my own. "Bernie's got my number if..."

"I won't."

Adrian kisses me on the cheek, then leaves. The sensation of his lips warms me long after he's gone, but I know I've done the right thing.

Forty Three

Winter in the Rocky Mountains is no joke. I don't know what's been going on in my mind. Somehow, I've managed to minimize this whole snow thing in my mind, convincing myself that yeah, I'm a native Coloradan and I can handle it. Right? Not really. I might've been born in the stuff, but I've never driven in it and I've never had to shovel it and I've forgotten how cold it is and how quickly a good set of toes can freeze up if you don't put on enough socks, and how much of a necessity a hat and scarf are and hot chocolate and firewood and four wheel drive and...hell! Does anybody sell extra strength moisturizing lotion by the gallon? My skin's so ashy if I rub my legs together long enough I can set a forest fire.

My little cabin doesn't have central heat, so I rely heavily on my fireplace, electric heaters in all the rooms and thousands of pairs of long johns. So, maybe I'm going to have to rethink this little log cabin thing. When I moved into the place I really thought about someday buying it, but then again that was back in May and it wasn't bad then. Soon as my lease is up, I'm going to find me a nice little place with lots of knobs and buttons and electrical this, central that, washer/dryer hookups and reliable whatevers. Roughing it just isn't in my nature.

My fire is burning down and I cringe at the thought of having to go back outside into that Tundra to get some more wood. But what choice do I have? If I want to keep the feeling in my fingers and toes, none. I throw on my boots, scarf, hat, gloves and set out to brave the elements in my thermal underwear. I load up my wheel barrel with logs and roll it back to the front of the house to unload. As I'm piling the wood onto the porch, a big black SUV pulls up into my yard slash driveway. I stare at the truck trying to make out who's driving, but the windows are tinted and I can't see inside. I'm not expecting anyone and I don't know anybody with a truck like that. I ease my front door open, ready to grab that rifle sitting idle and loaded just inside my cabin. The door opens and he steps out. Adrian. Looking like a spokes model for *Mountain Man* Magazine, wearing a big black parka, plaid flannel shirt, way too expensive hiking boots and a grin a mile wide.

Needless to say, I'm shocked, and that's putting it mildly. "What are you doing here, Adrian?"

He walks over to me and kisses me smack dead on the lips, "Came to help you bring in this wood." Then he begins unloading the firewood, taking it into the cabin, throwing some logs into the fireplace. He doesn't say another word to me until he's finished. Meanwhile, my shocked self just stands here, in the cold, freezing my booty off, watching him, utterly speechless.

"Baby," he says from the doorway, "you'd better get inside. It's freezing out there."

Like I know it's freezing, but what I don't know is how he found me, why he found me, and what he plans on doing with me. So, when I get inside, I ask again, "What are you doing here?"

"We need to talk." Adrian takes off his coat and makes himself right at home.

"You came all the way out here to talk?"

"Well, you wouldn't talk to me in Jacksonville."

"Because I had nothing to say to you in Jacksonville. Like I have nothing to say to you here."

"But I have things I need to say."

"You could've called me, Adrian."

"You would have hung up on me, Ruth. Which is why I'm here."

"This is crazy," I say, nearly falling down into my chair.

"You came all the way out here to say...what?"

"That I love you and I think we can, should work things out."

"That's crazy, Adrian."

"Why is that so crazy?"

"It is because I don't want to work things out."

"You don't love me anymore?"

"I don't want to be with you."

Adrian grins. "So you do still love me?"

"This whole thing is just..."

"Crazy. Yeah, I know. You already said that."

"How can you think... Adrian, you dumped me. You broke my heart. How can you possibly believe I'd want to be with you again?"

"Because I'm admitting I was wrong, Baby. I made a mistake. A big mistake at the expense of your feelings. And I love you, Ruth. I've always loved you and I always will."

"Since when is that enough?"

"Then tell me what is enough and I'll do it."

"It's not that simple."

"It's not that hard. Not for me."

"You're willing to do anything for me?"

"Damn right. Just name it."

"It wasn't that long ago when I was willing to do anything for you, Adrian."

"I know."

"Then you also know, it's not that simple."

"Ruth...," he looks disappointed. But that's not my problem.

"I honestly don't know what to tell you. There isn't anything I want from you and there's nothing that's going to change the way I feel right now."

"So, you're cool with this? Living by yourself, in the mountains, alone."

"It's not about that. It's about taking care of me, making sure I'm okay. I can't depend on you or anyone else to do that for me. I've got to do it."

"And being with me isn't taking care of you? That doesn't make you happy? I didn't make you happy?"

"Yes. You made me very happy, but I can't depend..."

"On me? Is that what you were about to say?"

"I shouldn't have to depend on you."

"That's fine. Then don't. But does that mean you have to deny yourself, Ruth?"

"I'm not denying myself. I'm learning to live with myself."

"And you're denying yourself, Baby. Don't you see? It's not about having one or the other, Ruth. You don't have to choose between me or you. You can have me and you. All you have to do is take it. Take me."

But then that would mean losing me in him again. How can I have both? That's asking for too much. Isn't it? That's wanting to have my cake and eat it too. Isn't it? If I allow Ruth to disappear just one more time, I won't be able to get her back, because I know her. She won't come back.

"I'm human, Baby. I made a choice and it didn't work out. I hurt you and me. But I learned a valuable lesson. It was hard, but I learned that a man needs to go with his gut instinct and mine told me not to let you go. To work something else out so that I could have both you and my son in my life. I opted to go with my head, lost the woman I love and ended up being the kind of father I didn't want to be. Long distance."

"Those are your consequences Adrian, not mine. If I've learned anything in life, it's that we all have to be held accountable for the decisions we make, good...bad..."

"Fine, then hold me accountable, but don't make me liable for the rest of my life. Would you want to be held liable, Ruth? All I'm trying to get here is a second chance and correct me if I'm wrong but didn't you once say we all deserve second chances?"

Sure, I said that. Back when I was blissfully happy, I said a whole lot of things. The past is not something I've ever wanted to go back to. Not even a good past because it's left behind for a reason. He stares at me with deep, black eyes and all I can see is sincerity and honesty. I wish he'd never come here.

"I'm not obligated to give you anything, Adrian. I don't

owe you a damn thing."

"No, you don't. But you owe yourself."

"You're right. I do and that's all I'm trying to get you to understand. I'm taking care of me. I'm making me happy now."

"Who are you trying to fool, Ruth? You call hiding out up here in the middle of nowhere, taking care of yourself?"

"I'm happy."

"Bullshit. You ran away from home, Ruth. Away from everybody and everything that ever hurt you. There's nothing out here, Ruth."

"I want it that way, Adrian."

"No..."

"Yes."

"No! You want what you had with me, Ruth. You want to be back in my arms, in my bed, in my life."

"I loved being with you! But you're the one who walked out on me, remember?"

"Hell, yeah, I remember. Every day you're not in my life, I fuckin' remember, Ruth and that's why I'm here, Baby. To fix what's broken for both of us. And don't stand there and try to tell me you're not broken because I know better."

"So?" Brilliant comeback, Girl. You tell him.

"So...," he smiles, "let's get married."

That man must be out of his mind. Married? Where did that come from? Why in the world would I, being in my right mind for the first time in ages, agree to marry Adrian Carter? Yeah, he trekked all the way up here in the dead of Winter to apologize, but it isn't about his apology. It's about me taking care of me. I'm in control and I like it. I'm not being driven to do or be anything or anybody else because of a man. Not even this man. From this point on, it's my way, or the highway. Period.

"Of course I'll marry you," I say with tears in my eyes. I throw myself into his arms and lose myself in that intoxicating flavor of this man like I've done so many times in the past. "If you ever let me go again..."

"I won't, Baby. Believe that."

Questions

1. In your opinion, why would a woman to remain in an abusive relationship for as long as Ruth did?

2. Her excuse for staying was fear. Do you think there was more to it than that? Explain.

3. Why do you think Eric refused to let go of Ruth when he obviously didn't love her?

4. Do you think he had fears of his own? Why or why not?

5. In your opinion, were Adrian's reasons for leaving their relationship justified?

6. Given the choice, would you have taken Adrian back?